planet quest

BOOK
TWO

PLANET QUEST

BOOK TWO OF THE PAWN QUEST TRILOGY

by

KATE HARRINGTON

To Nathan and Alisa,
my computer gurus

Day One

Planetfall

Ran

The planet hung below, its crescent edge growing and brightening as the landing shuttle sloped down into the full light of day. Streaky clouds veiled wrinkled mountain ranges and a snowcapped pole.

Ran stared at the view screen while listening to the ongoing computer analysis. Two moons. Breathable air. Slightly lower gravity than Earth. Shallower seas. Why send him *here*? And *where* was here? The ship had spent half the six-month voyage accelerating out of the solar system, followed by a period in hyperspace and a somewhat shorter period decelerating to this planet.

No one had told him the reason for his exile, not that Ran was the only one. The ship's medico said his fellow passengers were all fosterlings being returned to their parents. What parents? Ran knew he didn't have parents. He didn't want parents, not after battling with every foster father he'd ever been assigned.

They circled into night and back into day, the planet surface much closer now.

Aside from his seat near the view screen, the entire compartment was filled crates. He wondered why he'd accepted Second Mate Gumption's invitation to ride down with the cargo. He should have waited to finally meet those dozen or so fellow passengers. He hadn't seen any of them during the voyage, all of them undergoing space sleep while he stayed active to heal his extensive burns.

Their descent brought them closer to a black scar whose unnatural straightness cut through a range of hills and continued into the bluish-green waters of a large sea. He lost sight of the scar as the landing shuttle slowed, dropping toward hilly lands broken by a single, high ridge standing lonely above the rest.

With a slight bump, they were down. Ran stirred, uncertainty warring with an urge to get out and see the place for himself. Wait. Wait for the lander to cool.

The hatch slid open. Second Mate Gumption grinned up at him. "Hop down, Pawn Boy. We'll dump the cargo and take off. Next trip will bring you company." *Pawn Boy.* Gumption's latest nickname for him, all because Ran said he felt like he'd been shoved out onto a cosmic chessboard. And why not? He hadn't asked for this journey.

Dust blew in Ran's face as he dropped to the ground, small bag in hand. *Oof!* Gravity pulled at all his parts, as if eyelids, skin, every bone were coated in lead. He fought the planet's drag to look around.

"Where are the people?" No one around to boss him for a while at least.

Gravity sagged the second mate's features, aging him beyond his middle years. "Since you're here," he said, "you can take charge of the next group till someone comes for you. Did you spot the building?" He waved toward an overgrown trail climbing out of the landing area. "Off that way."

"Take charge? Is *that* why you wanted me down with the cargo?"

Gumption grinned. "You've got time to scope out the place, and you're not recovering from space sleep." With a wave, the second mate climbed back into the shuttle.

But the second mate hadn't answered his question about people.

"All right, Gumption," Ran muttered. "I'll check things out and babysit." With a scowl, he added, "Pawn Boy moves onto the board."

Used. Maneuvered into taking charge. Annoyance obliterated the other questions Ran had wanted to ask. He crunched across the baked landing surface and up out of the bowl. *Oof!* What *lesser* gravity? He might as well be walking on Jupiter for all the effort it cost him.

Sparse plant life in depressing shades of yellow-greens and red-browns covered the hills. The trail was overgrown as well. He dodged a grabbing branch with curiously fat leaves and jerked back from another. Everything had thorns. Lots of them.

At the top of the slope, he turned in time to watch the shuttle rise and hover over the platform at one side, where it disgorged the crates that had filled the compartment. Then, belly resealed, it rose steeply to skim the hills. Dusty air rushed to fill the shuttle's void, making him cough. The vehicle would already be reconfiguring the compartment into seats for its next load.

A slight descent led him to a creamy-gray structure. Smooth walls bore clear evidence of it having been grown, like the arcologies back in Kansas. Eroded nodules for gathering solar and wind energy covered the exterior walls. The planet's strong winds probably accounted for the pockmarking of its high-set, grimy windows.

He rounded the near corner, and then the next, to find a door. Entering the single, large room, he dropped his bag and looked around. Near the door, empty floor-to-ceiling shelves shaped one wall of a partitioned area, enclosing a toilet and sink. No water came from the taps. He headed back out and continued around. On the next side, he found an attached utility room containing a small tractor—land transport only, useful for moving cargo; also a valve to power on the water.

But where were the people? *Blast* Gumption! The man could have been more informative about what was going on. Had the ship notified anybody? Where were they?

Restless, unwilling to sit around waiting, Ran chose a direction relatively free of plant matter and headed out. The wind cut through his ship knits. He considered returning to pull on his coverall, but adding more steps in this gravity seemed too much effort. Besides, most smart cloth failed to protect from windchill.

Sidestepping between low, prickly plants, he labored down and then up a long gradual rise, huffing and puffing to the top, only to discover more hills. In the opposite direction was that high lonely ridge—maybe thirty-five or forty kilometers distant.

A planet was a big place. Big and all natural.

Ran was a machine guy. He missed the ship's comforting sounds. He missed his pet cleaning bot, that palm-sized, roach-shaped mechanism that came out during sleep cycles to sweep his tiny room. He missed vexing—the virtual exercise necessary to keep muscles and bones in shape—and was sorry he hadn't done lots more.

A rushing noise caused him to turn. Fernlike plants below his perch fluttered, then flattened a microsecond before the heavy gust reached him, full of grit and dust. Agitated plants flung themselves at his legs.

Time to head back,

At last the pale building came into view. A muted roar announced the returning shuttle. Ran panted up toward the shelter. A tall, spiny shrub blocked his way, its stiff branches held out in all directions. Avoiding an inch-long spine, he touched one of its thick leaves. "*Sludge!*" Why did a plant with huge thorns also need invisible prickles? He circled it, continuing past the shelter for a view of the landing area. The others would be arriving soon.

Correction. They'd already arrived, milling around in the dusty air while the shuttle, bucking against the heavy wind, dropped bags beside the cargo and took off. Ran watched it go with a deep sense of loss. He'd felt more at home in the *Orpheus* than any other place he'd ever known.

He had his orders. Time to meet the passengers, whoever they were. Taking a deep breath, he forced his legs again into motion.

"Ran!" came an eager shout.

Pel? Ran's jaw dropped. It couldn't be! Pel was safe back on Earth.

What the *sludge* was Pel doing here?

Hallie

Last to get on the lander, Hallie and Pel were also the last to get off. Wind whipped at the two guys in the lead as they shuffled stiffly down the ramp, exactly how Hallie felt. Those months of hibernation had done this to them all.

Her view of the planet from the open hatch looked no more inviting than that seen through the lander's view screen. An alien world, the sky bluish, the vegetation sickly browns and reds and yellows. Her mother, who prided herself on combining beauty and usefulness in her horticulture, would have been horrified.

There were twelve of them, all zombies wanting only to return to a state of dormancy. "You'll get over it," the ship's medico had said. "Keep eating, drinking and moving, and the remnants of hibernation drugs will dissipate." He had made it sound simple and ordered them to take turns exercising virtually, but Aryn was the only one Hallie had seen going beyond their limited access to virtual exercise. Every time she woke or fell back to sleep, Aryn had been standing on her head or doing a slow tai chi or stretching. Why bother? All Hallie wanted was to go back to bed in hopes that the ship would turn around and take her home.

Home! The other teens expected to find parents here, but not herself and not Pel. Desperation gripped her throat. If only she *knew*. Why include the two of them in this exile? If only she could remember. How could a simple picnic have sent them across the galaxy?

Pel touched her shoulder, a reminder that she'd stopped moving. A hail of windblown particles hit her face as she stepped onto pebbles in a wide depression bare of plants. Taking a deep breath, her nose wrinkled at the creosote-like smell. It was real. No mistake, this exile.

The lander retracted its ramp, rose, and hovered briefly to drop their bags beside a load of containers resting on a shelf at the edge of the landing area. It then took off with a roar, stirring up more grit-laden gusts.

Hallie pushed short, ragged hair out of her eyes, blinked away dirt and who knew what, and sent a mental command to her tooth phone's record switch before remembering—*again*—that her journal wouldn't work here. The recording utility had been a phone add-on for her thirteenth birthday, a gift from her father, who died just before she turned fourteen. That was two years ago—two and a half now—but how could she be any older after sleeping all those months?

She reached for her braid—gone with her memory. Sleeping Beauty with the bad hair job—that was her. Standard airboard instructions were *Find your balance and brace for forward momentum.* No airboards here, but still good advice. She pushed back at the churning in her stomach and forced her heavy feet to move. After the ship's light gravity, this planet business was going to be difficult.

"Ran!" Pel's eager shout brought her whirling around. *Ran.* Engrossed in her miseries, she'd forgotten Ran's unseen presence on the ship.

From the top of the slope, Ran strode down into the landing basin. He wore turquoise, like the ship's crew, but without trim or insignia. Narrowing her eyes, she studied his movements, which were smoother, more graceful than she remembered. Something about him had changed.

Pel grabbed Ran in a hug and Hallie hurried to join them, though even in her rush she wondered at Aryn's wide-eyed stare at Ran.

"Pel, why are you here?" Ran said in amazement. Over Pel's shoulder, Ran's eyes caught hers. His jaw dropped in shock and horror. "Hallie too? What the sludge are they playing at?"

Hallie recoiled. *Filthy spamguts!* What had she done? So busy playing the victim of memory loss when—

On the ship, she'd had nightmares of being chased. Twice she'd been wakened out of space sleep, and a shivering Pel was brought to talk to her. Etched in Hallie's waking memory had been this senseless exile and her sister Liz's words that it was out of her power to change the orders. "If I could, I'm not sure I would." Pel had suggested that her sister was protecting her. Though even now, Hallie couldn't understand a computer logic that demanded kids be *returned to parents forthwith*, and at the same time could tear her and Pel from their own parents!

It always came back to her picnic with Pel and Ran. Pel had been so comforting, telling her of their discussion, of the delicious food, of Ran sailing his model boat. *But she didn't know what happened after!* There'd been some kind of explosion. *What?* Why didn't Pel say? She must be— she *had to be*—the reason the three of them were shipped so far from home. She'd done something horrible. No wonder she couldn't remember.

"Hello, Ran." Brushing hair from her face, Hallie turned back to collect her bag, back to her exile. She grabbed her orange case. Behind her, Ran shouted for everyone to collect their stuff and follow him.

Pel grabbed her arm. "The guy saved your life! He kept you from being burnt to a cinder and you—"

"You never told me! What did I do?" spewed out like vomit. "Did I cause that explosion?" But he just said Ran saved her life—and now she'd hurt him again. "*Filthy spamguts!* I wish I was dead." A gust of wind tried to knock her over.

"Come on." Pel pitched his voice over the wind's sudden howl. "You didn't do anything. Let's get out of this."

The others were streaming up and out of the landing area. "*Ow!*" Something stabbed her shoulder blade. Another hit the soft flesh of her side. The air was full of flying objects.

Darts. More stabbings. More darts.

"Hurry!" Pel pushed her ahead of him. She ran, hugging her bag to her chest. The frond of a bushy plant, forced over by the wind, lashed at her leg making it sting and prickle. The planet's warn off. Some welcome!

They raced along the side of the building and around to a door that thudded shut behind them. The room was large and square. Even in her misery, she recognized the creamy shell-like walls of a building grown, not built, curving up, up out of the matching floor.

Faces, her fellow travelers, turned to look at her.

Mom would tell her not to be impulsive. Well, Mom wasn't here. She marched across to the far wall and hammered on it.

"This. Is. A. Horrible. Place." Every word a thump. "I want to go home."

"We need that wall," said a soft voice. Hands pulled her away. Through tears, Hallie saw the curly red hair of Reba, from the bunk above hers. "Hang on. You'll be okay. Remember what you told me. We're in this together."

She'd said that to Reba during those horrible moments back on the ship while they were all recovering from the oxygen being shut off in their sleep compartment. She'd meant it too, but now— There was nothing okay about this place.

"Hold still," said Aryn. "We've got to remove these thorns."

"Darts," Hallie said. "The planet throws darts. It hates us. I hate it back." Forget *forward momentum*. Brace herself for total misery.

Outside, wind rattled debris against the walls. The planet— shooting more darts.

Pel

Pel watched the girls surround Hallie. *I want to go home*, she'd said. So did he, but his mystery was here. He yanked a plant missile from his left calf—the only one to hit him, even though he'd been behind Hallie during that barrage. It was all his fault, this assault on their lives. Hallie was right. He'd avoided telling her of the explosion and of Ran's horrific burns. She should blame *him*, not herself.

How could he have imagined his *disappeareds* to be off-world when no planets had been approved for colonization? But then, why assume someone capable of stealing people to be law abiding?

Pel snorted. He lacked imagination, that was his problem—one of many problems. He'd only wanted to solve a mystery and get back to classes. But when he got his chance to ask a question of the NODE, that all-knowing computer, he'd jumped at it. So in a way, he'd caused this exile. But for Hallie to be included—*Hallie!*—the victim of an attempted kidnapping that had robbed her of memory? He groaned.

The planet dragged on them all. Hibernation drugs and planetary pull and flying projectiles. *Frass.* What a combination.

When Ran headed back outside, Pel followed, wary of shooting plants. The wind still howled, but its missile warfare had stopped and a rumble of thunder sounded overhead.

Ran leaned against the building, and looked at him. "You knew I was being shipped out?" he said. "What did they tell you?"

"Yeah, but we never caught sight of you. All I knew was that the NODE issued a writ that superseded everything else."

"That much I know. So if I ever get back, I return to the same trouble I left."

"Maybe not." A surge of memory energized Pel. "We have an eyewitness. Jeb got Typhus to make an affidavit of what he saw. I don't think it could be used as evidence, but— Sending us here, they've allowed us some time. No rushing into zombihood, at least."

He blinked at the darkening sky. Here and there clouds broke apart to reveal stars.

Ran said, "Why didn't they just transport the adults back to Earth? *If* they're here. Why send *their* kids?"

"That's had me wondering the same, whether we've been disappeared too."

"Except someone didn't want the ship to arrive," said Ran. "If we're being disappeared, why stop us?"

"Is that why we almost died of carbon dioxide poisoning? They wouldn't tell us what happened."

"Yeah. Someone tried to poison hydroponics to get the ship turned around before we got into hyperspace. When he got caught, his crony got more creative and tried to murder all you sleepers and then me."

"Man, you did have adventures! They woke me a couple of times because Hallie kept having nightmares. That's why we were awake when it happened. Hallie was the one to hit the alarm."

"Thank the stars for Hallie!" said Ran. "If you'd been killed. . ." He blew out his breath and looked skyward. "Problem is, I don't know if they'll manage to repair the original damage to the ship."

A half-shrouded pair of moons hung on a pale horizon. "Spectacular," Pel said, of the interlocking crescents.

"Two moons," Ran agreed. "One smaller, faster and closer, orbits in a third of the time of the more distant one."

"Yeah, when we heard that, I thought one moon could mark a week, the other a month. But I can't remember their orbital periods." Pel rested his head against the wall.

"Pel the analyst," said Ran. "You shouldn't be here, but I'm glad you are."

Pel straightened as a fierce spattering of rain hit them. "The three of us need to talk."

"Sure," Ran said.

The girls had settled beside Hallie against the wall she'd pounded on.

Some of the guys were tossing what looked like a shoe back and forth in a game with no discernible rules.

Pel went over to Hallie and touched her arm. "Hallie, come talk. We need to get this settled. Can't let it go, undertow. It'll grow bigger with time." Yeah, he was nervous, rhyming again. To his relief, she got up.

They headed toward Ran, who was talking with Aryn. Pel remembered meeting Aryn months ago—though it felt like only a few days—while on their way to the space dock.

"We have water," Ran was saying. "I got the pump started earlier. Be nice to find food in that cargo outside."

Aryn knelt beside the floor to ceiling shelves enclosing the toilet nook. "Will this do?" From the bottom-most shelf, she pulled out several stacks of wafers, each contained in edible wrappers.

"I didn't see those!" said Ran.

"They were pushed way back. They're sealed." She opened a packet and tried one. "Dry, tasteless, but edible."

"Emergency rations, maybe?" Pel suggested. "I see you two have met. Sam Suzuki was one of my disappeareds. I'm sure Aryn's his daughter." Dragging himself back to his purpose, he said, "I'm calling a meeting. Let's find a place to sit."

Pel waved toward the nearest empty section of wall. They *had* to be friends again. But when he opened his mouth to apologize to Hallie, Hallie moved to touch Ran's arm.

"I'm sorry, Ran. When I saw you today, I just suddenly felt so guilty."

"*You* guilty? You were the one being carried off. It was my actions that caused—"

She cut Ran off. "But I don't know *why*. No one would tell me any-thing! Only that an aircar exploded. And that you were in the hospital, burned."

"My fault," Pel said. "I spooked them off the ground. Without my interference, Ran might've stopped them."

"Not." Ran's flat denial allowed no disagreement. "They had all the fighting skills I lack." He sank onto his heels and looked up at Pel. "You called this meeting."

Pel slid down the wall and scrubbed hands across his face. Keep them on track. "Okay," he said. "Let's start from the beginning. The picnic, I mean." He glanced at Hallie where she sat, her legs crossed, her back against the wall, and shook his head to dislodge distractions.

"Let's stick to the picnic for now. The kidnappers sprayed Hallie with Doramnis, leaving her with no memory of what happened. On the ship, she had nightmares"—Pel noted Ran's intent face—"and they woke me a couple of times to talk to her. I didn't want to give her worse dreams, so I didn't tell her everything. If I left the wrong impression, I'm sorry, Hallie."

She threw him a half smile.

"Truth is, I didn't want to remember those parts either. But we need to pool our stories."

"All right." Ran drew a breath. "Hallie, at the park, I was sailing that model boat. You stopped to tell me Pel was asleep and you were going for a walk. I don't know how much time went by. Quite a while. Then you screamed. That's when, suddenly, I remembered hearing an aircar. Some-thing about it had bothered me. I started running."

He rubbed his neck. "If only I could've gotten to you faster."

"Faster?" Pel broke in. "Man, I've never seen anyone move as fast as you did. I was still hearing that scream and you were gone!"

"No spam?" Ran's eyes looked as haunted as Hallie's.

"For real. Those *perversos*—Jeb's term—weren't about to waste any time." Hallie's brother-in-law had been Pel's only source of information and sanity. "If you hadn't stopped them, they'd have gotten away with her. Jeb had nothing but good to say about you."

That brought Ran's head up. "Jeb?"

"Yeah. He came to see me while I was locked up. I guess they wouldn't let anyone talk to you in the hospital." He detected a slight easing in Ran's expression.

"Anyway," Pel picked up his end of the tale, "after we ate, I fell asleep." He stifled a yawn. "I hadn't slept well all that week. When I woke, Hallie, you were gone. Ran was sailing his boat. My head was still full of that question I'd made to the NODE, but I should have gone to look for you. Ran leaped up and took off before I even registered your scream. I was on the far side of the pool. I followed, but got tangled in the shrubs. When I finally caught up, two guys were trying to load you into their car. Ran appeared and fought them. One threw him down. I was still too far away. I yelled. They tossed you on the ground and took off." He shuddered. "I can still see it happening. The car disappeared, then reappeared, and exploded. Ran threw himself on top of you. I tried to put out the flames." He looked at his hands.

Ran said, "I cut straight across and saw a Harly Spark. Obviously a direflier. I'm sure it was the same one that nearly killed me the day I first met Jeb. Two guys were carrying you, Hallie. I had to keep them from taking off and there wasn't enough light left to find the car's brain"—he looked directly at Hallie—"so I cut the fuel line. I needed time for the fuel to drain out. I tried to stop them. But they both had fight training.

I couldn't—"

"The newscasts said they were Peacers," Pel said. "They'd had plenty of training."

Ran gave a nod. "With only me to fight, they'd have taken her. *Your* appearance caused them to leave Hallie behind."

"So if I knew why they grabbed me," Hallie said, "we'd have the whole picture. If they had something to do with the bombing—"

"*They* were the ones at fault," Ran exploded. "Whatever you did or didn't do, *they* were the criminals."

"But I felt it!" Hallie said. "When I first saw you, I felt so guilty, so despicable."

"Are you sure those were *your* feelings?" Pel said. "Maybe it was that amnesiac spray they hit you with." He was glad they'd finally shared what happened—but that scene of chaos, Ran's body in flames, the smell of burning flesh— *Aargh!* "It's a miracle you survived, Ran. You look well."

Ran's crooked grin appeared. "While on ship, I was forced to come to terms with my virtual reality phobia. It took months, and the medico was threatening to space-sleep me for the rest of the trip. But I did it! Right before his deadline. After that I got in a lot of vexing."

Hallie broke into Pel's congratulations. "*That's* what I saw when you came down the trail. Virtual exercise smoothed out your movement patterns. That's wonderful!"

"What happened to you both while I was in the hospital?" Ran asked.

Pel let his eyelids sag. "Security kept me locked up until they signed me over to Turner. He's the InfoTech guy who logged my question with the NODE. He flew me to catch the shuttle and gave me a databank, on a time lock."

His eyes popped open; he slapped his pockets. "It's supposed to have the NODE's answer to my question. And Ty's affidavit. You've got to see it."

Pel scrabbled through his pack. "Here. Just watch this. Affidavit." He waited for the gold-backed device to unfold into a cube the size of his fist. It remained flat.

His mouth opened, closed. "Is it dead?" He handed it to Ran.

Ran held it, his eyes narrowed in concentration. "It's definitely alive. An expensive one. With that surface, it ought to charge itself almost anywhere, from any source." He returned it.

Pel stared at his databank. "So it's still viable?"

"It's working," Ran said. "You said a time lock? What will it produce when time's up?"

"Wish I knew," said Pel.

Hallie had pillowed her head on his pack. Pel awkwardly tucked the device away. "Maybe it was a trick to get me to go quietly. We were in the air heading for Denver Spaceport before Turner told me where I was going. I was freaked. But I *did* see Ty's affidavit."

"Tell me again what you asked the NODE," Ran said.

Pel swallowed a yawn. "The reason we're all here is my fault. Because of my question. I meant to say that in the first place."

"What was your question?" Ran urged.

"How do the following . . ." He stifled another yawn. "No. It was *'How do these words— Whistlestop, ThymeSage, Crumbling Pyramid, and Rosemary—relate to the disappearance of the following people: Sam Suzuki, Geraldine Ramirez, Father Dominic Rivera, Taylor Layton, and Gabe Fletcher; where are these people now, and where are their offspring?'*"

They were here because of that question, whatever logic the NODE had fixed on. The other teens were the offspring of his *disappeareds* and of others he hadn't identified. He was sure of it.

Pel wanted this mystery resolved. He wanted to get himself and Hallie back home again. He wanted to get back to safe, peaceful studies and his familiar village. But his mystery was here, and he was finally going to get some answers.

Ran

Pel had settled against his backpack beside Hallie. All the teens seemed to be under a sleeping spell, most of the girls along one wall, the boys on the other side. Lights were dimming due to the lack of movement.

Ran forced himself to his feet, muscles stiffening from his earlier explorations. Lights brightened again. Their talk had reminded him of his physical shortcomings due to his previous inability to learn from virtual reality. While vexing on the ship, he'd been obsessed by that mountain, wanting only to reach its top. Too bad he hadn't been obsessed by martial arts instead. He'd failed to stop that ship saboteur and, before that, those kidnappers at the park.

He went out and circled the building, but nowhere could he spot manmade lights. Only those two moons, now masked by clouds, and a few stars. He needed height, maybe from the rooftop.

Ran went back inside. The wind's patterings against the building were quieter now. He found a spot near his friends, glad to succumb to gravity.

Tomorrow he could examine the cargo.

DAY TWO

Decisions

Ran

Daylight filtered through the pockmarked windows of the shelter.

Ran stifled a groan as he pushed himself up from the hard floor. Gravity again. The only way through that weighty battle was to fight it. The other teens still slept, some huddled together, some solitary. Hallie's left arm rested on Pel's chest, her head against his shoulder, with Aryn, finder of those wafers, nearby.

Where were the people who were supposed to be here? Second Mate Gumption had waved him off as if the shelter was the answer. Thanks for nothing, Gumption!

Ran longed for the familiar surround and machines of the *Orpheus*. When boarding the shuttle, Gumption had said, "We've been ordered to do some survey work out here. We'll swing back by, but I don't know when." Survey work? First they had to clean out the damage done to hydroponics by those saboteurs.

He pulled on the gray coveralls he'd worn back in Dodge over the ship knits he'd slept in. Outside, the wind blasted at him. He started up the little tractor, drove down to the landing area, and stacked three of the meter-square crates on the tractor's bed. On his return, the tractor treads completed the job of clearing intrusive plants from the trail.

He dragged the crates inside and pried one open, not caring if he made noise. It was daytime after all. The others should wake.

The first crate held powders for a food fabricator. Even if they had one, he doubted if the eroded energy paints coating the building would be sufficient to run it. The shelter barely powered its water pump and dim lighting. Nor were the food fab inserts useful without a fab; since those chemicals and reagents required machine processing.

The next crate contained packets of seeds. The third held nourishment for an organic computer. What blockhead had chosen this cargo? Unless someone knew a lot more about the place than he did.

He grabbed a couple of wafers and drove again to the landing site. Parking the tractor, he crossed the depression in the opposite direction from yesterday's explorations, soon regretting not driving, since the tractor would have protected him from grasping thorns.

Like yesterday, he saw little from the hill he climbed. He shivered even in his doubled clothing. Stringy gray clouds gusted overhead. No signs of people. In the far distance, a line of purplish blue had to be one of the mountain ranges striping the land. Reluctantly, he turned back, stepping over low-lying plants. The taller ones whipped at him, often contrary to the wind's orientation.

He drove back to the shelter with the next batch of crates. This time he stacked the three in a rough staircase against the outer wall, clambered up, and pulled himself onto the roof. Good! He'd guessed right about the ridge's direction.

Leaving the steps in place, he went inside and rubbed his chilled fingers. A tap on his shoulder startled him. Aryn collected a dry wafer from the shelf behind him.

"You're the only one up?" he whispered.

She nodded. "Find anything?"

"Nothing. They could be on the far side of the planet for all I know. How're we supposed to find them?"

"Someone's here," she said. "We're not alone."

"How do you know that?"

"I dreamed about finding them, just before I woke this morning."

He stared.

Aryn's cheeks reddened.

"Yeah. Well, why are you the only one not sleeping?" Ran asked.

"They said to eat and drink and move. I know my body. I guess my training has been more extensive than theirs."

Ran considered. "In other words, they need to work off the drugs? We'd better wake them."

She agreed and went to the closest sleeper.

Ran turned the other direction. Groans met his efforts. He grabbed a container from the food additives crate. The cloud of particles made him cough as he poured the granules into the edible—but not waterproof—wafer packet they'd emptied the night before. Then he filled the empty container with water.

"Okay," he told Aryn. "You take some wafers. We'll force-feed next."

He shook a shoulder roughly. When he got a response, he said,

"Drink." After a few swallows, Aryn followed up with a quiet "Eat," and pushed a bit of wafer between jaws, leaving a larger piece in their hands. By the time they got halfway around the room, a few were sitting up and munching. Others lay back, jaws moving.

Ran shook Pel. "Okay, Mom," Pel groaned.

"Not your mom," said Ran. "Just drink and chew."

Accepting a wafer, Pel's eyes closed again. "How could they dump us without even notifying anyone? What's going on?"

"I wish I knew," said Ran.

Pel's eyes opened. "Didn't you ask?"

"The second mate waved me to the shelter and flew off to bring the bunch of you," said Ran. "Didn't *you* ask?"

"They said someone would be along—but that someone was you."

"Aryn dreamed about people and says we need to find them." Ran didn't trust dreams, but he sure agreed with the searching part.

"Hmm." Pel looked at Aryn. "Did you dream about where to look?"

Aryn shook her head.

"I went exploring this morning," Ran said. "I couldn't see anything from the near hills. Aryn is the only one of you who doesn't sleep all the time. How come?"

"Good question." Pel propped himself on his elbow to address Aryn. "What's your secret? Let's call a meeting of minds."

That was a start. Ran headed out to collect more crates, satisfied that Pel would put his brain to work on the problem. And maybe he'd get some help with the crates.

Hallie

Hallie stared at the ceiling. Morning. The act of sipping water and eating that tasteless wafer had broken some kind of sleep spell. Too bad. Nothing had changed. They were still here, wherever *here* was.

That picnic—*her idea*—had left her life in shambles. No matter what Pel and Ran said, *something* had happened to turn her entire world upside down and inside out, and she wanted to know what and why. *Spamguts!* That was the same thing she'd said when Liz told her not to investigate that bombing, and she'd gone ahead and done it.

A bustle of activity caught her attention, and she rolled over to get off the floor.

Aryn the active was leading them in yoga. "Keep reaching high; send all your energy up through your fingertips."

Hallie groaned. Her arms fell to her sides like lead weights, but everyone else was obediently following Aryn's direction. What made Aryn the leader?

The one who does, leads, of course. Aryn had been exercising since they first woke on the ship. *Forward momentum*, remember? For now, just do.

Hallie reached her arms high. Fight the planet's gravity. Fight her desire to be moss or amoeba or anything that didn't get uprooted and shot across the universe.

Some rapid rounds of sun salutations left her breathless, more alive and awake.

When Pel called them all to a meeting, she joined the lopsided circle, leaning back against a crate.

Pel scowled at his little device for note taking and recording, and returned it to his pocket. "I don't know everyone's name. Are we all strangers to each other?"

The tall, dark-haired teen with hawk-like nose and narrow face waved at a couple of others. "Not the same school, but I saw some of us in music competitions."

"Get together later." Pel cut off a discussion of what music they'd brought. "Anyone else?"

Strange, thought Hallie. She knew the girls were all from near Dodge. It looked like the boys were too.

Pel continued. "Why don't each of you say your name and tell us how you feel."

The tall musician snapped his fingers. "No. Let's start with a game. Say your name and some word that describes you, beginning with the same letter. Easier to remember. I'm Rhythmic Ramon because I love music, especially the beat. The next one repeats my name and says theirs."

"Rhythmic Ramon, I'm Artsy Aryn, because I love to draw."

Hallie ran through words—*hallowed, hollow*—empty for sure.

"Romping Reba. My mother—foster mother—called me that because I like to run." Short Reba with her red hair had the palest complexion.

Hungry, haunted, hung up. Oh, help! She needed a dictionary.

"Lizard-loving Leif." Leif, the other red head, had light mocha skin.

"Persistent Pel, because I've followed a mystery all this way."

Dear Pel. Persisting last night to get the three of them to talk, persisting today to get them working together. *Harmless, hurried*. Just in time. She took a breath.

"Hurried Hallie. I wanted to push through tertiary asap. Now in a hurry to get home."

"Dancing Dacey." The slim, dark girl's hair straggled out of a messy bun.

"Lutenist Luisa, but I could only bring my flute."

As tall as Hallie, Luisa had thick, black hair in a single braid. Hallie wanted her own braid back, the one she'd lost along with her memory.

"Tired Tesia," was next smallest, after Reba, with dark hair as long as Luisa's.

"Not good enough," said Ramon. "You need something more unique."

"I'm too tired," Tesia said.

They repeated, "Tired Tesia."

"Manager Manuelo, because I like to take charge."

Maybe so, but Pel had taken charge of this meeting, Hallie thought with satisfaction.

"I love all animals, but *Aminal* Amado sounds more mellifluous than Animal Amado."

"Nimble Nick," said the smallest of the boys. "I got hauled out of an airball game and told I was being returned to my parents. So where are they? I had to miss the tournament."

Ran was last, standing near an unopened crate, looking impatient, neither with them nor apart. "I don't know. All I can think of is robotic or rocket, and neither is me."

"What about Repairman Ran?" Pel suggested.

Ran repeated that and all the names along with the group.

The teens still sprawled in their circle. Everyone looked as mopey and dopey and anxious as Hallie felt. Action was needed. She straightened.

"We need a plan. We've got to find the adults who are supposed to be here. Did anyone bring a com?" She'd never had a toothache, but the tooth with her embedded phone ached with her longing to call home.

"They don't work," answered three in unison.

Ran opened the crate he'd been leaning against. "There may not be infrastructure to support communication," he said, peering inside, "or it may be because of the magnetic storms, enormous ones, on the star here."

"They wouldn't let me bring my airboard," complained Nick. "With airboards we could go look."

Almost in unison several said, "No way to charge them up."

"So how do we search?" Hallie asked.

"The only ones who seem physically capable of running a search," Pel said, "are Ran and Aryn."

Ran opened and closed his little utility knife. "I want to go search, but first we need to take inventory. Find out what we've got to work with. I could use help bringing up the rest of the crates."

Hallie stiffened. "You can't go out there. Those flying darts will murder you!"

"No signs of poison in anyone—" said Aryn.

"How do you know?" Hallie broke in, remembering her friend Cass's medical studies. "It could be a slow, systemic infection or something. We know nothing of what's here."

"We'll put on layers and take our chances. We need to find the people," Aryn insisted.

"Those thorns don't fly all the time," Ran said. "Only that once, so far. I think it was the sudden wind shift that did it."

Hallie settled back against her crate, pushing short hairs out of her face. No going back. No shuttle returning to say, "Sorry, wrong planet," or

"Let's make sure someone's home before we maroon you here by yourselves." She wished again that she could record on her tooth phone's journal-function, a medium that would accept her turmoil without screaming back about its own. Talking to others was different. They answered back, leaving no time for her own words to reverberate.

Stop whining. Survival came first. Make a list: Inventory the crates. Find food.

She pushed herself up off the floor and went to help.

Pel

They took turns hauling crates with Ran, and Pel discovered how very out of shape he was after space sleep. Maybe he should do rounds of push-ups instead of yoga.

Inventory completed, the teens gathered for a second meeting. Pel was grateful for the lack of panic. Maybe they were all too tired. *He* certainly was. Hardly anything to eat, gravity to adjust to, drugs to work out of their systems.

"We were told someone would come for us. What if something went wrong?" Nick, the youngest as well as the smallest, asked the first question but far from the last.

"Those cracker things won't last long. Then what?" said Ramon.

"What if the ship's message wasn't received?" "Are we in the wrong place?" "Are they all dead?"

"Okay," Pel interrupted. "We're all wondering. Meanwhile, what can we do to draw attention to our being here?"

"Stand on the rooftop and everybody scream," said one of the girls.

"No one within earshot," said Ran. "I've gone off in two directions and found nothing. I want to explore further, taking that tractor to cut through the plants."

Red-haired Reba said, "Show us which directions you already went. We could go out in teams for half a day, turn around and return."

"It's all hills around here. We need higher ground. That's why I want to head for that ridge, and it's a lot more than a half day away," said Ran.

"Not alone," said Pel. "It needs to be two. If you run into trouble, you need one to go for help or bring back a report." Even with his eyes closed, Pel knew Ran was scowling. Ran would want to do it on his own. "Two," Pel insisted. "If one gets lost, how do we know where to find you? Or if you fall in a hole, who'll pull you out?"

"And if both fall?"

"One boosts the other out. You know what I mean. Two, sticking together, can keep each other on target."

"Not again!" Ran yelled, jumping up. "If you lose me, you're still okay here. If I take someone else along and lose that person, I have to live with it! And that person's parents have to live with it."

Pel straightened. The guy was a hero! He'd rescued Hallie. He'd done *nothing* to feel guilty about, just as Hallie had done nothing wrong. How could he convince Ran how wrong he was? Pel opened his mouth, but Aryn spoke first.

"You won't lose anyone."

"I can move faster, farther, on my own."

Pel stood to face Ran. "We won't be better off if we all starve. This argument is going nowhere. *Two* to search."

"Then let's get moving," Ran said. "We've wasted enough time."

"Better start asap," said Ramon. "I want out of here."

Not trusting Ran's sudden capitulation, Pel decided to stick close. "You plan to take the tractor?"

"It's slow, but it'll carry more water. That way, we can go farther. And it's small enough to get through tight places. Some of this plant life is lethal." Ran rubbed his fingers. "The day is already part gone. I want to head for that ridge. You can see it from the roof."

By midafternoon, Pel stood with the others to see Ran and Aryn off. The crates had revealed little of use beyond lengths of tough, hard-to-damage smart cloth that kept a body warm or cool, except in wind. Kansas winds, this planet's winds—all part of some cosmic joke, Pel decided.

The sky was a soft blue-green with only a scattering of clouds. Sharp gusts promised greater winds to come. The two searchers sat on the open seat, their supplies tied on to the tractor bed, including a length of gleaming metal to signal with, claimed from the crate of hardware fab inserts. But so many things could go wrong.

Pel dragged himself back inside the shelter. *On a wild goose chase, no humans any place; exiles lost to the human race.*

So-o-o-o tired. He wanted his own bed in his own quiet village, even with villagers telling him, "We told you so." He wanted nothing more than tertiary classes to worry about.

He'd made a promise to return home. Some day. Some way.

Would he end up breaking that promise too?

Aryn

Aryn took her place on the tractor. Ran thumped down on the seat beside her with a wave of hostility. "Why didn't you tell them no?" he snarled. "Let me go alone."

He threw the switch and the tractor trundled off. The little hauler that Ran called a tractor was all-purpose, with a front-end loader and a short bed behind, to which they'd tied their water containers, wafers, and rolls of smart cloth.

She waved at the teens remaining behind, hair whipping her cheek, then said, "Because Pel is right. Two can watch each other's backs."

As they crested a hill, she stood, clinging to the seat to drink in the shades of sky, textures of plants, curves of dunelike hills. Her fingers itched for pencil and sketch pad.

"What do you see?" Ran asked.

She knew the correct answer was *nothing*. "Beauty," she said as she sat down.

"Beauty? This desert place?"

She tried to see it through his eyes. Sparse plants. Rocks. Dry and barren land. A wind that wanted to blow them far away, but still— "The colors are amazing. So subtle. I bet that rock"—she pointed—"could be ground up into pigments for paint." She couldn't name the rocks, but their tally of colors included tones of olive, ochre, sienna . . .

"And you'd paint this place? No paper, no brushes?" His voice was dismissive.

Aryn stiffened. "I have a pad, back there with my things, but I'd paint on rocks with my fingers if that was all I had." Breathing fast, she surprised herself by her own vehemence. It was true. She had to paint. And she really did have to paint this place. Leaving Earth had cut her off from classes, art teachers, and especially her foster family. A longing for the only home she knew brought an ache to her throat.

"And you're not afraid to be here with me?" Ran's hostility seemed to have eased.

"It's my choice. And no, I'm not afraid of you."

"We're probably going to get ourselves killed. Aren't you afraid of anything?"

"Of course. Of coming all this way and not finding my parents. We all are. What if something has happened to them?"

"But we're here now. Stupid NODE with its orders. Where are they?"

"There *are* people here. I'm sure of it."

"You dreamed it. How do you know it wasn't wishful thinking?"

She shook her head. "More than that. A gut feeling."

"Feelings," he said.

"You have feelings," she challenged. "You have feelings for machines. What are your feelings telling you?"

The silence between them lengthened. His mouth twisted. "That I don't want to be responsible for any more deaths!" The last yelled word was swallowed by the wind.

He must feel guilty for the deaths of those kidnappers, she thought. Actions have consequences but what would have happened if he hadn't acted? "Pel told me what happened—and I listened to you three last night. But what about the living?"

"What do you mean, 'the living'? The others back there have food, water, shelter. If I die, no one else is hurt."

Ah. That was it. "You've been hurt—a lot."

"No, I haven't. My burns healed." He kept his eyes straight ahead. "Why are we here?" He sounded calmer. "It makes no sense."

"I don't know," she said slowly, "but Pel thinks he knows who my father is. He's so sure this place is the answer to his mystery." Her gaze lingered on Ran's profile.

"If we can find them." He threw her a glance.

His resistance to her presence shaped a wall between them, but the fragile thread telling her they weren't alone on this planet held. She'd wondered about her real parents for so many years, who she resembled, what had become of them, what sort of people they were.

The tractor rattled and rumbled over rocky ground.

"You care about art. That must be your strong suit." Ran sounded less angry.

They jolted over a stony, dry watercourse. She was very conscious of him beside her.

"Art is how I know myself. I feel crippled without it." She'd been able to pack only one drawing pad and a few pencils. Not drawing was like losing a limb, unable to understand what the wordless part of her brain wanted to say, except through pictures. After months of ship sleep, her art classes back on Earth seemed distant, yet almost like yesterday.

She looked again at Ran's profile and let memory take over, returning her to Figure Drawing class, with its warm scent of growing plants in that rooftop conservatory. She heard again the chatter of her fellow students as she threaded her way through the tangle of easels and legs to take a seat beside her friend Samantha. Immersed in her work, she'd been startled by the teacher's voice.

"I can't say you didn't look this time. But who is that?"

Her charcoal strokes portrayed the model's back accurately, but instead of the back of his head, she had drawn a profile: ear close to the head, straight nose, strong chin.

Ran's voice drew her back to the tractor and this strange planet. "How can you be so calm about riding off into nowhere with a stranger?"

"You're not a stranger. And your friend Pel trusts you."

"What does he know?"

"A lot, judging from the stories he tells. But there's another reason." She hesitated, but knew she had to tell him. "I never saw you until we arrived here, but several weeks before being told I was leaving, I drew your picture."

He turned to stare at her. "What d'you mean? How could you draw me?"

"In Figure Drawing class. I was sketching a male model, but I drew your profile, not the back of his head. I brought it along. I can show you when we get back. And one other time, I drew a landscape when I was supposed to be drawing a female model. I still haven't found that place, but maybe it's here. It tells me we're linked in some way."

"Huh!" He seemed more surprised than disbelieving. "Yeah, I'd like to see that. Several weeks before? I wonder if you drew me before or after Pel's question to the NODE." Shaking his head, he said, "That doesn't mean you should have come on this hunt for lost colonists or miners or whatever they call themselves."

"It will be all right." She itched for her sketchbook.

Hallie

They were in a no-win situation. Ran and Aryn had gone to search with no way of contacting the other teens unless and until they reached the ridge. Everyone was struggling to adjust to this new, strong gravity. They exercised to rid themselves of hibernation drugs, but exercise brought hunger. And their supply of wafers was limited. The rule became drink as much water as possible—both to wash out the drugs and to control appetite.

Hallie gulped down more water, but all she could think of were the lunches Uncle Jack programmed on the food fab—spicy, cheesy-textured dishes, hot and filling and tasty.

She groaned. *Don't* think of food. *Ha!* Do something.

While Tesia, Dacey, and Luisa practiced a series of dance moves, Hallie caught Reba's eye and waved. They met at the floor-to-ceiling shelves, empty except for those pitifully few wafers. "Let's figure out how long we can make these things last," Hallie said.

"Lucky they don't taste good enough to tempt," said Reba.

Hallie snorted. Small amusements were better than nothing.

Pel clapped his hands and announced a meeting to set up a watch from the rooftop; short watches because of the windchill. Tonight, assuming Ran and Aryn wouldn't reach their goal, the watch would end at full dark. There was always a chance they might spot lights in some other direction.

That settled, Hallie let Reba explain the wafer-rationing system they'd decided on. Munching her evening wafer, she ventured outside. They had water. Food was the main issue. On the least windy side of the shelter, she examined the closest plant—a long, yucca-like spike covered in prickles. Using a sharp rock, she carefully scraped off thick skin to reach the pulp. With a fingertip, she touched the moist interior and brought it to her nose. Its faint odor smelled of green, almost a grassy scent. She brought her finger to the tip of her tongue.

"Ugh!" Hallie began spitting. She rushed to rinse her mouth over and over. This was getting complicated. To test all varieties of plants, they would need teams to identify and sample. They should also try boiling those same plants to see if that removed toxins.

They'd probably end up poisoning themselves. Ran and Aryn had better succeed.

Ran

The tractor crawled along at a fast walking pace. Ran drove toward landmarks he'd noted from the roof, demonstrating to Aryn how he used the tractor's otherwise meaningless compass to keep them in a straight line until they could gain a visual on the ridge.

Aryn stood again, twisting one way and then the other, wind whipping her hair. The terrain leveled out through a wide but not really flat valley. Ran looked back.

"If the tracks last, we can retrace our route. Otherwise, it's the compass." That trail from the landing depression must have been carved by a tractor, but any tracks had been destroyed by wind. "Just don't touch anything. I don't think Earth deserts have anything on this place." His finger still throbbed from its first contact with a plant.

He steered uphill, downhill, trying to avoid all but the smallest plants.

According to the second mate, this was an illicit AstroMining project. AstroMining was an offshoot from the defunct Atlas Corporation. Was Earth even now going after AstroMining's solar system enterprises? The World Court's *Rules of Engagement with New Planets* said nothing was to be damaged, burnt, used for any reason until a full survey had taken place. Survey estimations ranged from fifty to a hundred years. If Astro-Mining had wanted something from this planet, it was no wonder they'd kept it secret. He wondered what they mined. And where?

Tired of circling thoughts, he said, "Talk to me."

"I'm not much of a talker. I jump from one disconnected thought to another. They connect in my head, of course. My mother used to say—"

"Foster mother?"

"Yes, but they loved me as their own. Their families came from India during the First Ocean Surge and stayed. She used to say my thoughts connect like jumps from star to star, leaving no trail."

"You lived in Dodge?" he asked.

"Yes, in the Indus Arcology, out near the Art Institute. I've been studying there since the end of secondary. What do you know about your family?"

"Nothing. I examined my chip more than once—no DNA, not even a name. Kenelm was the name of my first foster family. Ransom Kenelm? Sounds like begging to be rescued, doesn't it?"

"What about your foster parents?" she asked.

"I had several sets." Ran shrugged. "My own fault, I guess. Never a problem with my foster mothers; it was always the foster fathers I fought."

"I wonder why."

"Yeah." He wondered too. He glanced at Aryn before eyeing the countryside.

"Doug and Marge were my last set. For years, he hounded me about school, about how I had to work harder than the other kids because of my VR phobia. After secondary, he kept pushing me to apply for tertiary. I got fed up and left. But, living in Workless, I realized Doug had been right most of the time; I just didn't want to be bossed. Like, Doug pushed me to apply for tertiary, but he sure didn't tell me how to manage the virtual aspects of it. Pel and Hallie had some good suggestions and I was getting ready to put in a late application when the kidnapping happened."

He shifted his shoulders and was reminded of the healed skin beneath his coverall. "I wish I knew why those two were shipped out. I was all braced to be a zombie for the rest of my life. But there's no reason for—"

"You're still under age. I don't think they can do that legally." Her watchful eyes flicked in his direction. "What was schooling without virtual like?"

Ran grimaced. "Teachers learned to assign books and flat-screen time while the rest of the class were laughing or singing or wrapped up in whatever kind of VR."

"What happened whenever you put the contacts on?"

"It was always the same. I'd hear a scream and the connection would break. On the ship, the medico insisted I exercise virtually. I put on the contacts—three times a ship day—for weeks. I would hear Hallie scream and feel this rush of adrenaline to go to her rescue. But *Hallie's* wasn't the original scream. The ship's medico told me to figure out why it happened, but I could never find a memory. I think I was too young to remember."

"But you managed to overcome it. How?"

Ran checked the tractor's compass and looked around, scanning for signs of humans. Aryn was easy to talk to, maybe too easy. Distracting.

Aryn stood and turned, checking the terrain. *She* was watching. All right then.

"It still amazes me. If I listened to *Orpheus's* machinery and kept my focus on the ship when I put on the contacts, I could stay in. My tiny cubicle stopped feeling like solitary confinement once I started class work and exercise. I loved vexing. There was one mountain climb I wanted to reach the end of, but never did."

The tractor's shadow stretched out before them as it crawled across a slowly rising landscape. The ridge came in and out of view. Occasionally, they descended into a dry wash or arroyo and then climbed back up the other side.

"Let's keep going till dark," Ran said.

"We need to see the ground and what's around us when we stop."

"As long as possible then. You say when. We could dip into an arroyo free of plants."

"As long as there are no clouds," came her slow answer.

Ran agreed. During Earth's most turbulent climate periods, extreme drought had alternated with some terrifying flash floods throughout the world.

"Can you steer awhile?" he asked. "I'd like to get off and move."

"Sure. We can take turns."

He jogged behind, his head bowed against a steadily increasing wind.

He bumped into the tractor. "Why did you stop?"

"Look." She pointed toward the ridge. "Is someone actually out in that wind signaling?"

A beam of blinking light reflected off the dust in the air. Ran studied the ridge crest, memorizing the rock slide directly beneath the beam's source.

"It's not natural," he said, "with or without a human. But where are they aiming?"

There were too many hills in the way, and the wind had grown colder. Were they going in the wrong direction? He got back on the tractor seat and pulled part of a cloth roll over their shoulders. "Let's get as close as we can before dark."

When dusk cast deep shadows, they found a shallow arroyo with plants growing on its upper slopes. The sky was clear, but during a pause of wind the air felt heavy, sultry.

He estimated the ridge to be less than a half day of travel. They should be able to reach it and even climb to the top before nightfall tomorrow.

DAY THREE

Search

Ran

Ran burrowed deeper into his doubled roll of smart cloth, but the brisk wind funneling up the shallow wash cut through. He sighed and poked his head out. It was still dark. The faster of the two moons had passed overhead. One star after another blinked out. He sat up.

Above him on the tractor bed, Aryn stirred. "What's happening?"

"Weather moving in," Ran said. "Clouds."

"Uh-oh."

He leaned back against the tractor, scanning the horizon for lights until a short spurt of stinging rain and hail forced him back under his covers.

When dawn arrived with garish purple-red streaks, Ran got up. The brief rain had dampened the dust. The air smelled fresh, with a metallic taste. He climbed out of the wash to find a secluded spot to relieve himself.

On his return, he found Aryn shaking out his coverings.

"Sorry," Ran said. "You shouldn't have to do mine. I just needed to go."

She tucked the cloth neatly in the tractor bed. "You can dig out some food while I take my turn."

Wafers and water—*bleah!* Ran craved ship food or even the lousy meals at Workless. At least they'd been filling. A picture of Hallie's Aunt Bet, her hands full of greens and tomatoes, flashed into his mind. His mouth watered for one of *her* meals.

The sky was still heavily overcast, purples and reds fading to deep gray.

When Aryn got back he said, "Decision time. Continue or go back?" though he had no intention of going anywhere before climbing to the ridge.

"Weather passes." She munched her wafer and stretched, ending in a full back bend. Ran winced, wondering if she'd checked the ground for thorns first. Completing her flip, Aryn stood. "We're chasing that signal. Let's continue."

Once out of the wash, the wind blasted their right sides. A cap of clouds crawled down the ridge toward them. Occasionally Ran or Aryn dropped off the tractor to stretch and jog.

The wind shifted to their backs, along with an intermittent pelting rain.

Aryn was an uncomplaining companion. Ran kept wondering how she could have drawn his face. When he picked up a smart machine and knew whether it was live or not, he was actually touching it. But to draw something unseen?

They descended to a broad, sandy riverbed, possibly a mile across.

Plants had taken hold of all but the river's centermost meander.

"This must have shipped a lot of water once," Ran said as they started across. The wind whipped down the channel, chilling their left sides. They remained on board, letting the vehicle plow through loose sand.

Halfway across, Aryn leaned forward. "Stop."

Ran obeyed. "What?"

"That pool. I don't trust it. We need to go around."

"It's shallow," he protested. "Only a puddle." And a big detour.

"Maybe." She got down and wandered until she found a rock as big as her fist. She tossed it a few feet into the pool. The stone sat there.

"What—" Ran began. The rock disappeared with a *bloop*. "Okay. You win."

When he circled the pool and drove across wet rocks, she made no protest, instead commenting on plant colors. She broke off to point. "Look."

A ripple of movement crossed their path to dive into a hole in the far bank. Behind them came a shrill whistle. At least two creatures. Same species? Predator and prey?

Once out of the riverbed, Ran and Aryn resumed their upward trend. Midmorning, clouds lifted off the ridge. The wind blew colder and fiercer, even as the sky brightened. Their route grew steeper.

"Turquoise," said Aryn.

"What?"

"The sky has a turquoise tint to it. I wonder why."

"Looks blue to me," Ran said. "I wonder how high that ridge is." It loomed above them, dwarfing Dodge City's half-kilometer-high arcologies two or three times over.

The battering wind grew more furious. Aryn pulled out one of the smart-cloth lengths and wrapped it around their shoulders.

Another wash appeared, a steep-sided channel. Something pinged against the tractor.

Ran jerked. "Ow! Get down!" He pushed Aryn to the floor. More pings sounded. He steered straight down the side of the channel.

Aryn cried, "No!"

The tractor slid to the bottom and stopped. Gusts swirled around them but without those attacking thorns, to Ran's relief. "Why did you say *no*?"

Her eyes were wide, her breath fast. "There's danger down here."

He could barely hear her over the wind. "There's danger up there!" More thorns flew above them. "One got me." He pulled up his pants leg looking for it.

"Another of those shooting thorns." Aryn carefully pulled it loose and examined it before handing it to Ran. "Not the same kind that I pulled out of Hallie."

He turned the projectile over. "Aerodynamic. The plants must actually shoot them. I wonder how. Funny way of propagating."

"If they're seeking water, what happens when they find your blood?"

"Take your pick. I'd be herbicide or fertilizer." Her laugh made him feel witty. "Some change in wind velocity or direction must tell the plants when to let go."

She twisted around, eyeing the sides of the wash. "No wonder the creatures live underground. Are the people underground too?"

"Either that or running around in armor."

They sat while seed projectiles continued to fly, some lodging in the upper wall of the wash.

Finally, the wind shifted. "Ran, we've got to get out of here." Aryn's voice bordered on shrill.

"All right, let's climb out." He put the tractor in reverse and attempted to back up and out. The six-foot walls were too steep. "*Sludge!*" More time lost. "I'm going up channel."

"We're going deeper?"

"In a way, but we're still climbing."

"We need to get out!" Aryn shrieked. "Now!"

A groaning roar slammed at his ears. The tractor tipped. Ran grabbed at Aryn, but touched only air. Rock cracked beneath them.

He pitched forward against the steering column.

Deafening noise. Piercing pain. Rocks bounced and crashed around them.

Hallie

Hallie woke to a howling wind trying to tear off the shelter's roof, but the roof—grown seamlessly out of the walls—provided no protruding edges for the wind to pry against.

She rolled over, ignoring the movements of the others, to consider her dream. She'd carried a basket of food until Pel removed it from her grasp with some laughing words. The dream had felt sunlit and happy. A piece of her lost memory?

Pel and Ran insisted what happened at the picnic wasn't her fault. Pel had researched his disappeared people; she had disobeyed Liz's orders not to investigate the bombing she witnessed. The dead woman had been aide to a congressman; after the bombing, that congressman had changed sides on a bill to make it easier for planets to be settled. None of which explained why the NODE had included her and Pel with the teens who'd lost their parents.

"Get up." Pel nudged her. "Time to exercise. Ramon's going to give us a beat. We'll do some dancing before we eat."

Ramon pattered out an intricate rhythm. A fast waltz. The wind howled louder. The animal-lovers Amado and Leif crashed inside from wherever they'd been exploring. Nick was ignoring the dancers to run at the wall, executing midair twists. Airboard dismounts. His last attempt ended in a stumble and he collapsed, dramatically clutching his belly. "I'm starving!"

Hallie shuffled to the beat, waving her arms and rolling her shoulders. She'd had no chance to say good-bye to Cassandra. Cass would call her tooth phone, get a "disconnected" message, and call Mom to find out why; Hallie could feel her mother's reawakened grief—aching and heavy—just like those months after her father died.

After dancing, she leaned against the wall, listening to the others set up a schedule for watching from the roof. Her old desire for independence felt childish in the face of starvation on an alien planet. She'd give anything to be back home with Mom. After their fights, she'd too often escaped to stay with Aunt Bet, who might now be gathering tomatoes for one of her fresh salads. Or, when Aunt Bet gave one of her lectures on using food fabs, Uncle Jack had charge of the food fab. He liked spicy.

Hallie swallowed. *Food!*

The discussion had turned to food. Their supply of wafers was almost gone. Even rationed, there were only enough for today. Then they could fight over who ate the wrappers.

"Hallie had the right idea, trying raw cactus," said Nick. "But there isn't much variation around this building. We need to try farther out. I'll be the guinea pig for all of us."

"Scrape off the stem and sniff. Only if it smells okay do you touch it to your tongue," Hallie said. "*Don't* eat it, whatever you do. You have to give your body time to react."

"That's step one," Manuelo agreed. "We can start a fire and roast bits, and follow the same process. Or some poisons wash out by cooking in water. But what do we use for a pot?"

A loud discussion followed about the possibility of building a solar cooker using material from the hardware fabricator supplies. The end result was a single rule: any fires built would be kept outside in a firepit. The challenge would be finding and handling dry plant matter for burning.

Hallie said, "I'm going to try mixing fab reactants to make nutritional drinks. We've got to keep up our strength."

She wished she'd thought of that before trying that *filthy spamguts* plant. But when she lined up one container of each color and content, she felt more like a mad scientist about to create a monster. Reba came to see what she was doing, and Hallie looked at her in relief.

"Any idea how to turn ourselves into a food fab?" Aunt Bet would know exactly what each chemical was and and how it interfaced with the others. But even Aunt Bet had never tried to use them outside of a food fabricator, with its intricate processing.

First came the problem of mixing. The powders didn't stir; they clumped.

"Try shaking it," said Reba. The resultant foam smelled terrible and tasted worse—a disaster of gagging proportions. Maybe they should try heating their drinks. *If. If* they had a fire and *if* they had a pot to cook in.

The door slammed open. Ramon and Pel supported Nick—a gasping, choking Nick—into the room. "He didn't follow instructions about only touching the tip of his tongue," Ramon said.

"And it's starting to rain," Pel added.

Hallie groaned. So, no fire. No food. They'd be safer if they all went back to hibernating.

Ran

The tractor lay at an odd angle, nose down in a sinkhole, rear treads almost overhead, the seat beside him empty of Aryn.

"Aryn!"

The deafening roar of shattering rock had ended, but Ran could barely hear himself croak. He took a breath and coughed; his left temple pounded; something weighed on his legs. He twisted, trying to move, unable to see through the fog of rock dust.

Shadows pooled. A ray of light sparked against sharp edges of a jagged crystalline wall, then faded. He struggled to identify what he'd seen, even as his ears registered an ominous rumble. Another collapse? They had to get out!

"Aryn!" He heard his voice crack. His ears were clearing. He looked up. The tractor wasn't going anywhere. A foot or two above the rear treads was the floor of the wash.

He shoved rock bits from his lap. One leg wouldn't move, so he yanked, releasing a small avalanche to free it. Nothing broken. Find Aryn.

He stepped off the tractor onto a large—and he hoped steady—rock. His chest blossomed with pain. So, *maybe a broken rib.*

He wanted to wipe his eyes free of the shadows and dust. "Aryn!"

A step. That deep rumbling nagged at him, but the base of the sinkhole seemed stable.

The nose of the tractor rested against a boulder; a moan came from its far side. Spotting her pale sleeve, he wriggled over the big rock. "Aryn." He coughed. A jab in his chest forced him to straighten. *Don't cough!*

Another soft moan. Aryn sat up. His hand reached hers and worked up her arm.

Her voice came in a whisper.

"What?" he said.

"We've got to get out of here."

"Can you stand?"

"We've got to get out."

"Yes. Can you stand?" The rumble was louder. A nearby trickling distracted him. Water flowing.

With a groan, a muted cough, and "*oof*," Aryn stood upright. "The food fell when I did. Under this big rock. We've got to get out of here."

He reached down, his ribs screaming, and touched a corner of the food packet. "You climb out. I'll get it." He wondered if he could budge the boulder.

"It's too big. I'll push too." Aryn braced herself. With both pushing, the boulder moved slightly. The rumbling lent desperation to his efforts. The boulder rocked.

Ran grabbed the packet and handed it to Aryn. Above the shadowed sinkhole with its amazing faceted walls, the air was lighter but still full of dust.

"Hurry. Climb out. I'll untie our water."

The ominous trickle became a gush, filling the sinkhole. As he'd feared. This morning's rain. *That* was the source of the rumbling.

Aryn climbed onto the tractor bed, their remaining wafers under one arm, crossed the gap from sinkhole to channel floor, and splashed to the wash's steep bank.

Ran stepped onto the seat back and untied the water container. *Just the ribs*, he kept telling himself. The tractor was about to drown. He grabbed at the loose lengths of cloth and bundled them under his arm.

The rumble grew to a roar. Ran stepped out on the floor of the channel. The flood washed sand from beneath his feet, knocking him to his knees. The flow of water strengthened, heavy with gravel and sand picked up in its rush to obey the laws of gravity. Someone should invent an emergency anti-grav lift for humans caught in flash floods.

Ran struggled to his feet, clutching the container and cloth to his body.

Only a step—easy enough when dry—to the side of the channel. Aryn was halfway up the side wall. He met her eyes and read her intent to come help.

"Go on!" he shouted and slipped, landing on his hip, water roiling over him, dragging the cloth from beneath his arm, tugging at the precious water container.

He landed facedown in the torrent. Choking, clinging to cloth and water container, he fought his way to the bank where he surged upright. Frantically, he strove for a foothold in a shower of rocks and dirt. One length of cloth slipped free and washed away. He flung the other length up toward Aryn, who snatched it.

Ran heaved himself and the water container up and over the channel wall, where he collapsed. Below them, the thunder of a higher wave drowned the sinkhole.

"*Ow!*" He forced himself off the plant he'd landed on. "Are you okay?"

"No, and neither are you."

"Break anything?"

"I don't know." Her arm cradled the small packet of wafers. Her voice quivered. "My hand. Maybe a finger." She shivered in the wind.

"First aid," Ran said. "Then we figure out what to do next."

Smart cloth was tough; its tight construction allowed Ran to cut only single-directional strips with his small knife. His long, narrow strip turned Aryn's hand into a clumsy ball. He didn't want to bother cutting a second one for his ribs, but she insisted.

One-handed, she helped bind him up. "We're the walking wounded," she joked.

"So we go on?" They were so close to the ridge with its mysterious signal.

"We go on." Aryn rolled up what remained of the fabric and gathered the food.

"What have we got?" Ran said. "One piece of cloth. A little food." Their reflective bar for signaling from the ridge was below them somewhere. He sloshed the water in its container. "A tiny bit of water. I wish I dared capture that flood."

"We'll look for a spring." Aryn picked up the wafers. "Lead on."

"And if no one is there when we reach the top?"

"One step at a time," Aryn said. "We'll still have a view."

She was right. They might spot the settlement from there.

Their way steepened, then dipped. Aryn limped steadily, following his detours around ominous thorns. An hour later, he stopped to catch his breath and looked back and down at the wide riverbed they'd crossed. Seemed long ago. Everything pre-sinkhole felt ancient.

Moving again, they descended into and climbed out of another wash still wet from its own flood. Then they met a rock wall. Impasse.

"Can't go over it," he said.

"Can't go under it," chanted Aryn.

"Have to go around it," they agreed in unison.

They descended to a more surmountable section of the same rock face. Aryn got up easily with only a minor lift. Using the smart cloth as a rope, she helped Ran. He rolled onto the ledge and struggled upright, ribs screaming beneath their tight binding.

The ridge's crest seemed to have receded.

"Eat first," Aryn told him.

Dry, dry, dry. He forced down crushed wafers. "We've got to keep on." His thighs and calves burned. This reality was nothing like the virtual climbs he'd done on the ship. That Colorado mountain trail had been without thorns, and a hundred times more scenic—though no doubt Aryn would disagree. And the VR monitor had always ended the climb before he reached his limit. This was only their third day of bucking this gravity.

He pushed himself to his feet, ribs aching. "Let's move."

They had to cross a low gray-green plant topped with round spiky balls, reminding him of the grass seeds that used to stick to their school clothes on the playground. Beyond the low plants, taller, long-stemmed branches blocked their passage. Each branch ended with a single fleshy, hairy brown leaf, its lobes armed with villainously sharp claws.

"How fascinating," Aryn said. At least she didn't call it beautiful.

"Bear claws or big cat paws," Ran agreed.

Aryn wound the cloth around him and moved close against his back. Partially protected, they tore through and rerolled the cloth.

Resuming the climb, Ran's ankles itched and burned from prickly contacts. Against a roaring headwind, he worked around a stone knob and stopped, blocked by a steep canyon, its bottom coated with red plants. Why red, he wondered.

Thin cloud streamers covered the sky.

"Have to find another way," he said. He turned. No Aryn. She'd been close behind— *How long ago?* He hadn't looked since that headwind. Plants in his wake lay prone from the gale. His heart thudded. Not again!

"Aryn!" He retraced his steps. He should have taken better care. He couldn't even see his own tracks. He stepped on their almost empty food wrapper. "Aryn!"

A faint, sharp cry came in answer. Ran found her higher on the slope, sprawled facedown, caught between rocks and thorns, hair stirring in the wind.

He crouched beside her. "What happened? I got to a dead end and you weren't there,"

She shivered. "I was following my inner guide. But I got distracted and my ankle gave way. It felt so good to not move, I just stayed."

"Hold still." With a stone, Ran held back a threatening branch. "Okay. Now."

Aryn rolled over and sat up, wincing. Her face showed lines of strain. Her wrapped hand and clothes were embedded with grit and thorns. With her uninjured hand, she clutched her ankle. She'd been limping since they climbed out of the wash. Whatever was wrong then had worsened.

"You can't go on."

Realization struck. Aryn had been one of the hibernators. She should never have come.

See Pel? I told you I should go by myself! They weren't going to make it, in the middle of nowhere, no water, no food, no way to signal . . .

"We've got to find you a protected place where you can rest."

"No. First you have to mark an arrow in the direction I fell."

"You can't go on! What good will an arrow do?"

"You have to go without me." Aryn's pinched face hardened. "Mark it!"

With the stone he'd used to move the thorns from Aryn, he dug a deep arrow. Its direction might actually lead higher, avoiding that canyon that had stopped him—but what good was that?

"You've got to get out of this wind." He helped her up, stifling a groan of his own.

She winced again as she took a step. "We're about halfway. You'll have to avoid dead ends and pick the right path every time."

"*Hah!* How do you pick a path when you can't see that far ahead?"

"You saw the ridge from below. You do know which way to go. Start in the direction I fell."

She was the one with the artist's eye for detail. "I need you for my guide."

"No, you don't. You're the one with the strength. You'll find your way."

"I can't leave you alone! I can't risk losing you."

"I won't let you lose me. You will get there and back."

"How do you know?"

"Just let your body do the work."

"You think I'm not?" His body *was* doing all the work! He ranged up and down, searching. Beside a boulder, he scuffed away rocks and plants to shape a tiny room, dropped the cloth, and helped her hobble to it. He then went to work walling her in—feeble protection against shooting thorns and wind. His ribs shrieked every time he bent to pick up another rock.

"If I leave you here, how am I to find you again?"

"You'll find me. Eat and drink now. As much as you can hold."

He shook his head. "I'm leaving the supplies with you."

She frowned. "I'm not the one expending energy." She divided the wafer crumbs in two piles. He didn't have time to argue. He crunched them down and swallowed some water.

"Take the cloth," she said. "You may run into weather."

"*No!*" Fed up with wind and thorns and the whole struggle, he shouted, "I will go as fast as possible, as lightly as possible, so I can get back to you as soon as possible."

She might have an inner guide, but he had no such thing. Let his body do the work?

He had to get going. The sun was dropping nearer the horizon.

He leaned over the stone wall. "Will you be okay?" This little protected space wasn't enough. He should've—

She levered herself up and kissed his cheek.

"You'll be all right?"

Her nod gave him the reassurance he needed, her face almost peaceful. "I'll wait for you."

"Stay alive."

She smiled. "I'll do that too."

He wanted to make some gesture—but he didn't know what, and so turned away.

No more false starts. His cheek felt alive where she'd kissed him.

Pel

Pel shivered on the roof beside Hallie. Their third night on this planet. Ran and Aryn had been gone since yesterday. It had been a mistake to send them off. *What? Better we all starve together?* Their wafers were gone.

Some traces of dusk remained. The eleven at the shelter had alternated watches in short relays since midday. Nimble Nick was now Limping Nick after twisting his ankle in an attempt to use the bottom-most crate in one of his "airboard" dismounts. The early-morning rainstorm had been only a brief squall, but constant wind gusts defeated all fire-starting attempts. Maybe tomorrow during a lull, they could—

"I thought I saw a flicker," said Hallie.

Standing on her windward side, Pel had seen nothing. "Maybe a rising star. Right at the edge of the horizon?"

"It wasn't east," she objected. "More like northeast."

"Still, stars will be appearing."

"Maybe." She sounded doubtful. "But it wasn't that kind of flicker."

The wind wailed, occasionally ending in a shriek of despair.

"There's the smaller moon," Pel said, as it came up far to the right of the ridge. "I wish I could stargaze instead of watching one place. It takes me out of my worries."

"Hardly." Hallie's arm was warm against his. "Maybe the worries feel smaller but they don't go away."

Amado and Leif climbed up. "Our turn to watch."

Though chilled, Pel was reluctant to go back inside. Time there moved too slowly. Lack of food, lack of power, lack of solutions had them bouncing off the walls, or fleeing outside only to be driven back in by wind and darkness.

Hallie returned to the girls' side of the cluttered room where, using a crate top for their work surface and with Reba's help, she was attempting to concoct something more palatable than their first attempt using food-fab chemicals.

Ramon drummed a rhythm against the wall.

Manuelo said, "It's been too long! We can't stay here with no food."

Reba looked up from their chemical lab. "Where would we go?" she asked, reasonably.

"We have to wait for Ran and Aryn," said Hallie. "They're out in this!"

Hallie's thoughts matched Pel's own. Small comfort, that.

Accompanied by tall, quiet Luisa, Pel climbed to the rooftop for his second after-dark watch to relieve Ramon and Nick.

Nick shouted over the howling air, "I spotted a gleam of light up there."

Ramon leaned in to focus his voice. "It happened right after we came up. Whatever it was, it wasn't the signal we agreed on."

People. There had to be people there. But none of them spoke their hope aloud. Pel hugged his arms against the constant gale and stared into the blackness beside Luisa. Clouds obscured most of the stars. The wind reminded him of Kansas blizzards and tornadoes.

"I hear something," said Luisa. Must be her musician's ears, to distinguish anything over the wind. Then Pel heard it too, the thrum of a heavy-duty air vehicle. "I'm going to tell them." Luisa slipped down and around the building.

Pel's heart raced as vehicle lights settled in the landing area. *Have we been found? Or are we bound for someplace worse?*

Aryn

Aryn stared at the stacked rocks surrounding her. She could no longer hear Ran's footsteps. She bit her lip, overwhelmed with doubt. The day was too far gone. Ran had expended too much time and energy building her shelter. She'd been wrong to encourage him to go. If he didn't come back— Her heart missed a beat.

He *had* to go and he *would* be back.

The walled area provided barely enough space to curl up in. She wriggled around. Her hand ached. Her ankle throbbed, its swelling much worse. She feared she'd broken something in that second fall, but the only available remedy was to elevate it.

A rock poked her hip. She shifted, trying for a comfortable way to raise her foot. The rock still poked. With her good hand, she felt for it and discovered a lump in her pocket—an angular crystal, its facets reflecting a tinge of purple in the fading light. She'd forgotten those sinkhole walls glinting behind the dust, as if the tractor had broken through into a giant geode. She had no memory of dropping this broken bit into her pocket.

Propping her leg up against the stones, she held the crystal. *Stay present,* she told herself over and over. *Be here for Ran.*

She'd been so tired. While focused on the best trajectory to reach the ridge, she had allowed herself to anticipate meeting her parents. That brief, *so brief,* break in her concentration was all it took. She'd stumbled.

And her fall slammed her back into her body—

All because she'd relapsed into her old habit of dreaming about her real parents.

See! She was doing it again. She'd promised Ran to stay with him in spirit. A lie, but she had to tell him something hopeful. Except it was also true. Why else had she drawn his face back on Earth—the same profile, the same set expression as he'd worn on the tractor?

Because he's the cause of my death? If he doesn't come back, if he dies, I'll die too.

No! She drew a deep breath and let it out. As if her broken finger hadn't been enough to keep her in her body, now her ankle literally grounded her to this place—and she still daydreamed.

She ordered each muscle to relax, striving to clear her mind.

She'd told Ran she'd paint on the rocks if she had to. Not rocks. The ground itself. She twisted to smooth a space beside her, and using the crystal, she drew. By the time she finished, it was too dark to see what she'd produced.

She lay back again. The activity had kept her from worrying. With dusk, the wind held less force. A shrill whistle brought her head around, but Ran's wall of stones blocked her sight. Something snakelike glided overhead, its long, flat body rippling to maintain altitude, quickly out of view. Her throat tightened with wonder at the creature.

She rubbed the facets of the broken crystal, the motion calming and steadying her just as drawing did. She brought all her thoughts to Ran, picturing his determined expression.

He was well.

And something more. An unasked-for certainty grew, that only *one* of her parents was on this planet. Only one. But now was not a time for grief. It was time to remain connected, to Ran, to their goal, to the planet.

The planet supported her, in the same way it supported its thorns and secretive creatures. Adjusting her padding, she gazed at the sky, watching stars appear.

Ran

Ran verified his direction at the arrow Aryn had insisted on.

I told you Pel! I should have gone alone.

But it wasn't true. Aryn had an unerring eye for landforms. She'd been the one to catch sight of that beam of light. He trusted her information. He didn't trust himself, or his ability to return to her.

Keep moving.

He had to find her again. The light kiss she'd given his cheek felt like an old-time transmission wire between them. He shook his head, but the idea remained. Why not? A reminder of why he was climbing.

His legs burned. He pressed his arm tight against aching ribs, turning now and again to impress the area on his memory. One step at a time.

Plants were no longer whiplike; these clung to the rocks, but it was still an alien planet, full of leaves that didn't look like leaves. Even these rock-clinging plants appeared misshapen.

One more step. Another. Taking him farther from anything he'd ever wanted. On Earth he'd wanted a job, any job. On the *Orpheus*, he'd wanted desperately to belong to the ship's crew. Aryn was looking for her parents. He had no one.

It didn't matter. He had a job to do. Her dry lips touched his cheek.

Keep going.

Recriminating faces from his past floated around him. His foster father's disgust at his failure to plan for tertiary-level classes. Gumption's grim face blaming him for the ship sabotage. Hallie's expression when turning away from him at the landing site. He wasn't going fast enough. His ribs throbbed. He gasped, unable to draw a deep breath.

Slow down.

The edge of the cliff opened up, curving inward and then back around to face him across a rockfall—the scar he'd spotted when they watched the signal. The flashing lights had come from the far side—so close and so far—the steep canyon standing between.

He stepped out onto the scree. Loose stones slid underfoot. Careful.

Let your feet find the way. Let your knees know the way. Let your belly show the way. Give credit to your body's wisdom. Words like a Native American chant, almost as though Aryn whispered them. *That* was what she'd meant. Let his body do the work—the work of knowing.

His tongue stuck to the roof of his dry mouth. The wind blew hard and cold through his tattered pants. His body wanted to rest. Sure, curl up and become an ice cube.

He couldn't catch his breath. He stopped and hugged his ribs. Blasted nonsensical shifting of pawns across the board of the universe—*no, don't exaggerate*—across a section of the galaxy.

Aryn was waiting for him. He set his foot on the next rock. Pel was right. It takes two. Without her waiting, he might give up.

He let air fill his lungs and pushed forward a few more steps.

Can't stop.

Slow down, or he'd start a rockslide and end up at the bottom.

Have to hurry. Aryn'll be in the dark.

She'll be in the dark, no matter what.

No one will be on top of the ridge.

He took another step. And another, legs so heavy he couldn't possibly raise his foot over another rock. The top edge of the ridge grew closer, guarded by the worst section of loose scree. What if he started an avalanche?

He gulped air, looking over all possible paths.

On the clifftop, a brief flare caught his eye.

"Hey!" Ran yelled. His yell came out hoarse, from a dry throat.

Hey. His voice echoed back.

"Help!"

Help. Echoes. Illusions. Wishful thinking. Exhaustion.

He aimed himself at where the cliff face narrowed, its height less daunting, just below that flare. Rocks sank and turned underfoot. On shipboard, he'd never managed to reach the top of that virtual mountain, always ending at the beginning of a talus slope like this one. This time, it was real. No VR monitor to end this hike, telling him he'd reached his limit. He was beyond his limit, running on empty.

His lungs and every limb ached.

Aryn's warm smile assured him. *I will stay alive.*

Gingerly, he took another step, leaning away from the steep drop. Wind whipped up, down, in his face. *Concentrate on your feet.*

Two more steps. The scree sank under his weight. And another two steps . . .

The light flared again.

"Hey!" he yelled. His heart thrummed.

Careful. Aryn counted on him.

He forced leaden legs to move. His last steps were rushed, rocks sliding. An exclamation came from above, along with a blinding light.

"Careful there." The voice had a grating sound, as if from a sandpapered larynx. "Take it easy. Grab hold." A rope slapped at his shoulder.

Ran twisted it around his arm and clung with both hands. His feet climbed as he was towed up over the rock edge. Facedown, he clung to solid ground, gasping at stabbing ribs.

"Thanks!" He wanted to weep with gratitude, but every bit of him was dried out.

Light flashed in his face, then pointed away. "Who *are* you?" asked the grating voice.

"Name's Ran. The ship *Orpheus* . . . brought us." How good not to move. "No one to meet us . . . Aryn and I set off to look. Aryn's hurt. She's below. I've got to get back to her."

"We had no word about a ship. *Who* came?"

"Offspring," Ran mumbled to the ground, wondering if he had the energy to get to his feet. "Looking for parents. Aryn's hurt—"

"Well, I'll be spaced! What game are they playing at? Continents roll!"

Ran found the will to roll over. He clutched his ribs. "Thanks for pulling me up."

"Don't want to shine this light in your face. How'd you know to come here?"

"We saw your beam—yesterday."

"Yesterday? Wonder of wonders. I was supposed to be gone, due at my next station today. Got delayed." After a pause, the man said, "It'll be a week before I'm back."

Accepting the man's hand, Ran got to his feet and stood swaying. "Aryn's down below. I've got to get back to her."

"How bad's she hurt?"

"Ankle—sprained, I think. Her hand."

"Nothing life threatening?"

"Only the planet." Cold. Thirst. Unknown creatures.

"You came all the way from the Shed?" The grip on Ran's elbow steadied him.

"The building near the landing site. Eleven more kids are there. No food." Glad of the support, hoping every step to be his last, Ran stumbled behind the beam of light.

They moved farther from the cliff edge, down a ramp, through a door. Once the door closed behind them, instruments lit up, illuminating the room with soft light. Ran eyed the instruments—energy available here—before looking at his rescuer. Not a large man. Graying hair, shrewd eyes, deeply tanned skin; his paler forehead revealed habitual use of hat or helmet.

"There are eleven more kids there," Ran repeated. "We took the tractor, but it got caught in a sinkhole and a flash flood buried it. So we went on foot. I've got to get back—"

"You left her sheltered somehow?" The man turned away.

"A rockpile. She has the cloth we brought for cover. I've got to go back."

"You're out on your feet, boy. Take a rest. Eat something."

He returned with a cup. "Drink this. I'm going to beam the news so they can collect the others from the Shed." He rummaged in the cabinet below the instruments.

Ran sank down. He didn't feel like eating and hardly felt any thirst. He took a sip—*not water*—and gulped it down. "It's sweet!"

"Local brew from a native plant. Drink up. Looks like you need it. Best pick-me-up on the planet." The man refilled Ran's cup. "My name's Perk. I'm the planetary geologist. I'm going to beam the others now."

Geologist. That explained the tool belt and sturdy boots.

Ran tried to sip the second cup more slowly, but it was gone in an instant. He sat dazed, unwilling to move. Minutes passed.

Perk reentered.

Beneath the howl of wind, Ran felt a deep thrum. "Someone coming?"

The grizzled man cocked his head, then grimaced. "Blast." He rummaged on a shelf and brought over a container of orange-colored wafers, similar—other than their color—to what they'd found in the shelter—the Shed. "Prob'ly Wick. Here, eat."

Ran bit into one and coughed as spice met his throat.

"Heat gets easier after the first bite."

"Did you send word?"

"Yes, by laser. I got a response," Perk said. "Looks like just in time," he added softly.

The door slammed open and a short, stocky figure marched in. "What are you doing here, Perk?"

"Got delayed fixing the anemometer. The wind picked up, and I decided to wait till morning. Then this kid came climbing up the hill."

"A kid? Thought it was a scarecrow. Who is it?"

The man's dismissal chafed Ran like his chapped face.

"Seems we had a delivery." Perk's gravelly voice suited his occupation.

"A ship? When? We got no notice at the base."

Ran scowled. So. The ship *hadn't* sent a message? What was their game?

"I don't have the story yet, Wick. He just arrived. Left someone halfway down."

"The *Orpheus* landed us," Ran said. "Space Corps. This makes our third night. Some of the kids were told they have parents here."

Suddenly his stomach had no bottom. He crammed orange bits into his mouth as fast as he could swallow. Perk refilled his cup.

"Son of a quark if I ever heard such nonsense! What's your name?"

"Ran Kenelm."

"No Kenelms here. I know the list."

Ran kept eating. No reason there would be. It was the name of his first foster family.

"And the one below?" asked Perk.

"Aryn Suzuki," Ran said between bites.

"Sam's kid? He had a girl," said Wick.

"She have a mother?" Ran asked.

"Dead," said Perk. "About blew Sam's mind. This'll be a supercharge for him."

"Let's go get her." Ran staggered upright and turned toward the door.

"Not so fast," said Perk. "It's dark. The wind is howling. Gotta wait for daylight. We can't park on the slope. We'll need to fly down and climb up to her."

"But she's alone. Give me a light. I'll go back down."

"Chivalry flies again," said Wick.

What chivalry? She was as strong as anyone, but she was alone.

"Not many hours till dawn," said Perk. "Might's well rest awhile. Be easier to see."

"I'll go alone then." Ran took a step for the door.

Wick blocked him. "Perk's right. Wind's picking up. Virile and I could hardly land the two seater. Soon as things settle, I'll go back for the truck. Best take a rest."

The door opened. A pale-skinned man entered. Something about his cold eyes raised Ran's neck hairs. "Find anything?" Wick asked him.

The man shook his head. "Nothing, Boss."

Perk ignored the interruption to steer Ran to a bunk. "Lie down."

Ran sat up. But he was unable to resist Perk's insistence combined with Wick's thicker frame. Together they pushed him down.

All right then. He'd wait them out. He'd go as soon as they left. His legs throbbed. The bunk felt comfortable. Too comfortable. Had to stay awake. He rubbed the chafed skin of his face and listened.

"What brought you out, Wick?" asked Perk.

"I heard Delver was going to be here. False alarm, I guess. Didn't expect this."

Ran lay still. He'd leave as soon as Wick took off.

Pel

At the sound of a vehicle, Luisa climbed down from the roof to alert the teens. Pel followed, his breath quickening as he stopped at the corner to await these new arrivals. *Someone* had to be the official greeter.

A shadow crunched up the path, followed by a second.

"Who are you?" Pel called, blocking their way.

"Transport. We got a beam from the geologist's site that you were here."

"Any word on the two we sent looking for help? They were heading for that ridge out there."

"That's where word came from," the man called over the wind's howl. "Said to go asap to the Shed to pick up delivery of offspring. We didn't know what to think."

They made it! Success! Pel turned and led the way.

Ramon looked out of the door. "Sounded like a truck. Who are you?"

"Inside," urged the man. "I'm Ed, and this is Fletch." Ed was middle-sized, middle-aged, his face lined. "We got a signal, but it only said offspring arrived by ship. Are you all— No, wait. We have a large vehicle, but how many are you?"

"Eleven here," said Pel.

"Just let me get your names and we'll transport you to the Warrens."

The wind roared in response.

"Forget names," said the other man. "We have to hurry." He examined the wafer packaging—the only edible matter remaining—and shook his head. "Good thing we came when we did."

Ed looked around at the crates and picked up a container of nanopaints. "What have you got here? Fletch, check this one out."

Were they in a hurry or not? Pel wondered.

"Get your bags," said Ed, finally decisive. "And let's see how much of this we can fit in as well. I'm leaving Fletch behind to stand guard. Maybe the bigger boys too."

Fletch. The repeated name grabbed Pel's attention before he digested Ed's words. Cargo of greater importance than passengers? "Stand guard from what?" he asked.

Fletch scowled. "People first. Take the kids this trip. Then come back for this stuff."

"Survival is priority," Ed said. "We take as much of both as possible."

"What's the danger?" Pel spoke louder this time.

"No danger," said Ed. "It's the middle of the night. Wick won't be out."

"Don't be so sure," said Fletch. "I say people first."

"All you girls, get your bags," ordered Ed. "You boys, help us load.

We'll squeeze in as many as possible. Let's move!"

Pel returned from hauling the crate of nanopaints to find Hallie silently repacking food-fab containers. "I'll do that. You go with the other girls," he said.

"I'd rather wait with you."

"No, go! Be my eyes till I get there." Too bad his noter had no charge. She could be recording for him as well.

Reba and Tesia rolled up the scattered piles of smart cloth. Fletch reentered and gave a satisfied "Ha!" on seeing the cloth. "Bring that along, girls. Get aboard."

Reba, her arms full, loosened one hand to link with Hallie. "Come on."

Moments later, the airtruck thrummed upward. Nick and Leif had managed to fit in along with the girls, leaving four with Fletch. One of Pel's disappeareds had been named Fletcher, a government accountant. This Fletch, lean and tough, with bags under his eyes, didn't resemble a number cruncher, but then the planet might change anyone.

First though, "Who's Wick?" Pel asked.

Hallie

Hallie squeezed in among legs and bodies and sat on the flat truck bed. Be Pel's eyes? All right then, she had a purpose. They'd been rescued—but where were Ran and Aryn?

"Good thing we're packed so snug," Luisa said, as the airtruck juddered upward.

They landed after a short, jerky, nauseating flight. Last one in, Hallie climbed out first, disoriented by darkness and wind. She huddled with the others, unsure where to go.

A brief flash of light accompanied a woman's voice. Ed took a few steps into the dark to meet her. They exchanged some words, ending in Ed's "Don't start till I get back with the rest." With another flash of light, Ed called for help unloading, and several people dashed out.

"Come in, all of you," said the woman, neither welcoming nor unwelcoming. "We'll wait in the gathering room." She stood to one side, holding open the long, stiff, overlapping slats that covered the entrance.

What a relief to move underground. Hallie trailed the others down a ramp into a large, excavated space. Rock-hewn tables occupied the center. The woman, seeming as disciplined as her tightly bound hair, herded them to a stone bench at the back of the room. Hallie took her place on the end, feeling alien, a spy to this homecoming of long-lost children.

A short man stomped out of a nearby room. "What's happening? What's Ed up to now?"

"A ship," said the woman. "Ed says wait till he gets back with the next batch. They arrived with supplies."

People erupted out of a stairwell. Ed's orders to wait didn't stop them from filling the room; many appeared to have just awakened. Well, it *was* night, Hallie admitted, but she hated the eyes, everyone staring, her hair so like a scarecrow's. Along the bench, the other girls and Nick and Leif were equally disheveled, all wearing their school blues. A good thing Nick had recovered from his poisoning so quickly; she'd have hated to be the one to tell his parents the planet had killed their son.

The adults mostly wore undyed, patched coveralls; a few wore equally battered brown ones. Smart cloth lasted well, but not forever. All the clothes were gathered at ankles and wrists, probably to protect from gritty winds.

Adult expressions alternated from horrified to longing to disbelief, back to horrified. Hallie knew that swooping airboard ride—she was still disbelieving and horrified at being here—but she didn't understand *their* horror. What did they fear?

The stream of people from below continued. Whispers buzzed. "Who are they?" "Why?" "Why now?" "Are they ours?" "Why now, of all nights?"

Of all nights? Something had been interrupted.

She played a game with herself. The quick turns of heads, never quite staring—those were the childless, merely curious. The ones who couldn't stop looking, displaying anticipation and dread—they had lost children. One small woman with curly red hair—hand covering her mouth, tears streaking her cheeks—stared at Reba. Another woman examined each of them before turning away with the faintest hint of disappointment, as if she hadn't allowed herself to hope. Who was she looking for?

How would her own mother have looked at a time like this? Hallie's mind skittered from that thought. She should have been a better daughter.

Pel

In the shelter, the four remaining boys listened as the airtruck took off with its full load.

Pel's question "Who's Wick?" hung in the air.

Fletch glanced around the room taking tally of what remained. "Grab your bags," he said. "Help me haul the rest of this shipment down to the landing site. Then I'll answer your questions." He scowled at the remaining crates. "We can't fit it all. It'll take a third trip to finish. I don't know if the winds will let us, so let's get the ones that matter most."

Pel grabbed his bag and Ran's. One of the girls must have taken Aryn's. The wind almost blew him over as he fought his way down the path. They stacked the bags on the raised cargo platform and returned, passing Fletch dragging a crate. Too bad they didn't have that little hauler. But Ran and Aryn had succeeded!

Once all the crates were back down on the flat, the five returned to the emptied shelter. Amado and Manuelo sank into squats. Pel leaned against the wall beside Ramon.

"You were going to tell us what danger we're in," Pel reminded Fletch.

"All right. Listen for the Trilby's return."

A Trilby? Named for the ancient trilobites they resembled, those airtrucks hadn't been manufactured in years, but they were sturdy and still flew Earth's skies.

Fletch's long face gave him a mournful air. "No communications worth a quark on this planet, which can sometimes be good news, but right now we're missing a person—believed dead—and what he set out to do is still undone."

He rubbed his mouth and started over. "All right. Basic information. Most of us were co-opted for this exile. Ripped from lives and homes, stuck out here to keep us quiet. You'll find us the most ill-assorted group of miners you ever saw."

How else, if Atlas Corporation had been getting rid of whistle-blowers? So they weren't picked for their skills. *Get on with it.*

"Nowhere to run once they dumped us here. Forced to work in order to eat. In particular, those who had their children stolen were controlled by threats against them." Fletch's mouth quirked downward. "Something's changed, that's sure."

This man had stories to tell and Pel was impatient to hear them. "And the danger?" he prodded, but Fletch proceeded at his own pace.

"They sent pictures of kids by the first couple of ships. And the ships only ran every two to three years. More of us came with each one."

Pel nodded. That agreed with his research. They hadn't all left at the same time.

"Then the mine started killing people, including the command head. They had to move the mine. Life at the base grew more difficult, living all cramped up. Bad blood and fights. The women pushed for better living space. That resulted in building the Warrens, underground near the new mine location. Most of us moved there. Wick and his guns stayed at the base."

Wick and his guns. That was the danger then.

Ramon nudged Pel, his head tilted. The Trilby rumbled overhead. Blast the windy fellow. Too late to hear about Wick and the guns.

"Let's go," said Fletch. "Everyone, hurry."

They arrived beside the stack of goods just as the Trilby landed with a sideslip. The men got to work loading crates with the boys' exhausted help—far more exercise than the ship's medico had prescribed.

A deep rumble cut through the relentless whoosh of wind.

A large black mass hung above them. Another Trilby.

Ed swore. "That does it. Leave the rest. Get inside."

Pel grabbed his bag and Ran's. A sudden gust caught and pushed him into the thorny slope. Ramon grabbed his arm and yanked.

The same gust tilted the heavily loaded truck. Ed shouted, his words blown away.

The truck righted itself. "Inside, inside," Fletch urged. "Let's go—if we can."

They scrambled through the cargo door, braced themselves against crates, and waited. *Wick and his guns.* Was Wick after lives or cargo?

The truck vibrated upward, then thudded down.

"Wait for the wind to ease," muttered Manuelo.

On their second attempt to lift, a gust slewed the truck sideways. Through the front view screen, Pel glimpsed the other truck looming—way too close.

Ed's swearing cut off. "Now," said Fletch. They lifted with a lurch. The heavy propulsion engines surged them forward.

"It's going to be rough," yelled Ed from the front, "but we're clear.

Rough but short. They landed with a tooth-rattling thud, scrambled out, and followed the men through slats and down a ramp into a lighted underground space, full of people.

Ed waved them to the bench along the wall. Pel let Ramon, Amado, and Manuelo precede him past the woman counting. "Ten. Eleven. Is this it?"

"Two more went off to look for help," Pel said. "I understand they got word to you."

She nodded, then turned when Ed yelled, "There wasn't time, I tell you!" Ed was facing a short man with a graying beard. "We got the message. It read 'asap.' I notified Fletch and we took off to get them."

"But what if it had been a trap? You'd have lost our transport, just like that." The man's cheeks reddened above his beard.

"It wasn't a trap," Ed said through his teeth. "The important thing was to get these kids."

Hallie shifted to make space for Pel at the end of the bench. "We interrupted somebody's plans," she whispered.

Pel leaned closer. "There seems to be major strife between them and the base. A man called Wick arrived before we took off and we barely got away. How'd he know we were there? Plus, someone's gone missing."

He looked up to meet the intense gaze of a dark-skinned woman. "Oh, frass!" Pel dropped his eyes but could still feel hers. He couldn't deal with this. *I'm not your son. I've nowhere to run, I wish I hadn't come.*

"What is it?" Hallie whispered.

Pel shook his head and swallowed hard. It was what he hated most about the research. What had been one more blip of data came with a flesh-and-blood mother attached.

Ed slammed his hand on a table. "Meeting is called."

With considerable chatter, the crowd settled, some on benches around the perimeter, others sitting at or leaning against tables. The talk continued.

Ed said loudly, "As current moderator, elected by you, let me run this meeting. You can choose a new leader tomorrow if you wish. Meantime—*shut up!*"

A gong rang out from the far side.

"Thank you, Bork." Bork was the bearded man who'd been furious with Ed. Maybe they weren't enemies after all. "We got all of the kids and most of the cargo. Wick was arriving as we left, so there won't be anything to go back for. Meanwhile . . ."

Several more women arrived, followed by a few men. They squeezed into the corner nearest the teens and stared—with twitching hands, twitching mouths, eyes shuttling between Ed and the new arrivals.

Into their restless silence, Ed said, "Thank you. Let us identify each child, one by one. Quickly, before mutiny strikes." He pointed. "Stand up. Give us name and birth date."

"Nicholas Robbins, born February 13, 2216."

A short, gaunt (they were all gaunt) woman stood. "Nicholas Robin Simms. That's our boy." Nick disappeared behind the woman. A weeping man pushed across the room to converge on them.

"Good," said Ed. "Make way for them. Next."

Reba addressed the teary woman with the matching red hair, her voice shaking. "Reba Reynolds, born Cinco de Mayo, 2212."

Hah! Almost eighteen. She might have been next to be killed.

"Rebina Reynolds, and they messed with your birth date a bit." Her mother shared Reba's small size as well as the hair color. She reached out to stroke her daughter's wet cheek.

A man rose and told them, "You girls go ahead and talk."

"Your stepfather," her mother told Reba.

And so it went. Pel and Hallie sat silently. Leif was claimed by a woman who told him, "I was your father's second wife. I guess that makes me your stepmother. He was the first to die in that mine. Your mother died shortly after she arrived here."

Pel met Hallie's horrified glance. Leif *had* no parents! The NODE had sent Leif here, unknowing.

Amado and Manuelo were claimed by both parents, Dacey by a woman with the same long, graceful, dancing legs. Hallie kept wiping her cheeks. Many adults were doing the same, but Pel also detected worry. And he had worries of his own.

"Geoffrey Ramon Ramirez" was claimed by an angular woman.

Geraldine Ramirez—one of his disappeareds; he'd have recognized her face anywhere from his research.

Pel looked around, hoping to identify others, and lost track of who claimed Luisa and Tesia. Then Ed's finger pointed at Hallie.

Pel stood with her and spoke. "I'm Pel Teague. This is Hallie Pollard. Both of us have birth families back home. We're not part of your offspring. We got drawn into this by a different series of circumstances. Two others went in search of help: Aryn Suzuki and Ran Kenelm."

With an exclamation, a man jerked upright.

"Sam." Ed gave him a sharp nod. "You'll have to wait a bit to meet your daughter."

But the woman who had been eating Pel with her eyes blocked his view of Sam. "You're not my son?" She had a deep voice. Her dark eyes reminded him of his own mother—and of the stark hopelessness he'd seen in her face the last time they spoke.

"No, ma'am," Pel said.

"I'm not *ma'am*. My name is Orenda."

Hallie nudged Pel. "What do you know?"

He bit his lip. *Bad news, no way to refuse* . . . But he had to be sure.

"Tell her what you know," Hallie insisted. "She'd want to know sooner." Hallie seemed to be reading his mind.

"Uh," he began, and swallowed. "Years ago, I started investigating disappearances. Recently, I got on the track of an increase in fosterlings. A couple of them, when they turned eighteen . . ." He couldn't do this.

But the woman was waiting, the entire room silent, intent on his words.

Pel took a shaky breath. "I don't know if he was your son. I'd need to access my data to be sure. There was a young man who died in an aircar crash, a hit-and-run. His name . . ." he dug into his memory, "was Owen something."

Orenda's hands flew to her face. "Owen Oakes."

That was the name. Pel sighed and nodded. "Another fosterling—a girl—also came of age and caught a strange virus and died. It seemed like coming of age was bad news, but Ran, who went with Aryn, also had a close call with a hit-and-run and he was only fifteen." He took a breath. "Is anyone else missing a child?"

Ed looked around. "Didn't Elena and Oro have a daughter?" At a general nodding, he said, "Might have been theirs then. They're both gone."

Relieved, Pel felt on a more stable footing. "Then, because of my research, I had a chance to ask the NODE a question. That's the National Online Data Exchange that keeps track of everyone. I asked about the few specific names I'd found with unreliable death details, and added the clause '*and their offspring.*' If your kids were all meant to meet similar ends upon coming of age, that might be why the NODE opted to ship them out here. Hallie and I don't know why we were also ordered to come."

Orenda Oakes straightened, pride and sorrow plain on her face. "Thank you, young man. And you, young woman. Your instincts are right. We've lived too long not knowing."

"But what about Ran?" said Hallie. "Doesn't anyone claim him?"

No one spoke.

Orenda joined a sad-faced woman against the far wall, between two doorways. Their hands clasped.

"We'll have to find space for you two," said Ed, wearing a guarded expression. "It's late. We'll have another meeting tomorrow to resolve questions."

"When we boarded the ship, all of the others had extra data loaded on their chips," said Pel. "It would be useful to read them."

"Very useful," agreed Ed, "but we might have a problem doing so."

"Don't you have a scanner?" Pel asked.

Ed rolled his eyes.

The woman who had counted them approached Pel and Hallie. "You'll stay with Ed and me," she told Pel. "I'm Marney. I've asked Melody to take the girl, since she has space at the moment." At Marney's wave, the woman sitting with Orenda came across to take Hallie's hand.

Pel looked after them.

"She'll be fine," said Marney. "Melody is missing a husband, poor thing."

Missing. Was that the one Fletch had mentioned? Believed dead. Something unfinished.

"Come along," said Marney. "We'll find you a place to sleep."

At the top of the stairs leading down, Pel looked back. Ed, accompanied by several men, must be going to unload the cargo.

Pel followed Marney down curving steps and along a stone passageway. He didn't know what was most tired, his body, brains, or spirit.

Hallie

I'm Melody. Marney asked me to give you a bed." The iridescent patches on the woman's coverall drew Hallie's eyes as she followed her to the stairs.

"I'm Hallie. Thank you." She was tired, hungry, lost—and grateful. For the first time in three days she couldn't hear the wind.

"Hallie." Melody's voice was slow, calming. "You had a long trip, my dear?" as if she had just come for a visit. And yet something beneath the words caused Hallie's eyes to prickle. They descended stone steps and walked down a hallway.

"Here we are." Melody opened a door onto a sitting room. Lights slowly came alive.

Hallie stared. "*Oh*." A loom against one wall held an unfinished weaving containing the same iridescence as the woman's patches.

Melody picked up a spool of the fibers. "We call it silk plant, because it shimmers."

"You mean *something* on this planet is beautiful?"

Melody blinked. "There is always beauty if we look for it."

"We've seen nothing but prickles and darts. However did you find your silk plant?"

Melody was silent for a long, long moment, her hands unmoving. Hallie wondered if she'd been forgotten, but she felt a disquiet not her own.

"I'm sorry," Hallie said. "I shouldn't have asked."

Melody released a deep sigh, her shoulders slumped. "I try not to remember those times. Del had to leave work to come after me, and they hurt *him*, not me."

Had Melody been wandering? Running away? Looking for something? Hoping it was a safe question, Hallie asked, "What does a silk plant look like?"

"Very tall. Upright with stiff arms. They grow in protected places where the winds aren't quite so strong. Let me show you where you'll sleep."

In a short space of time, Hallie was tucked up on the other side of the room in a long niche cut in the wall, soothed by the clicking of Melody's shuttle. *Look for beauty,* she thought drowsily. She'd found beauty in Melody's weaving as well as a sorrow in Melody equal to Orenda's.

Poor Pel, having to give Orenda such horrible news. And poor Mom. Who would ever want a child, knowing what mothers could suffer?

DAY FOUR

Work

Ran

Someone shook Ran's shoulder roughly. "Time to go."

Ran stared up at Perk's grizzled face. He'd thought—*dreamed*—he was on his way back to Aryn. He swung his legs off the bunk.

"I'm up. Let's go."

"Not so fast. Have a drink. Fuel your engine. We'll head down soon as you're set, but we'll be methodical about this. Haven't done many rescues." Perk handed him a cup.

Much as he wanted to gulp it down, Ran hesitated. "Aryn will need some of this."

"Already packed."

"Where's the other guy?"

"Wick? He flew off to change vehicles. He'll be back." Under his breath, Perk added, "Prob'ly too soon."

Ran set down the empty cup and stood. *Oof.* He rubbed his thighs. "Where's the toilet?"

"Collection station's out that way."

When he hobbled back, Perk handed him more of the spicy orange wafers and led him through the brisk wind to a two-seater Mini. "Squeeze in there."

A tight fit, with all the equipment crammed behind his seat. Perk took off with a bumpy lurch. Ran stared down, trying to decipher landforms previously seen from the ground. The talus slope he'd crossed. That tall pyramid-shaped rock. The outcropping of white quartz in contrast to some green boulders Aryn would have admired.

Where was Aryn's arrow? They'd gone too far.

Flapping cloth. "There she is!" *Alive!*

"Smart girl," said Perk, "to realize how hard it is to spot one more stack of rocks." The Mini shuddered. "Too much wind to hover." They landed on the nearest level spot lower down.

Ran stepped out of the aircar and gasped at muscle spasms. He headed up.

"Slow down," came Perk's raspy voice. "No point in rushing."

A stiff climb, though nothing like the day before. Ran's thighs and calves howled that they'd worked too hard already. His legs burned from all the plants he'd brushed past on his way to the ridge.

Aryn sat beside the boulder, her cloth flag already neatly rolled. "You found someone!"

Ran captured the warmth of her smile and stored it.

"Little lady, we're here to help," Perk said in his gritty voice. "I'm the planetary geologist. Call me Perk. And who might you be?"

"Aryn Suzuki," she said in her light voice. "Do I have a parent here?"

Ran gave her a sharp glance. She had spoken of *two* parents only yesterday!

"I know Sam. Fine man. You have a look of him. Never knew your mother. Can't tell you a thing about her." Perk handed her a container of the planetary drink.

Ran asked, "What do you call that stuff?"

"Sugar nettle tea. Made from ground nettle, a low plant with fat, little leaves. Very hard to find these days."

Aryn's eyes widened with appreciation as she drank. "I bet we crossed some."

"That spot guarded by what I called bear claws," agreed Ran. "Too bad we didn't know."

"You'd have regretted it," said Perk. "Besides the challenge of picking it, is the challenge of preparing it." He looked at the slope they'd just come up. "Now, let's see how best to get you out of here. We don't have a clear path for a chair carry."

"I can walk," she said. "I'll be fine." She limped forward.

"Just remember, both of you," Perk said. "I don't take sides. We didn't have a chance last night for explanations, and we don't have much time now." He nodded his head upward where a Trilby circled. "That'll be Wick."

"You said you don't take sides," Ran said, "like there's a war going on?"

"Only a struggle." Perk's gravelly voice was calm. "No fear. In geologic terms it's a minor quake. Your group looks to be providing another tremor. I wonder . . ."

They began their descent. Perk, close to Aryn's height, acted as her crutch. Ran had only to keep his feet moving and avoid plant life. A crackling came from the device on Perk's belt—a walkie-talkie—really old tech. Garbled words ended with a questioning uplift.

Perk answered, "We're walking down now."

He looked back at Ran. "The sun storms prevent normal communication most of the time. We're entering wind season now. That's when plants go crazy."

"Last night I saw a flying snake," Aryn gasped out as she hobbled. "A long, flattened-out shape."

"A seraphim. They're rare. Generally, they hole up in the strong winds."

"And something whistled at me, both then and again in the early light. I couldn't see it, but I heard it run across the rocks." Her voice came in jerks. "I never felt alone."

Ran walked close behind Perk, wishing he were supporting Aryn, though it was struggle enough to keep his own legs in motion. He shook his head. Comforted by a whistler and a flying snake? Strange girl, putting her faith in the local wildlife.

"You had a determined rescuer," Perk said. "Took two of us to hold him down and force him to rest."

"What will happen next?" Ran interrupted.

"I beamed the news to the Warrens last night. Luckily, Ed was watching and responded. They will have collected your fellow passengers." Perk glanced back. "Problem is—my Mini is tiny. I can't squeeze you both in."

Which meant he'd be riding with Wick. "Who were you talking to last night?"

"You met him. Wick."

"No, before Wick arrived. While I was crossing the talus slope. I could hear you."

"Must've been talking to myself," said Perk. "I do that, you know."

Ran knew what he'd heard. Two voices. He also remembered that Wick had been searching for something. For *somebody*? "What was that about a false alarm?"

"Wick's got someone at the Warrens feeding him info, but as I said, communications are a problem. He might've got it wrong. I don't get involved."

Ran switched gears to ask, "And who is Wick?"

"Wick was DeWarg's top aide. DeWarg died early on, during the first mining operation. Wick took over as boss."

"What do they mine?"

"Beijingite."

Ran stopped in surprise, then hurried to catch up. "*What?* That's impossible! Beijingite is a complex, manufactured compound." Required for spaceship hulls. Very costly too, made of rare materials.

"Yup." Perk's thin shoulders jerked. "Hello, Wick."

Wick chugged up the slope toward them. "Thought you might need some help there," he said genially.

"Doing all right," said Perk. "Brave young lady here. I'm going to transport her to the Warrens for care and to meet her father."

"I'll take the boy with me, then. We'll drop by the base. Find him some clothes that don't look like a scarecrow's discards."

Perk grunted.

Aryn threw Ran a glance over her shoulder, biting her lip as she turned away.

The remainder of the descent passed with Wick maintaining an intermittent stream of chatter about nothing.

Ran followed Aryn to Perk's Mini. Once seated, she released her clutch on her injured hand to grasp his arm. "Watch out," she said.

Ran nodded. She hadn't been wrong yet in her warnings. "How did you know you only had one parent?"

Aryn shook her head. "After dark I felt really peaceful—some sense told me you were all right, and somehow I also knew *that*." Her eyes flickered in warning at the crunch of steps.

"The pawn steps out onto the game board," he muttered. Raising his voice, he added, "Get better. I'll see you at the Warrens."

Her smile was rueful. "I wish you were coming with us."

She'd survived. That was what mattered.

Ran turned away, almost bumping into Wick. Two men leaned against the big Trilby, the pale-skinned one from last night and another, muscular and black bearded.

"Get in back, men," said Wick. "I need to talk to the kid."

Mindful of his ribs, Ran carefully folded himself onto the wide seat beside Wick. They took off, their flight paralleling the ridge line.

"Judging from Perk's Mini," Ran said, "I thought you'd only have tiny vehicles here."

"We brought in two trucks. The Warrens has the other one."

Perk's Mini headed in the opposite direction. Ran stared after it. "Where *is* the Warrens? We didn't know which way to go."

"You wouldn't have found it," Wick said. "They're dug into the ground. We're heading for the base, the original settlement."

"That landing spot's not the original?"

"The Shed was temporary, for storage, and it's got a beacon for landing shuttles. The base is my headquarters, the command center with the records and the Brain."

He made the Warrens sound like it held second-class ranking. "Who lives at the base?"

"Me and my men."

"And at the Warrens?"

"Everybody else. Should never have shipped those women out here. Someone thought the men'd be more amenable with them along, but the women make too much trouble. And now kids? Whose idea was that?"

Ran kept his eyes on the hills below. "The NODE ordered us here. Now that this place is known to exist, there are charges of slavery against AstroMining."

"What slavery? They'll just make AstroMining pay back wages. That's the way it works. Not my worry. I only work for them."

"Didn't AstroMining kidnap them to work here?"

"Who told you that? That's not the way it was at all. Perk tell you?"

"Perk didn't say anything. It's what the kids thought. If their parents weren't kidnapped, why would they have left babies behind with no knowledge of their families?" Pel's research indicated faked deaths behind those disappearances. The parents had been *abducted*, not rescued through some protection racket.

"We couldn't bring brats to a new planet. The only slightly illegal part was not reporting this place. That was company policy. I came as foreman to manage the mine. Had to get the stuff out before protectionists started screaming about planet inviolability. It's the only way."

"So you imported unwilling workers to do the mining."

"What d'you mean, unwilling? They had to go somewhere. We gave 'em safety and put 'em to work. That's all. Ungrateful bastards."

Ran looked down on clumps of prickly plants or rocks covering the hills. Probably both, he thought. He changed the subject, "You've been here since the first?"

"Like I said, I came to see things got done. When my boss died, I became boss. I take care of my people. Early days, a few got hurt, till they learned the setup."

Sure they did, Ran thought. The ones in power make the rules.

"The women complained, wanting protective suits and masks, wanting better everything. I told 'em, 'Of course the work is dangerous, but we don't get supplies unless we produce goods. You can make whatever living quarters you want, so long as you do the work.' So, they dug out their own living space. And they work the mine."

"You have only one mine? For what?" Ran wanted confirmation.

"The rarest—Beijingite."

"An actual deposit? It can't be natural."

"Lode is a treasure trove."

"*Lode?*"

"Lodestone's what they called the planet. You'll see the long, black scar when we get close to base."

"I saw it coming down in the lander. What caused it?"

"Perk's still trying to figure that one out. Says it looks like the land is trying to split, but it doesn't show the usual signs. Maybe a meteorite strike. That's where the best deposits are."

A meteorite strike like no other—scraping across miles and miles of planet to end up in the sea. Perk *must* know it was a shipwreck. Did alien ships also use Beijingite as hull covering? It must have been *huge*! If this crash site were public knowledge on Earth— Yeah, the planet would be deluged with scientists of every kind, wanting to know everything about the planet and the alien ship. World Court would get involved. No wonder AstroMining kept it secret.

"The other group also lives near that scar?" Ran asked.

"Nearer the other end. Shorter trip for 'em, hauling the B'ite to the Shed."

He and Aryn could have reached the Warrens if they'd known which way to go. But he hadn't noticed anything waiting for pickup. "Is there a ship due soon?"

"It's overdue. What ship brought your lot?"

"The *Orpheus*." He'd said so last night.

"Never heard of it. Not an AstroMining ship."

"No, Space Corps." Didn't the man listen? He'd said that last night too. "One of the new hemispheric design. They brought us in a hurry. I think it was before the government could complain about the cost."

"Brought in a new crop of workers is what it looks like to me."

"If AstroMining is being charged with slavery," Ran said, "won't they be forced to bring everyone back, rather than send out new workers?"

"Charged is not convicted," said Wick.

"Yeah, right." He hadn't been tried yet for the deaths of those two kidnappers either. Lying in the hospital with his burns, he'd been sure he'd end up a zombie. According to Pel, the families of those dead men were influential. If he managed to return to Earth, they wouldn't have forgotten. "So, you're the boss."

"I'm the boss. You do as you're told, and we'll get along."

Like some foster fathers he'd known. "And if I don't?"

"You'll do as told. I've got the food."

"The Warrens will need more food now they've got their kids."

"They'll have to work harder, is what. What're you good at, kid?"

"Machines." Ran's answer was automatic, he'd said it so often back in Dodge while looking for work. "I'm a fixer."

"No lie? We can use you for sure. What'd you say your name was? Kenum?"

"Ran Kenelm." If he could find a scanner at the base, he could access the data loaded on his chip at the spaceport, maybe learn his real name.

"No Kenelms here, but you look like someone."

"Why should I? I don't have any parents." He'd also said *that* for years.

"Then why are you here?"

"Don't know." Ran concentrated on the Trilby's rough growl. Might be dirt in the propellant drive causing that.

"Don't know or won't say?"

"I got into a little trouble."

"Some trouble—ship you off Earth."

"I always wanted to space out." This dusty planet could make trouble for vehicles.

"You should fit right in. A fixer you say? We'll find you plenty of work."

Big mistake, giving Wick a reason to keep him. "So where are we headed?"

"The base. Over there." The Trilby descended. Nestled among light-brown hills, the double dome resembled a paler hill formation. "We'll find you a bunk and put you to work."

"I want to go to the Warrens—make sure everyone arrived safe there."

Wick didn't respond, nor did his face reveal anything. Ran glanced over his shoulder at the guards in the back. His eye snagged on three crates. Wick *had* been to the Shed. No mention of kids, so they'd gotten out. He was glad.

A short, paunchy man opened the hangar door, hugging himself against the wind's blast. The truck hovered inside, shuddering until out of the wind.

"Park," Wick ordered. All was quiet as the Trilby settled. "We're down," he called to the two in the back. "Bring those containers. Let's see what we got."

Ran climbed out, caught his breath at the stab in his ribs, and looked around. The large area could easily fit another Trilby, but held only two Minis; the one in the far corner had been in some kind of accident, its dented hatch sagged. All the vehicles were wind peeled.

"Gooney!" Wick shouted.

"Yeah, Boss?" answered the paunchy man as he pulled the door closed.

"A job for you. Find this fellow some clothes and a bunk. Put him in the Mechanics' section. He's going to do some fixing for us."

"Fixing? You trust him to fix things? Where'd he come from?"

"What's to trust? You'll watch him work. See that he gets settled."

Gooney canted his head toward a far doorway. Ran followed him through a passage into the connected dome. A left turn brought them into a room lined with bins. Gooney measured Ran with a glance and reached for a drawer marked Tall.

"Clothes, the boss said. Here, try this." Gooney handed Ran a dark-brown coverall like the other men's. "How'd you get so torn up?" he asked. "No, I can figure out *how*. Where'd you meet up with bull-whips?"

"Bullwhips?" Ran pictured the tallest of the whip-like thorn bushes.

"That's the one that tears clothes. Smaller ones we call cat-o'nine-tails. You like rubbing up to the nasties out there?"

"We got dumped on planet, and two of us went out to find people. Hard to avoid plants, especially when the wind whips them around at you."

"They don't need wind. They do it to be nasty. What's your name?"

"Ran. Wick called you Gooney? Is that short for something?"

"Don't question a man's name. Don't ask how a man came by it neither. Most just go by one name here. Get that in your skull, boy."

"Ran. Not boy."

"All right then. You got the idea. We'll find you a bunk."

Enclosed in a spray of warm water, Ran relaxed. *Nothing happens by accident* had been the medico's philosophy on the *Orpheus*, but accident or not, he wanted to be at the Warrens with Aryn and the others. The recycling shower was a good place to think while it cleaned scratches and warmed his bruises. Too soon, the water cycled off and began drying him.

The strangest part of his arrival on the ridge—Perk said he should already have left. *Who* had the geologist been talking to, and had that person's arrival caused Perk's delay? If so, Perk had lied to Wick about a repair.

Gooney was waiting when Ran stepped out of the shower and pulled on the clean coverall.

A bell sounded. "Follow me," said Gooney.

From the central room came a grumble of voices, reminding Ran of his month spent at Workless, the unemployed men's housing in Dodge. He'd grumbled about that food himself. This room felt far too large for the few men assembled there.

Wick sat at the head of a mostly empty table. The men grew silent as Ran entered. "Listen up!" said Wick. "We've got a new recruit, fresh from Earth. He says he's a fixer, and have we got work for him. Talk to

Gooney if you want him to do anything. Name's Ran—until we find a better one."

Wick rattled off the names of his two guards and the three men on his management team. "And you already know Gooney."

Each place held a bowl containing an unidentifiable brownish mound. Certainly a change of texture from those wafers but . . .

Ran looked at the now silent and expressionless faces bending over their servings. He spooned up a bite and resisted the urge to spit out the gluey, tasteless mouthful. A faint bitter aftertaste accompanied his first swallow. "What's wrong with your food fab?"

"First item for you to fix," Wick cackled.

Ran was too hungry not to finish the meal. And too tired to fight with Wick about whether he belonged here or at the Warrens. He got up from the table, circled the room once, examining the hexagonal arrangement of rooms leading off from the common space, and went to find his bunk. His eyes were closed almost before he hit the mattress.

He should have kissed Aryn good-bye.

Pel

A firm hand shook Pel's shoulder. "Food upstairs. We're going now."

Pel took a bleary look at his sleeping niche carved into the sitting room wall. He was in Ed and Marney's rooms. He vaguely remembered hearing a gong.

Ed had said food. *Food* was a reason to move. A good reason. Something, anything other than those tasteless wafers—or that awful wafer wrapping. Pancakes would suit—a food fab could produce quite decent ones.

Pel dressed and pulled from his pack the gold-backed, palm-sized databank for which he'd had such high expectations. It supposedly held all his data, plus the answer to his question of the NODE.

He'd researched disappearances for years, ever since his friend Mik disappeared from the village when they were both ten. He'd had nightmares of disappearing himself. Only the act of searching for Mik on the Net had staved off the bad dreams. Then, the day before he asked his question of the NODE, he'd located Mik on a ship halfway around the world on the Kara Sea.

He should've gone home then. But no! After investing so much time and effort in his searches, he couldn't quit. And so here he was, far from Earth, holding a mute databank in the very place his disappeareds had vanished to. Far more disappeareds than he'd identified.

If these fosterlings had been due to be murdered when they came of age, then his question of the NODE had saved their lives. On the other hand, his question might have doomed them all.

Morbid thoughts. Hungry thoughts. He was starved for food and data. Those people upstairs could provide answers. Plus food. Geraldine Ramirez. Sam Suzuki. The man called Fletch. They'd all have stories.

"What's on the menu in this venue?" he muttered. Ed and Marney's rooms opened onto the foot of the curving, stone-carved staircase leading up to the communal room. Muted voices drew him.

He reached the top step just as a woman announced, "Perk's here."

The room grew quiet. Pel peered between heads to view the ramp. A slender man with graying hair entered with a limping Aryn on his arm. One of her hands was wrapped.

Injured. Where was Ran? He met Hallie's eyes asking the same question. She joined him and squeezed his arm.

Sam Suzuki rushed to his daughter. The man supporting Aryn stepped away. For a long moment Aryn and her father looked at each other. Sam stroked her face, while seeming to ask about her injuries. Glowing, Aryn shook her head.

Pel was remembering his first meeting with Aryn aboard the shuttle heading for Space Dock and the *Orpheus*. She had said, *All my life I've wondered about my parents.* He'd been impressed by her calm acceptance of their voyage. Well, now she knew.

Sam said something and waved toward the kitchen wall behind them, causing Aryn to turn. Pel and Hallie intercepted them as they crossed the room.

"Where's Ran?" Pel asked.

Aryn's smile faded, her brow furrowed. "Perk only had room for one. The other man, Wick, took Ran to the base."

"Wick," said Pel. "He spooked us last night, when we were trying to take off. They say Wick has the weapons."

"And now he's got Ran," Hallie said. "As hostage?"

"Maybe." Aryn bit her lip.

Sam put his arm around his daughter. "Orenda is waiting. Let's get you checked out."

"We want to hear about your trip later," Pel called after her. He was eager to meet Sam Suzuki too.

The kitchen gong sounded. Ed yelled, "Attention everybody. Get your food and eat. Then check the assignment board. Everyone has to pitch in around here. I repeat, everyone."

"I hope it's real food," Pel told Hallie.

When they reached the polished stone counter, Hallie giggled and nudged him. "Watch out for what you wish for."

It was real. No disguise. Tubers. One of each kind. Sweet potato, white potato. Cooked, split open, and salted. They took their plates to a table away from reunited kids and parents.

Pel alternated bites between tubers. "It's better than those wafers," he said. *Far* better than the potions Hallie had brewed. But he'd be hungry again—too soon. "How was your night?"

"I slept. Melody is . . . strange but easy to be around. She weaves. She has this loom with the most amazing fiber. I've never—"

"They've got to go back!" A man at the end of their table clanged his mug against the stone surface. "I won't go through a second starving time. They can't stay."

"How can they go anywhere?" said the woman opposite him calmly. "They've been dumped on us."

The man didn't look like he was starving, but no one could get fat on this kind of food. "We can't grow enough to feed this increase," he said.

"If *we* can't leave, *they* can't leave."

"I tell you, I won't starve again."

Hallie stirred. "What about the food-fab inserts? Some of them came with the first delivery. Did the rest come on your trip, Pel?"

The woman raised her brows and the man said, "*Food* fab? Talk to Wick about fabricators. We don't have any here."

Turds! Pel wanted to whine too. Food fab inserts and no way to use them—other than that horror that Hallie had been inventing?

"Move out!" shouted Ed. "Check your assignments and get to work. Normal duty rotation follows breakfast. Those of you with offspring, plan to include them so they can familiarize themselves with the layout. Meeting at midday meal."

Pel got up. His disappeareds were here. And their stories, probably enough for several books. He needed to find a way to charge his dumb little notetaker-recorder for interviews. First, find out what happened to Aryn and Ran. Move on to Sam Suzuki. Learn more about this Wick. Discover who they all were and their histories. He was a researcher like his grandfather. Here was the perfect source material.

Meanwhile, duty called. He picked up his dishes and went to find the assignment board.

Aryn

She had met her father at last, seeing half of herself in his face, feeling his caring as he propelled her over to a small room beside the kitchen.

"You're left-handed?" Orenda asked. Aryn nodded. The big woman's gentle hands felt Aryn's right hand. "Your little finger is broken."

Orenda splinted three fingers together, leaving thumb and index finger free. "Sorry," she said when Aryn winced. "We're short on pain-killers." She chose a packet from the stone shelves behind her. "This will help bring down the swelling in both your hand and your ankle. Stir a spoonful in a cup of water three times a day. I'll check again in a few days to be sure the finger is properly aligned."

Sam thanked the healer. "You'll want to rest," he told Aryn as she followed him down the stairs. "Third door on the right."

Her hand and ankle ached; she did want rest—but not yet. "Tell me about my mother. What was her name?"

Sam's eyes took on a more distant focus. "Rowan. You inherited my hair and features, but you have your mother's blue eyes. She saw more, knew more, than anyone else. She had a gift of knowing. When you were born, she caught that slime flux virus that no medicine could touch. You either survived it or not." His lips twisted. "She was doing better. We were so sure she was overcoming it. A big story was about to break and they wanted me for an interview. Rowan urged me to go. I should never have left the two of you. That was the last time . . ."

He focused again on Aryn. "Seventeen years? I knew nothing from the time I got captured until we landed here. Others did arrive with spouses, so when they told me Rowan was dead, I had no reason for doubt. The next two ships brought news, teasers—even a picture of you once—as warnings that if we didn't behave, something would happen to our children. All I knew was you'd survived somewhere. My daughter."

And here was her father after those same seventeen years. "I used to sketch how I imagined my parents to be. Do you have a picture of my mother?"

He crossed the room to a little niche in the wall above his bed. "Just this. I'm glad I had it when they grabbed me, something I could hold."

Aryn drew a soft breath at the small oval. Smiling eyes looked out as if responding to a question. "Why did they?" she asked.

"Grab me? I never found out."

"Pel has a theory about that."

"Tell me later. You must be tired and Orenda wants you to rest. I have to get to my assigned duty. Is that your bag?" He pointed to her small case beside a padded ledge.

She nodded.

"Will you be comfortable here?" He patted the ledge. "Maybe you can rest until the noon gong." He offered her a worried smile and left.

Her mother. Aryn looked again at Rowan's face before replacing the picture in its niche. Her mother's *real* face. That particular hole in her knowledge was now filled. The wall of portraits back in her bedroom on

Earth—guesses as to what her parents looked like—she could release them all now.

She pulled the purple crystal from her pocket and placed it beside Rowan, then crawled onto the padded ledge to elevate her ankle for the first time since waking in the tiny stone fortress Ran built. With the coming of day, she had finally seen the sketch she'd drawn in the dirt. Only a few rough lines, they had shaped an aircar. It might have been any aircar, anywhere, even back in Dodge City—but looking at it brought a return of the evening's calm. Someone would come; she had no doubts that Ran had succeeded.

Her mother had had a gift of knowing. A new particular to fit into an old grief.

Now sheltered by different stone walls, Aryn lay back. *Be well, Ran.* There must be some reason for him to be at the base. *Be well. Stay on guard.*

Hallie

Hallie ran fingers through her short hair. The two tubers on her plate were gone. People carried dishes to the counter, their breakfasts finished. The room was fast emptying, kids accompanying parents, Leif with his stepparents.

Her stomach churned. Important questions remained unresolved.

"Duty roster." She picked up her plate and cup and followed Pel to the smooth stone counter separating the kitchen from the gathering room to study the names chalked down the front of the stone supporting the counter.

"Kitchen cleanup," read Pel. "Both of us."

Marney bustled up. Her severely tied-back hair was not especially becoming, but Hallie felt a twinge of envy at its length. She wanted her braid back.

What a baby! Whining about hair. Here were people stolen from Earth, finally reunited with their children—and Leif discovering he was an orphan all over again. Her own losses were so minor—hair and the memory of one day—compared to their ginormous problem of getting back to Earth. And another thing—

"I'm your mentor this morning," Marney said. "We'll get this work done and then you can help gather food for lunch."

"They took Ran off to the base," Hallie said. "How do we get him back here?"

"You don't," Marney said sharply. She picked up a plate and cup from one of the stone tables. "Not till they're ready to release him. We need dishes washed, counters scrubbed, and the gathering room swept out."

Hallie gave Pel a quick look. He gave a brief head shake and asked, "Is there enough food for everyone? We overheard some concern."

"We're working on that. The base is supposed to supply us according to how much gets mined, but we've received nothing for a very long time. We grow what we can."

Already incensed on Ran's behalf, Hallie burst out, "It's inhumane to withhold food! Food is one of the basic rights."

"Right." Marney surged before them into the kitchen. Hallie had the impression the woman was rolling her eyes and thinking, *Get with reality!*

But what *was* reality? Ran was trapped at the base. She and Pel were alone here with no parents to advocate for them. *And Ran too!* No one had claimed him. This was more independence than she'd ever imagined.

An hour later, Hallie stacked the last plate while Pel wiped down the high stone table running the length of the kitchen. Stone pipes for water. A well-thought-out, intricate construction. Three big ovens occupied the narrow back wall. Hallie opened one and received a welcome puff of warmth. That was how they'd cooked the tubers.

"How do they heat?" said Pel. He pulled out his little gadget. It blinked. "Hah! It's charging. There's power here."

Hallie eyed the surrounding stone. Sources of power were commonplace back on Earth, but stone would block transmission of ambient energies.

"Sporadic," said Marney, returning from sweeping. "One of the work crews is planning to apply a new coat of nanopaint, since your cargo included it."

Marney's words sent a surge of bile to Hallie's gurgling stomach. Nanopaint? Marney was talking about a longer stay, an indefinite stay. *Leave yesterday already!*

Hallie's sight glazed. The ship had left them, after dropping off nanopaint, and seeds, and fab inserts. And a bunch of kids. For how long? Years? A lifetime? She'd been living in a dream. Of course, nanopaint and seeds and— *They were trapped.*

Marney eyed their work. "Looks good. Let's go to the greenhouse now."

Hallie bit her tongue and followed. The wind snatched her breath, sanded her face, and drew tears during the brief walk to another ramp leading into a greenhouse and hydroponics space. Toward the back, small groups bent over plots of some kind of grain.

Marney steered them to rows of greens and handed each a basket. "Fill these with salad greens. Leave the roots and some leaves on each plant. Then you can thin those carrots and lay them on top. After that, we'll go back and wash them." She strode off toward the distant workers.

Hallie bent to snap red lettuce leaves from the nearest bunch.

By midday, they had two heaps of colorful greens topped with thin orange, white, and purple carrots. And backaches. Hugging the baskets, she and Pel braved the wind to deliver them. In the Warrens' kitchen, Bork, the stocky man who'd yelled at Ed last night, ordered them to wash the vegetables.

When they finished, Bork released them. Hallie sank onto a bench, pressing her hands into the small of her back. "My hibernation pod sounds good right now." Her skin felt cracked from dirt and wind.

Pel slumped beside her. "Yeah. I thought of it as my casket. Very undemanding place. I've no energy for interviews."

The lunch line began to form, and they joined it to collect plates of food. Hallie tried to chew slowly to make the salad and bland mush on flatbread last. "Better than wafers." At least it was real. Like breakfast.

Ed brought the crowded room to order. "First," he said, "you newcomers, stick together. Never go off alone. Do what you're told. We all have to work to survive. None of you are allowed in the mine. Don't go off with anyone not your own flesh and blood."

"What about our friends?" Ramon challenged.

"Yes to friends. Stick with them or family, is what I'm saying," said Ed. "Meanwhile, the rest of us have a lot to do. I want to get you newcomers trained to help out with the non-mine labor. Bork, can you train helpers?"

Bork stood in the kitchen entrance. "I can always use helpers, Ed, but they can't waste anything."

The woman who'd shared their breakfast table stood up. "How are we to feed these extra mouths?"

That topic drew Hallie's mind from her backache. She bobbed up. "We arrived with lots of food-fab inserts. I was starting to experiment with them when those wafer things ran out."

Some of the teens groaned.

"It's a good thing you got found," said Bork, "before you killed your-selves. That stuff needs to be precise to the molecule."

Her face heated. *Unfair!* She hadn't poisoned anyone. Pel patted her arm as she sank back down. And no one had *found* them! Ran and Aryn had achieved that.

"Send the kids and the fab inserts to Wick," said the man who'd complained about starving. "Let *him* feed them!"

"*You* go to Wick, Satch!" Nick's mother, no taller than her son, glared at him. "You think Wick'll do anything but blackmail us with our own children?"

Satch looked startled. "I was joking," he said feebly.

"What should we do?" another asked. "Steal Wick's food fab?"

"Why not?" Hallie thought it was Tesia's mother speaking. "And his Brain too. These kids have no chance to continue their studies."

"Everyone can learn by doing," said one of the men.

"Learn to survive, sure, but not how to thrive!" She put her arm around Tesia. "I want my daughter to get back home, and us too. If Earth is sending our children, it's no secret we're here."

"Unless it was a gesture of good riddance. Ever think of that?" The woman sounded bitter.

"We don't know that," Tesia's mother said. "To my mind, it's the first sign of hope I've had in thirteen years. Somewhere out there is a ship. How do we reach it?"

Reba's stepfather stood to interrupt the discussion that followed.

"We're no longer merely trying to survive. We've got to consider our children. They need their educations; they need to stay healthy; they need hope for their futures."

The talk circled, worries with no answers. Beside her, Pel played with his little note-taking gadget. He must be thinking of interviews; he was lucky to have a purpose. The others had parents to get acquainted with. *We're in this together,* she'd told Reba on the ship, and Reba had said it back to her in the shelter, but Hallie had never felt so alone.

The meeting broke up. She and Pel again performed kitchen cleanup and then returned to the greenhouse. This time Marney introduced them to Gardner, the tiny woman in charge, who guided Pel toward the beets. Hallie tagged along, waiting to learn her assignment.

"How did you happen to come here?" Pel asked Gardner.

"Talk won't fill bellies. Do you know how to thin beets? Bork wants them two hours ago."

Pel nodded, sighed, and got busy.

Honestly, thought Hallie, Pel had no sense of timing.

Gardner led her to another area. "I want you to tie up these straggly beans."

"Do you have bees?" Hallie asked. "The ship had bumblebees for its hydroponics."

"Ships have specially bred pollinators. Unfortunately, our original insects didn't survive that first year. We've done it by hand, since."

"My mother is a horticulturist. I could help with pollinating." A chance to prove herself.

"Thanks," said Gardner, "but I've already recruited Aryn for that." Aryn, in spite of her injuries, was at work two rows over. "She has a fine, steady hand with a brush. But as you know, there's plenty of work here."

Hallie busied herself tying up bean plants. Aryn's fine, steady hands, broken finger and all, curdled her insides. Aryn the calm, Aryn the brave, Aryn with the well-behaved hair.

At supper beside Pel, she forced her eyes to stay open to scoop up the yeast and vegetable dip on her plate. Eat, work, eat, work, eat, sleep. Not enough food to satisfy. How soon could they get back home from this pestilential place?

She'd wanted to do important things with her life. If only her tooth phone worked. With a word she could connect to her sister Liz, or her friend Cass—Cass who was even now immersed in medical studies. Or she could record in her journal, listen to her own words.

Lucky Pel. He'd made his move to independence when he biked to Dodge. She'd done nothing at all. She sighed.

Beside her, Pel said, "Hard day?"

"Not hard, just—" She sighed again. "Yeah. Super hard. Hard to work on so little food."

"A meeting!" someone yelled. "Meeting now." The room became a hive of movement.

Ed stood. "What's your topic, Jay?"

Leif's stepfather rose. "Our kids have just gotten out of hibernation. We're not feeding them enough. And to schedule a full day's work is far too much in their current state."

"Remember when we got here?" another parent shouted. "None of us was capable of a full day's labor."

Moving to Ed's side, Marney said, "You're right, of course. I can schedule time off. The food question is harder to deal with."

Bork, from the food-service window, announced, "I'm doing all I can to increase yeast production," which brought a groan from some of the kids.

Hallie called out, "It's good. And Bork has a fine touch with his seasonings."

Bork smiled. "Thank you, miss. And to give you credit, I'm studying how we might use some of those food inserts—particularly the protein additives—to see if we can't make some judicious increase in our offerings."

Hallie smiled back. She was beginning to like the man. Bork said what he thought, like last night when he yelled at Ed, and this morning when he reacted to her suggestion. She relaxed on the bench beside Pel.

"There's Aryn." Pel waved her over.

At her approach, Hallie leaned forward. "What happened with you and Ran?"

Aryn told them. A soft smile curled her lips when she finished. "Perk said Ran fought to turn around and come back in the dark. He doesn't give up."

At a wave from her father, she stood. "See you later."

Ran had done so much—the search, the climb, the rescue—only to be stuck off by himself. Alone again. *So unfair!* Pel's warm presence comforted her. Everybody else had someone. And they all looked worn down, all battling for survival. But Ran had no one.

She ground her teeth, wishing her journal were still live. Her thought accidentally triggered an old recording: *Went virtual jogging with Cass. We had a good talk, only why didn't I mention Ran working for Uncle Jack? I mean, there's nothing to hide—so I must be hiding from myself. . . . I didn't want to admit to my own selfishness. That's why his presence bothered me!* Hallie shut off the sound of her voice. Selfish and petty, objecting to Ran's helping Uncle Jack. She ought to grow up!

A surge of decision swept her to her feet. Pel, fingering his maroon-striped noter gadget, had purpose. He didn't need her holding him back. "You'll want to be doing interviews," she said. "I'm just a drag on you right now."

She'd go downstairs and think while watching Melody weave. At Pel's soft "*Hey*" of protest, she almost turned back. Halfway across the room, a man blocked her path. She took in bushy eyebrows, strong jaw, white teeth. It was his smile, she decided, that made him attractive. Not nearly as old as most of the adults.

"Lovely lady, how can we cheer you up?"

She shook her head. No one could do that.

"A challenge, then. I like a challenge. How about telling me why you're so sad."

"Other than being marooned here?"

"Maybe you'd like a tour of the Warrens."

"What's there to see? I know the kitchen, the greenhouse, Melody's rooms."

"Other work areas. The mine office. I bet you haven't seen the yeast vats." He chuckled at her wrinkled nose. "Maybe so, but necessary for our well-being. And the algae pools. And the mills for oil and grains. Hmm, what else? Maps?"

"Maps of the planet or this area or what?"

"All of them."

"That might be interesting." She could find out where the base was. "Who are you?"

"My moniker is Rumbo."

She wrinkled her nose again.

"Just a shortcut name, easier to say and remember than my whole label. And you are Hallie, one of the unexplained presences among us."

Unexplained to her too! How could one lost day have caused this exile?

He tilted his head. "Homesick?"

"That's an understatement." She pressed her lips together to keep from crying. "I miss my family. But even more—no, not more, but—I've lost my phone connection; it had a journaling function that helped me process my thoughts."

He blinked at her thoughtfully. "People used to journal on paper."

"Is there paper here?"

"Nope. And plastic flimsies are scarce. Why not make some? Paper I mean. Cellulose, isn't it? Plant matter. You'll need to talk to Gardner."

Talking on paper seemed really old-fashioned, but it was an idea. "Thanks."

"*De nada.* Engineers like to solve practical problems. If you locate the material, I can help design a way to roll it flat."

"You're an engineer? Then . . . you're not one of the exiles?"

"Actually no. I'm a mining engineer. I grabbed the chance to come, straight from school."

"Don't you feel trapped here, unable to go home?"

"We knew we were in for a long stay when we signed on."

"How many of you came by choice and how many were shanghaied?"

He rubbed his nose. "Can't tell you that. Each person owns his or her own story. Meanwhile, do you good to learn the layout. Come on." Rumbo led the way up the ramp.

"But—" *What about that rule: Don't go anywhere with a stranger?*

Hallie sniffed. Rules! Everyone but Pel was a stranger. At the top of the ramp, Rumbo pulled on a long overcoat and handed her one. She followed him out through door slats into the dark. A blast of wind tore away her breath.

"Cover your face." Rumbo's shout came muted through a strip of cloth he held over his mouth and nose. He pulled up her coat's attached hood, and she captured the flap to cover her own face.

Relief—though the wind still cut through.

"Behind us, the Warrens. Over that way"—she followed the wave of his arm—"is the greenhouse." A glow of light seeped through the rounded, semitransparent domes protecting the food crop. "We get some energy from the domes, but most comes from the wind farm that powers the mine."

"Where's that?" She had to half shout through her face covering.

"You can't see it from here. It's maybe a half kilometer past the greenhouse. Probably still too close to human habitation but—"

Light flared from the top of the ramp.

"What are you doing out here with that girl?" Ed yelled, his voice almost drowned in the wind. He hadn't put on a coat.

With a hand on her back, Rumbo urged Hallie back toward Ed and pushed through the slats. "Now how much trouble could I cause by showing Miss Hallie the layout of this place?"

"Do it in company, not as a twosome. You—"

"Your rules are impossible!" Hallie raged. "You warn us against strangers but almost every single person here is a stranger. Why don't you put signs on people, so we know who we can talk to? Even the kids who came to join their parents are with complete strangers. Why not give us the whole story and have done with it?"

Rumbo chuckled.

Ed's mouth opened and closed. He finally said, "For now, stay in groups. Please."

Hallie pulled off her wind coat and handed it to Rumbo, who saluted and went back out. She scrubbed her hands through her hair and glared, furious at so much more than Ed's rules. The utter unfairness of the journey, the wind's constant chafing . . .

She wanted her journal function back!

Marney hurried over. "No harm done," she said. "Hallie, come talk with me a moment." Hallie followed her to a table. "Ed is taking his *in loco parentis* duties very seriously. You're new here. We don't know you; you don't know us. It hasn't always been easy maintaining a civil society in these close quarters. We've been in survival mode since the beginning. We're still in survival mode, but we try our best to remain fair and decent."

Hallie looked down. She'd been none too civil. Liz would've told her to back off and look at the big picture. Liz managed a whole city, but her sister knew nothing of the Warrens. And neither did she.

"Rumbo was only being helpful," she said in his defense. "He suggested I ask Gardner about making paper to journal on."

"You are a beautiful young woman," Marney said.

Ha! With her hair? She clenched her fists to keep from smoothing it down again.

"Some of these men have had little contact with available women and might consider you fair game." Marney tilted her head. "What is the age of consent on Earth now? They were starting to put a national rule in place, rather than state-by-state laws. Did that get instigated?"

"Yes, eighteen."

"And you are?"

"I was sixteen when I left."

"So not eighteen any way you look at it. Nor are the others, if we disallow hibernation time." The line between Marney's eyes deepened.

"The news that two children died when they reached maturity is very disturbing. Ed . . ." She shook her head. "All of us feel the need to protect you young ones."

"But you don't know what to do with us," Hallie said.

Marney nodded agreement. "If I had a child, I'd want her as bright and quick as you. Meanwhile, I'm teaming you up with Melody for your assignments. I hope that's agreeable?"

"That's fine. I like her. Her weaving is lovely. But something's wrong, isn't it?"

Marney sighed and rubbed her hands across her thighs. "She's grieving her husband. When she grieves, she shuts down and does nothing but weave. If you can distract her, that'll be a big help." She rose. "Can I count on you?"

"I'll try." Marney was trying to distract *her* too. "But I want to go home more than anything."

"So do we all," Marney said decisively. "For now, what we have is right here."

Cold congealed around Hallie's heart. Like an ocean wave, her situation kept surging back. She had independence—too much independence—but still no sense of purpose or direction. And she was so *filthy spamguts* tired! She and Pel and Ran had had no idea what they were getting into.

Ran. *There* was a purpose. She should have asked Rumbo where they parked their vehicles. The big Trilby had been gone when they headed out to the greenhouse this morning. They must park them somewhere. Maybe there was a smaller vehicle they could fly to go get Ran. She'd go watch Melody and plan.

Pel

Pel remained slumped on the back bench, chilled by Hallie's departure. Why had she called herself a drag? Didn't she know how he felt? Oh, so now he expected her to be a mind reader. And why *should* she care? He was the cause of her exile.

Frass! Some guy was smiling down at Hallie. Pel's fist tightened around his noter. If he had given up on his obsessive mystery when he found Mik, Hallie might be safe at home. Arriving at the Warrens—*only last night*—they'd been immediately thrown into work. Oh, to be home in the village. Especially for a Sunday dinner, the family working together on the meal, cornbread dripping with real honey, piles of vegetables, slabs of meat—mostly *near-meat*—filling every crack and cranny of his hungry body. He'd left that comfort to solve this mystery.

The mystery was all he had left. He might as well make a start, even with no way to record. The room was emptying, but Fletch remained at the end of a table with another man, both sipping from cups. Pel walked over.

"Excuse me, sir. Ed called you Fletch last night when you came to get us at the Shed. Are you Gabe Fletcher?"

"Why should I be? Excuse me, I've nothing to say." Fletch upended his cup and stalked out. The other man stood as well. "Don't ask personal questions."

Pel stared after them. *What?* Back when rescuing them from the Shed, Fletch hadn't hesitated to talk. He'd been the *good guy*, giving priority to lives over badly needed supplies.

Mouse turds! He should have thanked the man for coming for them, and for valuing lives over supplies, especially now that he saw how important any and all supplies were for the Warrens. *Blundering idiot, not a whit of wit!* Lurching into that put-down. A total stranger, arriving with their kids. Why should they answer his questions?

Hallie was nowhere in sight. And where the hell was that big guy she'd been talking to?

No, there she was, coming through the slats at the top of the ramp, wearing a long coat and looking totally furious.

Pel slumped against the stone wall. He didn't know what to do next.

Ran

Ran took a bite of his second gag-inspiring meal. Every muscle that had carried him up the ridge ached, but his nap had revived his mind. "So who discovered this place?"

"Atlas Corp," said the bald one, Einstein. Was that his real name or was he supposed to be a genius? "Back during the Atlas dismantling, it renamed itself AstroMining and moved headquarters to the asteroids. We ship them the Beijingite. AstroMining turns around and sells it as if they manufactured it."

"So some unknown ship crashes into the planet," said Ran, "ends up in the sea, and you mine the Beijingite scraped from its hull? It must have been *huge*." Ran waited. No one spoke but neither did they deny it. "Did anyone search for the ship?"

Capshaw, Wick's minerals expert, stretched out his legs. "If the first arrivals did, no one told us. They IDed the B'ite and named the planet Lodestone in its honor."

"You get this close to an alien and no one cares?"

"Perk figures the crash to be about a century ago," said dark-bearded

Noland, Wick's other guard.

"So? Didn't anyone wonder about their ship? Like how its propulsion works? Or whether they'll come back for it? Even a hundred-year-old ship under the sea ought to be looked into."

"It's death now to consider it." Noland didn't seem to be defending any position, just stating a fact. "The ship's revenge, maybe."

"Death? What d'you mean?" Ran looked around the table.

"Fairly early on, something killed the miners. Whatever it is stops the bots too. So, we moved farther up the Rift and established a new site and new rules. Only bots go in. No telling how long that site will last. But the farther from the sea, the better, since the 'creeps' come up from the wreck, near as we can tell."

"Creeps? What could kill both people and bots?"

Capshaw said, "We've imagined everything from tiny bots shooting death rays to a virus. Perk is fixated on nanites. Nanites don't make sense to me."

At Ran's look of disbelief, Capshaw held up a hand. "And no. No one has tried to find out. Delver wanted to, but—" Capshaw returned to his yucky mush.

Nanites? Ran rubbed his chapped face. How do you build a nanite trap? You'd need an analyzer to identify what you caught. These men weren't curious about what the alien ship looked like, how it had functioned, or anything else he wanted to ask. He finished his glop and pushed away from the table to prowl the big room, with Gooney following.

Aryn would be at the Warrens. His hand-carved chess set was there too, unless his bag was still at the shelter—the *Shed.* Lucky his smart tool and little knife had traveled in his pocket; doubly lucky he hadn't lost them in that sinkhole.

How was he to get to the Warrens? Walking would require a map and a pack for food and water. Better to fly. Three choices: the big Trilby, the Mini, or that other battered Mini.

First, try for some cooperation. Wick's men remained slouched around the table.

"So, what needs repairing?" he asked Gooney.

"Food fab, for one."

"Let's see it. You have consistent energy?"

"Good enough. Needs improving, but wind tears it off as fast as we get a fresh coat on the roof."

"You ever make trips to the Warrens?"

"*You* won't, long as Wick wants you here," Gooney said.

"Huh." The opposite to cooperating was to become too much of a pain to keep. That would be Plan B. "What's wrong with the fab?"

"Programming is what Einstein says."

Ran popped open the lid of the waist-high fabricator; its row of chemical inserts looked to be in order. The hologram menu refused to pop up. He pulled out the inserts to check their housings. No problems there.

His smart tool remained his last hope. If the fab retained its programming, the tool could identify the problem. But the smart tool only brought up a list of food qualities. Well, he could try.

"What do they want it to make?"

"Hey, Einstein," Gooney yelled. "The kid wants to know what you couldn't program this fab to make."

Bald Einstein wandered over. "Those crunchy things Perk eats."

Ran's mouth watered. "I like those too. Had some on the ridge. Where does he get his?"

"Perk's got his own fab."

"Do they have a name? Or did you try to duplicate them by guess?"

"They're called 'spicy crisps.' My guesses haven't been good enough for this piece of shit." Einstein aimed a kick at the fab. Ran's fists tightened, but the bald man's foot didn't make contact. "You have a try then."

Scrolling through the descriptors, Ran ordered crunchy, cayenne spicy finger food. The fab hummed and clanked. The other men wandered over to see the results, but what came out wasn't orange or crisp or spicy. More mush.

"It needs to be reprogrammed." Ran said. "Perk mentioned sun storms?"

"The fab's been like that forever," said Einstein.

Gooney disagreed. "No, only since the others decamped. We had plenty of those crunch things when the women were here."

"Yeah, well that feels like forever," said Einstein.

The other men nodded agreement.

"Are you saying they sabotaged this when they left?"

"Sabotage," muttered Gooney. Einstein gave him a sharp glance, and Gooney shut up.

"Your Brain would hold the specs. Why haven't you requested it to reprogram the fab?"

"No can do," Gooney said.

"Wick said the base has the only Brain."

"Wick won't let you anywhere near." And no one disagreed with Einstein's statement.

Ran displayed open palms. "I don't do miracles. You need proper specs."

"No Brain access." This time Einstein said it.

"Why can't Wick request the specs?"

Silence met his question. Clearly a mystery here.

"All right. Tell me about the beginning. You landed at the Shed and set up your basecamp. Where was the mine?"

"Used to be southwest of here." Einstein's gesture was toward the side of the dome away from the connected hangar. "But after those deaths, Perk ordered it moved."

"Who died?"

"DeWarg—he was boss before Wick—and three other men."

"What went wrong?"

"Never found out. Perk said we'd gone too deep, but he didn't know what could eat both humans and robots."

"*Eat?*"

"Not the bots as far as we know; they froze up. But the vids showed human bodies dissolving," Einstein said. "Here. I'll show you." He pulled a vid-cam from a clutter of instruments and ordered, "Play back."

Ran moved closer as a hologram formed, displaying a dimly lit area with a glassy, melted surface. The floor of the Rift, he decided. A low-slung robot with a rounded back and front scraper worked away.

"That's a turtle," said Einstein.

The turtle froze in place. A man stepped into view, went down on his knees to check the bot—

The hologram came to an abrupt end. Einstein swore. "I could kill that damned Brain. It's eating memory now." He stomped off, shouting for Wick.

Ran picked up the vid-cam and examined it. Not dead, but not responsive. The Brain eating stored vid memories made no sense. As their master computer, the Brain held specs for all the machinery in order to run everything. Why would it destroy data?

And why couldn't Wick ask the Brain for reprograming?

The management team surrounded Wick in the doorway to his office. Wick's voice rose. ". . . that son of a . . . He's dug his own grave if he's not already in it."

Capshaw jerked his head in Ran's direction and Wick lowered his voice.

Wick blamed *somebody*, but what had that *somebody* done? Curiouser and curiouser. Ran ground his teeth together. He didn't want to be here.

Back on Earth, all he had wanted was to work with machines. This place should be heaven. But machines did nothing to fill the hole created by his missing friends. *Holes.* An Aryn-shaped hole. A Pel-sized hole. A Hallie-sized hole. He hadn't had a chance to get acquainted with the others, but they were all part of an even bigger hole. The sooner he got to the Warrens, the better. He was tired of being alone.

Whatever Wick expected of him, it wasn't going to happen. No way was he staying. He'd borrow that Mini and find the Warrens on his own.

ooney's snores filled the sleeping chamber they shared.

Ran inched out of bed to avoid triggering the lights. His fingertips against the wall, he crept slowly into the central room. The sleeping rooms were arranged off four of the six sides of the hexagon. Wick's office, the door to the right of the entry, was Ran's target.

His foot banged into something. He jerked back, gasping as his ribs flared. His sudden motion brought up the room lights. He froze. At a count of thirty, the lights dimmed. He moved forward with a clear image of his route.

Resting his head against the office door, he detected the faint gurgling of a circulation system. An organic computer was being fed there. So at least it was being maintained. Also confirmed: the door did not respond to his palm print. For now, he had no access to the Brain.

Stifling a yawn, Ran inched back to bed.

DAY FIVE

Secrets

Ran

Enough light came through the translucent ceiling to tell Ran it was morning, while wind attempted to shake the solid dome overhead. The men at breakfast grumbled more about the wind than the food. That made a change of sorts.

"Well, blow me down, mates."

"No trips today."

"Shitty planet. Shitty food."

"Wind season, what's to love?"

"Muck to eat, muck to breathe."

"Good day for the boy to fix your toys then," said Wick, leaning back in his chair. His management team left the table, and Wick smiled at Ran with satisfaction. "Well, my boy, we can keep you busy for quite a spell."

My boy. Ran's jaw clenched. "Your Brain needs to reprogram the food fab. I don't see why you think you need me."

"You'll see, son," Wick grunted.

Son. Ran gritted his teeth. No chance he'd get away from here today, with that gale outside. Play along. More than one foster father had treated him like a half-wit. If Wick and his men underestimated him, so much the better.

Mineralogist Capshaw returned and tossed Ran a 3-D chess control. Ran thumbed it on. No holograph display. A reasonable challenge.

Saxon, his perpetual squint a sign of too much time in the wind, dropped three virtual helmets on the table. *Why not just one?* Bald Einstein carefully set down a battered interactive Psycho Spy Wars game. Virile flopped what looked like a lightweight spacesuit on the table.

"What's that?" Ran asked.

"A full-function stim suit." Virile's face revealed satisfaction at Ran's reaction.

Pleasure bot. They'd been hawked on Dodge's streets—half virtual, half live-stimulus from the suit's many contact points. To work on that would be like handling someone's underwear.

"This is all entertainment," Ran said. "I thought your repair needs were more serious."

"You think keeping us sane isn't important?" said Capshaw. "Everything's breaking down and no replacements coming in."

"You don't want to be around this bunch when they're bored," said Wick. He stood. "All right, men. Get to work." They filed out, leaving Gooney behind to watch Ran. "Never fear," Wick added from his office door, "there's other repairs too, boy. The food fab, motion sensors, tools, Gooney's still— The list is endless."

Ran collected the items and moved to examine them at one of the work stations spaced around the room. VR helmets were merely headbands with contacts. Each of Saxon's helmets included a small knob holding stored programs and a battery. Maybe one held exercise options.

"Hasn't anyone tried cleaning these things?" Ran asked.

"Only so many times you can clean them," said Gooney, leaning back with his feet on the corner of the large central table.

"I'll start there anyway. Where do I find solvent? And if that doesn't work, where's your hardware fab?"

"Hardware fab needs repairing too."

Ran growled. They could have taken better care of their machines.

Gooney got up with creaking joints. "Come on. I'll show you the cleaning stuff."

Ran tried out the first VR helmet he cleaned. The contacts were worn, but an index of offerings came up. *Porn.*

He tossed it aside and reached for the next, letting his thoughts turn to Aryn and the teens at the Warrens. Were they in danger near the current mine? People and bots had been killed by some unseen force. And after all these years, why had no one ever investigated the cause? That alien ship, wasn't anyone curious about what had crashed into the sea?

The second helmet index revealed virtual dreams. He pulled off the headband. The third held virtual sports—the violent, adrenalin-inducing ones. No exercise on any of them.

Einstein's Psycho Spy Wars game was also virtual, with handheld controls for two players. Einstein had cared for his game. The gear was stowed neatly, the box only slightly battered. The first handheld control felt alive, almost eager. Ran shrugged. No. Machines had no feelings— or did they? When he picked up the other one, his hand tingled. After a moment—during which it seemed to be going through a reset—it purred with an almost imperceptible sensation of a machine in top condition.

Because of his VR phobia, Ran had never had a chance to play anything like it. Psycho Spy Wars even included a low-level mind scan for players to read the thoughts and emotions of their opponents. While he'd been in the hospital after that explosion, Security had used their mind scan *to verify the truthfulness of his statement*, they said. He wondered what being on the receiving end would feel like. He repacked the handhelds and set the box gently on the big table. Psycho Spy Wars. He wanted to experience it for himself.

He turned to Capshaw's 3-D chess game, thinking of his wooden set. Was his bag containing his few belongings still at the Shed? Those two chess games he'd played with Pel back in Dodge had shown them to be evenly matched. He wished he were with the other kids. With an internal growl, he turned his attention back to Capshaw's set. It wasn't dead, yet the holographic image wouldn't come up, no matter what he did. He finally put it aside.

Virile's pleasure bot received only perfunctory attention. Ran then picked up Capshaw's chess game again. "Where's the other control? Shouldn't there be two?"

"It went to the Warrens," Gooney said. "Capshaw plays against himself—or did."

"Maybe it got confused," Ran said. "Something's gone quarks here."

Doors slammed as the men gathered in the main room. "Lunchtime," Gooney said.

Ran stretched, felt the stab of sore ribs, and went for a quick wash. By the time he got back, his work station was stacked with a pile of tools.

While eating, Wick said, "Better make the food fab your next priority, son."

He *wasn't* Wick's son. "I already tried. It needs reprogramming, which means you need your Brain to do the work."

"Not allowed," said Wick.

"And if it needs parts, you need a working hardware fab."

"Another item to fix," Gooney cackled.

Ran looked at Capshaw. "Your chess game isn't dead. I'd like to work with it some more." Just maybe his smart tool could do the trick; he should have thought of that before.

About midafternoon, Ran needed to move. Ignoring muscle aches and sore ribs, he headed for the hangar. Gooney galloped after him. "Where are you going?"

"I need a walk," Ran said, "unless you have an exercise room."

"We did once. It got dismantled."

"Dismantled at the same time everything broke down, or for some other reason?" What was wrong with these guys?

"We needed more sleeping space. And some bits were needed for other things."

Ran pushed through the door between living quarters and hangar and made a walking circuit of the area. The Trilby's hatch stood open. He climbed inside to sit in Wick's seat. "Access?"

"UNAUTHORIZED VOICE," responded the truck.

"What d'you think you're doing?" Gooney yelled.

Ran climbed back out. "It was running rough when we came. I thought if it gave permission, I might clean it up a bit."

"You thought wrong. And stay out of Wick's Mini too."

That left the wrecked one. Ran circled around to examine it more thoroughly and smelled leaking anti-grav fluid. "What happened to it?"

"Happened?" Gooney said. "*Happened* Delver crashed it."

"What's the story? How did he crash?"

"It was after they all moved to the Warrens. One day Delver came back for something. Wick caught him. Del ran. Wick chased him and brought him down. We hauled him and the car back and patched him up. Locked him up. He didn't say nothing. Clammed up good. We all started to feel sorry for him. Then one day he was gone."

"Doesn't he have a chip?" Ran said. "Couldn't you track him with a scanner?" though he hadn't seen any scanners in that pile on his table. The chip on his right scapula itched with his desire to know what data had been added to it at the spaceport.

"Only if the body's nearby and if your scanner works. Nothing at a distance."

"How did he escape?"

"We never figured that out," said Gooney. "He was on foot. The plants shoot you full when wind blows hard. Nothing to eat out there."

"So, he's dead?"

"Dunno. Prob'ly, but . . . dunno."

Ran mapped out a route, trotted the length of the Trilby, past Wick's Mini, around the wrecked Mini to the far wall and back again, noting a pile of rubbish in one corner. He slowed his jog to check the crates from the Shed. One held hardware fab inserts, including inserts for nanoassembly. *If* he could get the hardware fab working, he'd print out a scanner from scratch and read his chip. He took another look beneath the wrecked Mini.

Gooney asked, "What are you doing?"

"Just curious." Ran brushed himself off and picked up speed. Turning at the big Trilby, he misjudged his angle and sideswiped the corner.

"*Ow!*" The impact seized his chest. Already his legs were complaining. Breathing heavily, he slid the hangar door open two inches to stare outside. The screaming wind tried to force the door wider. Clouds scudded past at an incredible speed.

"There you are!" said Capshaw.

Ran threw his weight into closing the door. "Yeah?"

"We need you to repair my analyzer. What are you doing?"

"Checking out the sky. You ever feel shut in here?"

"It's a stir-crazy time. Don't worry, it doesn't last long."

"What happened to your other chess control?"

"My partner took it to the Warrens."

"Why split the game up?"

Capshaw shrugged. "His choice. I had a job to do here."

And of course Capshaw's analyzer needed programming, and probably parts from the nonworking hardware fab as well. This fixing job was going nowhere fast.

At supper, Ran put down his spoon and asked Einstein, "How about a chance to try your Psycho Spy Wars game to see if my adjustments worked?" He wanted a little fun.

"You ever play before?"

At his head shake, Einstein got up, rubbing his hands together. "Okay then. I'll slaughter you and still have time for a game with Capshaw." They settled at a vacant work station away from the group. "Once you begin, your assignment will be audible on your implant. Your challenge will be to keep your thoughts private from me and to reach your goal without being stopped."

Sounded simple. Ran pulled on the contacts and was in a penthouse high above a city. He recognized the Rocky Mountain backdrop of the Capitol, relocated from DC to the plains outside of Denver. On the rooftop sat a sleek Andromeda sports car. A voice announced that his job was to stop the Agent of Anarchy from his planned attack on the Senate. A map of the Capitol complex appeared with the Senate highlighted. A surge of adrenalin told Ran to move. The building in question pulsated. A sense of high glee, and *B-O-O-M!* the Senate blew up. Game over.

Ran pulled off the contacts. That disorienting whirl of explosion reshaped into the base's main room.

"You should have been running for your car even before instructions came through," said Einstein. "Easier than taking candy from babies. Now you've got the idea, you have to try again."

It had been Einstein's glee Ran felt. Not his own. Very strange. The adrenalin was catching, though. He could feel the rush. Ran put the headband back on. This time he managed to reach his Andromeda and get into the air. Behind him, his apartment blew up. And then so did his Andromeda. He pulled off his contacts. "I think I prefer a quiet game of chess."

"You're a straightforward thinker," Einstein said. "You've got to be devious to be a spy."

"Thanks for letting me try it." Ran took his straightforward thinking mind to bed. He needed to be well rested when the time came, but it looked like escape was going to take awhile.

Hallie

reakfast was flatbread made of something other than grain, topped with a brown goop, probably yeast or algae. Hallie checked the duty roster while collecting her plate and followed Melody to her preferred seat in the corner near the infirmary.

"We have greenhouse duty together," Hallie said.

Melody nodded.

"Is that where you usually work?" Hallie asked, but got no response. She gave a shrug and ate.

People came and went. No sign of Rumbo. Looking rather morose, Pel arrived, food in hand.

"Melody, this is my friend Pel. He's staying with Ed and Marney."

"Marney likes to take care of people," said Melody. "She took good care of me." She seemed to shake herself free of some thought. "Hallie takes care of me now. Where are we assigned?"

Hallie repeated, "The greenhouse." Her heart twisted. *She* was taking care of Melody? She'd never been able to ease her own mother's grief. "I guess we'd better go."

They stepped out into a ferocious, breath-stealing gale that tried to push them back inside. Holding her wind coat's hood to her face, her other hand clinging to Melody's arm, Hallie's back tensed in anticipation of darts but no shooting thorns came.

Inside the greenhouse, they lined up to receive orders from tiny Gardner. "Ah, Melody, good. I'd like you two to set out those wheat seedlings. I hope this batch is more blight resistant." Gardner turned to Hallie. "She'll show you how."

"All right," Hallie said, "but first, I wonder if you have any waste materials good for making paper. Rumbo suggested—"

"Paper!" Aryn stepped forward, her face alight. "Oh, *could* we? The small amount of drawing paper I brought won't last. I made paper once in art class."

Gardner looked harassed but faintly interested. "Plant waste?"

Aryn said eagerly, "We used onion skins, leaves. Any cellulose sources." Her face clouded. "It's messy work though, cooking, beating the pulp . . ."

"Rumbo said he could help with the equipment we need," Hallie added.

"After work then," said Gardner. "There's a low-light area at the back not used for plants. And enough energy for cooking. I'll see what's available."

Hallie followed Melody to their assignment. Aryn had all the talents: pollinating, art, even hair that behaved, but at least with Aryn's knowledge and Gardner's willingness, they were going to have paper!

Deep into their transplanting, Melody asked, "What do you want to do with paper?"

"A journal." Hallie delicately separated out a seedling. "I've lost the journal function on my tooth phone and really, really need to sort out my thoughts."

"You'll want to make a book then. With stitching on the spine."

"Oh, yes. That would be perfect!"

Paper wasn't only for journaling. No matter what Marney said, Hallie intended to rescue Ran. She could work out plans on paper. She needed to ask the others for ideas. And look at Rumbo's maps. And ask Rumbo where they kept their vehicles.

Pel

Bork worked away at the center table, stirring something that smelled of yeast, while Pel performed a solo breakfast cleanup.

That work was to be followed by serving lunch, lunch cleanup, and finally time off.

He doubted his chance of finding anyone to interview during their off-duty period. Besides, there was still that problem of no charge for his little noter and his databank.

Wash water cycled through a series of pools between kitchen and greenhouse, where it was used to water plants. It was good to see proper respect for water here.

"I like the way this place was carved out," Pel said. "It's practical and gentle on the eye."

Bork grunted, seeming in agreement.

Encouraged, Pel said, "Who designed it? Must have been quite a job."

Bork gave a derisive chuckle. "Designed by committee like everything else in the place. Not too bad a job, I agree. If you've finished there, you can mop out the gathering room before we dish up lunch."

Mopping was a hopeless task with the constant traffic, but Pel did it, then helped serve lunch, and finally carried his own plate across the room to sit beside Amado at what had become the teen table.

"Now that we've got time off, there's nothing to do," Amado complained. "They made such a big deal of our packing light, and for what? No power to charge *anything*."

"What kind of assignments have you been doing?" Pel asked.

"Cleaning crew so far. Inside hallways. All the dust that blows in—we sweep and mop and scrub rocks. It's a bore. I wish—" He grimaced.

"What do you wish?" Pel said, thinking of his own wishes.

"I wish my parents would talk about *themselves* equal time to me. They want to know everything I ever did, and tell me nothing about them." He leaned against the table, kicking his feet out to form a straight line. "And then they tell me to find something to do, as if I were five."

Aminal Amado, Pel remembered. "I overheard Gardner complaining about burrowing animals getting into the greenhouse. Maybe you should get reassigned."

"No spam?" Amado snapped upright, calling, "Hey, Leif!"

Pel picked up his dishes and headed back for cleanup. So he wasn't the only one shut out. Strange and ever stranger. Be nice if Amado got one wish.

Pel's wish required an energy source. Bork's ovens used power. A place to charge his noter? Struck by that thought, Pel quickened his steps only to stop abruptly when Bork shouted, "The kitchen is for food only! Get that thing out of here."

Ramon emerged, holding his music device.

"What was that all about?" Pel asked.

"My mother suggested I charge my music collection in the kitchen since there's not enough energy around here."

"I was about to do that myself!"

"Don't bother. Bork's a tyrant."

"Think Gardner would be more willing to charge devices in the greenhouse? Hallie and Aryn have duties there. We could let them ask."

"Good idea," and Ramon was off.

Once he'd finished the lunch dishes, Pel was free. He wandered into the gathering room, considering the ongoing secrecy. He was still determined to talk to Sam, but Fletch's turndown had left him twice shy. Anyway, Aryn's father hadn't been in to lunch.

What a blow; out of the know. He'd never imagined this difficulty. Researching on the Net was easy compared to getting information out of actual people. He'd thought he'd have no problem resolving his mystery. *Ha!*

Ramon returned from the greenhouse, rubbing wind-chilled fingers. "Gardner's providing one little shelf where we can set things to charge. She says we're not to interfere with her need to move the grow lights around."

"Fair enough." With most of the afternoon to charge, his noter might be ready to use by evening. Bent over to counter the wind, Pel carried his gadget to the allotted shelf.

Even following an afternoon of no work, Pel was more tired than he could remember. They were pinned down by real gravity. They were hungrier. And colder. Not seeing an available wind coat, he rushed back to the greenhouse through the gale to collect his partially charged noter, wishing he could forget his compulsion to uncover answers.

"Pel Teague," he muttered, "why don't you quit? Write a melodrama about a shipwreck instead." But back on Earth, nightmares had plagued him whenever he ignored his need to know. He snorted. Wasn't he *living* the nightmare this time? No one would talk to him. So close—and still so far.

Back at the Warrens, he pushed through rattling wind slats, headed down the ramp, and spotted Sam Suzuki only a few feet away. "Sir, could I—"

"No."

No. Without even listening to his question. Spoken with cold eyes and impassive face.

Pel's hope fizzled. Granddad, parents, the village—everyone had told him to leave off asking questions, leave off researching. Stick to his studies. They'd been so right. A zombie—*wrapped in a bow, nowhere to go, might as well throw* the whole project out. His eyes lit on Hallie, here because of his fateful question to the NODE. He stiffened. No way would he quit. He was going to find some answers.

Ed and Fletch sat at a table among what Pel guessed to be a group of leaders. *Something* was going on. He'd record them. *That* was where he'd point his noter.

If they wouldn't talk to him, his *recorder* would.

Ran

Ran woke to Gooney's snores. Careful not to trip the lights, Ran picked up his shoes. He wanted to look around outside. At least the dome wasn't shaking the way it had done all day.

Inside the hangar, he pulled on his shoes and headed to the Wreck's corner to grab the container of water he'd stashed. Since the hangar and living quarters were conjoined twin domes, the living quarters ought to also have a separate exit. Ran hadn't found it through any of the accessible spaces so it must be behind one of the locked doors. Not that it mattered, but he was curious.

Carrying the water, he slipped out through the hangar door, and closed it behind him. The dark was a problem. Should've brought a light. Keeping close to the dome, he felt his way along the curve. And the wind was still fierce. *Ow!* Something whipped out at his face, his hands, and through his coveralls. Dropping the water, Ran hissed and backed away. From the height and intensity of stings, he figured it to be one of those bullwhips Gooney talked about.

Back inside the hangar, he looked around. Time for some real work. His smart tool was about the same vintage as the Wreck. He could survey the Wreck's system and find out what it needed. Then he'd locate the hardware fab and check that out.

DAY SIX

Struggles

Ran

In the shower, Ran rubbed blood from the cut across his chin. Altogether, his night venture had been discouraging. Like everything else, the hardware fab needed reprogramming, which put a stop to his hopes of repairing the battered Mini.

His worktable was again piled with tools, including Capshaw's mineral analyzer—hopeless without a working hardware fab—and a scanner, the first he'd seen, plus several communicators.

Noland tossed another communicator onto the table. "No communication worth a nano."

Ran held it and sensed no faint vibration. "It's dead," he said and placed it with the discards. "I thought only close-in devices like Perk's walkie-talkie worked here. What are communicators good for?"

"As I said, even when they work, they're not worth a nano—but we keep hoping."

"Hoping for what? More communication satellites?"

Noland didn't answer.

Why not? Ran thought. The *Orpheus* might easily have planted some small, self-repairing com sats. Though what use com sats would be on a planet where nothing worked, he had no idea.

"When did the food fab go bad?" Ran asked. "I can't believe you've been eating yucky mush for years."

"It's been gradual," said Noland, leaning against the wall watching Ran work. "A progressive loss of menu."

"Weird. Really weird. Wick talked of feeding the Warrens, but I haven't seen anything he could feed them with—unless it's mush."

"Nope," said Noland. "They feed themselves now." He frowned. "The starving time—that was bad."

"But your hardware fab? Your food fab? Your tools of all kinds? What's going on?"

"*BR-I-L-L-L.*" A loud alarm came from the office. Wick's yell brought his management team rushing to gather inside, behind the closed door.

"What is it?" Ran asked.

"Ship." Noland's full attention was on Wick's office. Virile and Gooney stood frozen in place. Ran discarded two more small tools while listening to unintelligible voices.

At last Wick came into the main room, followed by his team.

"How far out is it, do you suppose?" Capshaw asked.

"We'll time it next time," Wick snarled. "And we're stuck here."

"Soon as the wind dies down, I'll need my analyzer," said Capshaw. "We'll never find the B'ite without."

Wick stomped over to the worktable. "Have you fixed that scanner yet?"

"It needs reprogramming." Ran wished he *could* get the scanner to work. He'd never known his real name, but data had been added to his chip at the shuttleport and he'd never found a chance to examine it.

"You're not getting anywhere near the Brain."

"If I can't fix anything here, let me go to the Warrens."

"There's nothing for you there," Wick told him. "We have work for you here."

"Without the Brain, I can't do anything! Obviously something's wrong, since you won't even let me see it." Ran nodded at the small pile he'd culled from the tools. "You also need more powerpacks. A working hardware fab can produce them easily."

He stood up, wanting to jog and think. "I need some exercise."

Wick protested as Ran started for the hangar, but Noland said, "Let him go. The kid's going to do things his own way."

A while later, breathing hard after an increase of laps, Ran stopped to lean on the Wreck. Peering beneath the aircar, he checked to be sure he'd left no signs of his middle-of-the-night work. He could no longer smell anti-grav fluid. Good enough.

Saxon sauntered across the big hangar.

Ran straightened. "Gooney tells me some guy crashed this. What happened to him?"

Saxon's squinty eyes narrowed further in memory. "Delver paid us a secret visit and then ran. Wick went after him and forced him down." He shrugged one shoulder. "He was hurt, lay around for a long time. Then one day he was gone. Wick was fit to be spaced, he was so angry."

A *secret* visit? Gooney hadn't mentioned that. Was it Delver who'd talked the Brain into sabotaging the weapons? Had he caused the other damage?

Saxon added, "We figure he hobbled away and died out there."

Everything was such a mystery. Ran itched to explore. Was the other outside door locked? If he accessed it from the outside, it might open into one of the locked rooms.

The wind gave a louder howl. "How often does wind season come around?"

"Regular," said Saxon. "Seasons don't vary much. A little cooler, a little warmer, but every time the shift comes, wind blows in the change."

"Seems like it blows all the time."

"Yeah. It blows cold down between the mountains, blows warm from the sea southwest of here. Sometimes it circles. Wind season is when it blows harder."

Ran yawned. The nights were taking their toll. He could do nothing more for the Wreck without a hardware fab. He guessed he'd have to hike to the Warrens. If he could climb to the ridge in the wind, he could handle the kilometers to the Warrens.

But he really wanted to see that Brain.

Plus, Einstein's phrase *straightforward thinker* kept bothering him. A chess game's goal was always the same, but the path was never direct. So, *hmm.* Maybe he needed to act on multiple plans.

Plan A. Line up another water container and a pack.

Plan B. Tweak the food fab, make the food worse, heighten the pressure for Brain access. And if Plan B didn't work out, go with Plan A. Leave tomorrow night.

Then again, when was that approaching ship due? That might change matters.

Pel

As the door closed behind Ed and Marney, Pel yawned and got up, hungry for breakfast and curious about what he'd recorded in the gathering room last night. It had been a tricky maneuver to keep the noter pointed toward the table where Ed sat.

Dressed and ready for breakfast, he brought the noter to his ear.

Ed: *Make do as best you can for now. We can revisit—*

[louder voice]: *But we're at a standstill until—*

Orenda: *Everyone's healthy. That's something to be grateful for.*

[same loud voice]: *I still want solid plans. We've had more time than expected but nothing's been accomplished. Don't think they're not pushing hard to get at us, and this time we're totally vulnerable.*

Ed: *You're forgetting the kids—*

That was when Ed had turned his gaze on the teen table. Pel's hand had immediately moved to cover his noter and shut it off. He was never going to make it as a spy—too nervous, too jumpy. And afraid he'd already given himself away.

What did that louder voice mean about being *vulnerable*? Because of the sudden arrival of the teens? Pel pocketed the noter and headed up to eat.

Hallie sat in her usual spot beside Melody. He almost headed her way, but instead went to join the other teens. Aryn slid into the seat opposite him.

"I'm sorry my father wouldn't talk with you yesterday."

The man's eyes—no, his whole face—chilled Pel still. He had found himself staring at the brick wall of a single word. *No.* "Has your dad told you anything about his past?"

"He doesn't know why he was brought here."

"I have a theory about that. Could you act as go-between?"

Aryn scraped up the last bit of food from her plate. "I don't get much time with him. He works really long hours and won't say what he's doing."

That sounded too much like Amado's complaint about *his* parents. "I thought they distrusted me as a spy or something," Pel said, "but if a father won't even talk to his daughter?"

"I've got to get to the greenhouse." Aryn picked up her plate, but paused. "I don't feel any distrust. It's something else . . . like he doesn't want me worried."

Pel went to find out his assignment. "*Digested wastes*. What does that mean?" Ramon would be his partner.

"Poop patrol," said Bork on the other side of the counter.

"Not many are listed for the mine," Pel said. The big guy, Rumbo, was assigned there.

"No one works *in* the mine," Bork answered.

"Then how do you get any mining done?"

"Robots, but they require constant monitoring."

Delighted that *someone* was talking, Pel asked, "Is that why the mine is off limits?"

"No, it's because it's a killer place and when it kills, that includes—"

"Shut up, Bork," said Ed from the doorway.

Bork shrugged and continued collecting ingredients for lunch.

Pel braved the winds to put his noter onto the greenhouse shelf before going back to find Ramon. He considered Ed to be his nemesis. Not only was he going to record Ed again, he was also going to make Ed into one of the villains in his melodrama. Words were already shaping in his mind . . .

Boss: *You're marooned, your arrival inopportune; we might keep you alive—*

Chorus interrupts: *It's impossible to thrive in this place of little food. We need to grow, to learn to know you. If only you'd talk; we're going to balk at being enslaved . . .*

Boss: *Dumped on us; you'll do as you're told; If you don't ask questions, then we won't scold . . .*

Yeah, yeah, Pel thought. All well and good, but he had no plot to wrap his thoughts around. He went to find Ramon.

The Warrens and the greenhouse were built on and into neighboring low hills. Ramon led Pel back toward the greenhouse, but turned left to head down between the two structures. They hiked to a low spot.

"The place drains out here," Ramon said, as he turned a lever to fill a two-handled container.

"Smells like shit," Pel said, hoping he sounded cheerful.

"I've been doing this since our second day here," Ramon said.

The wind helped carry odors away as they hauled the load uphill to a row of vats beside the greenhouse. Ingenuity had gone into this sewage system. Too bad it depended on humans for hauling. They tipped the contents into the first vat and headed back for the next load.

"Your mother is Geraldine Ramirez, isn't she?" Pel asked. Maybe this was a good assignment, in spite of the heavy lifting. "She was one of the disappeareds I was researching."

"Yes?" Ramon's dark eyes met his for a moment before he turned the lever to spill out the next batch of waste. "What did you find out about her?"

"She held a post in the Housing Administration and was a spokesperson when that Antarctic tsunami flooded New Zealand and Australia. She was 'lost' under suspicious circumstances, which caught the attention of several bloggers, but her disappearance was never solved."

Ramon shut off the valve. "She doesn't say anything about disappearing, except that it interrupted her plans to build arcologies for her refugees. Those governments had plenty of trade credits. She's wondered if they ever got built. And she worried about me, of course. I'd been left in creche while she worked." Ramon grunted as they hefted the load, an unhappy look on his face. "We'd do better to build a pipeline instead of this hauling."

They trudged back up to the vat, Ramon moving rhythmically in time to some unheard music, seeming impervious to the gale.

"What do you miss most?" Pel asked.

"My virtual friends."

Ramon's answer surprised Pel. "Virtual?"

"That's what I always called them"—his grin flashed—"because we only met on the SocialWeb. We could jam and rap and no one complained about the noise."

Interrupted lives. The Warrens was full of them.

"I'm calling a meeting," Pel said abruptly. "Pass the word. All the kids, tonight after supper."

Even if no adults would talk, there must be some way to make their lives easier.

Aryn

Aryn pushed against the wind on her return to the Warrens for lunch, to be followed by the now required afternoon break. She wondered about planet Lodestone's plants. How had they evolved to be so fierce? Did they protect themselves against the creatures of the planet? And what did the creatures eat? If plants, then how?

A yellowish-green bramble bordering the trail caught her eye with its tossing motions. Aryn knelt to examine its tiny triangular leaves. *Ran's mouth opened. He yelled something at Wick.* She blinked at the waving plant fronds, her vision gone as quickly as it had come. Only those two faces: Wick's impassive, Ran's impassioned. *Present or past or still to come?*

Her mother's gift. The thought warmed her; the vision chilled her.

Covering her fingers with her sleeve, she gently touched the plant. "Will you give me a piece of yourself?" She broke off the tip of the stem and stood.

After lunch, she got out her sketchbook, which held so few remaining pages. Carefully setting out the prickly stem, she began to sketch, wanting to connect her vision with the plant. Her idea seemed foolish, but she was curious to see if anything would come. An hour later, she gave up; her page contained only different angles of the plant, nothing more.

The greenhouse had an open area that would accommodate tai chi practice. Though very strict about adhering to the breaks ordered for the teens, Gardner wouldn't object to her practicing there. And she could check on their paper-making project.

Hallie

Hallie carried her supper to the teen table and slipped into a seat, wondering why Pel had called a meeting. He sat at the far end, with Aryn of the clever fingers beside him.

Turning her gaze away, she leaned across the table. "Leif, how is it going for you?"

Leif gave a slight grimace at his plate. "I never thought I'd miss those cracker things we ate at the Shed."

"Yeah, the food's not much for texture," she agreed. "But I mean, what's it like to have double stepparents? Have you learned anything about your real ones?"

Leif nodded. "There's something deadly about the mines. They moved the original mine because of it, but they're still afraid. My father was among the first to die there. Later, my mother partnered Jay. Then she died of some kind of cancer. Jay blames Wick for withholding his vita-med fabricator."

"Withholding? That's barbaric!"

"Or maybe Wick didn't keep it working, but yeah, Jay hates him. Layla, my stepmother, says there's other sides to the story. See, it was right after this group broke away from the base. Jay says the only thing they did was dismantle the Brain's access to the weapons system, nothing relating to health, but Wick blamed them for all kinds of damage and wouldn't help my mom."

Hallie made an outraged squawk.

Leif nodded. "Layla was my mom's best friend and nursed her."

"And you like them all right?"

"They try hard." He made a wry face. "It's the closest I'll get to my parents, so it's okay." He swallowed his last bite and got up. "Amado says he caught a creature in the greenhouse. He's not allowed to touch it, but I'm going for a look before he has to release it."

At least he had some enthusiasm for this place.

The meeting would begin as soon as cleanup was over. Hallie picked up her dishes, but before she could get up, Reba scooted in beside her.

"I was listening in. My mother says that because Wick wouldn't help Leif's mother, they stopped work to get him to change his mind, and Wick refused to feed them. They already had the greenhouse going, but plants can't be rushed. People were starving, until they gave up and went back to work."

Taking her dishes to the kitchen, Hallie remembered how on their first morning, Satch had said, *I won't starve again.* Actions had consequences, often unforeseen. She wondered if anything had been accomplished by their strike.

Amado and Leif returned, looking bright eyed. Others yawned, sagged, or rested their heads on the table.

"All present," said Pel. "I called this meeting because I think a lot of you are not happy with the status quo."

Manuelo pounded his fist on the stone table, which must have hurt, besides not delivering much of a thump. "They don't tell us what's going on. We're extra mouths and they won't even talk about getting outta here."

"I wish I had my music teacher," said Luisa.

Voices ran over each other as the stream of frustrations picked up speed.

"No connections . . ."

"Dance classes . . ."

"I need . . ."

"They tell me not to wander around outside, but I want to study life-forms," said Amado.

Hallie lifted her voice above the babble. "We've got to rescue Ran. It's not fair that he's stuck at the base and we're all here. I've been thinking about what it'll take to get him back."

"Aren't you forgetting the risks?" said Reba. "My stepfather says the base holds all the power."

"That's why it'll take lots of planning. I want—"

She stopped. Eyes were focused on something behind her.

"This meeting is ended," Ed said. "You're going nowhere. You don't know what you're putting at risk with this kind of talk. There'll be no rescue missions on my watch. Get to your rooms."

Filthy spamguts! She hadn't meant to be overheard, especially by Ed. Behind Ed stood a small arc of adults, some of them concerned parents.

Pel stood. "Wait a minute," he said. His eyes showed more white than usual. Hallie caught the desperation in his voice. "This meeting was called for an entirely different reason. What I wanted to suggest, before we got off topic, was that we have a lot of discontent and no school. People could pool their knowledge. Dance, music, science. And primary sources too. For xenobotany, talk to Gardner, see what she knows. For xenobiology, ask around. People must have information to share. We won't know until we ask."

Ed raised a hand. "Not with Miss Hallie promoting absolute starvation and ruin with her demands." He made her sound out-of-her-mind crazy.

Hallie's face burned. "All right!" She stood. "I'm out of here. Give the others a chance. Obviously I was out of line. Pel's idea is great. Give him a chance."

Behind her an eager discussion began. She'd just given the adults more reason to distrust her. *Impulsive!* She'd have to keep her mouth shut from now on. But Ed and the others were thick-headed slaves, no nearer freedom after more than a decade.

She stomped down the curving stone steps and paced the lower hallway until approaching footsteps drove her into Melody's rooms. As usual, her eyes snagged on the loom's gleaming treasure.

"How do you do it?" Hallie burst out.

"Do what?" Melody's fingers released the shuttle with seeming reluctance. She slowly turned to face Hallie.

"I'm sorry. I shouldn't have interrupted." But her seething mood prevented Hallie from settling. She paced, blinded by clamoring thoughts, until a touch on her shoulder startled her back into the small room.

"Tell me what's wrong."

How could she? Melody needed protecting. How could she tell the woman the violent thoughts she was having?

Melody pushed her weaving cushion over to Hallie's sleeping niche. "Sit by me."

Hallie sank onto her bed and words overwhelmed her. "Why does no one try to escape? All I wanted was to rescue Ran from Wick's clutches. And yes, I know! We risk starvation and Wick's weapons—but why not go down fighting? Doing their will, mining for those who brought you here, how do you bear it?"

"You children have your lives ahead of you. None of us wants to prevent that, and certainly not risk your futures," said Melody softly.

"We're not children. We're reasonable, thinking"—*impulsive*, added her mother's voice—"people."

"You each have unique histories and experiences that belong to you alone."

Why *shouldn't* she want to rescue Ran from that Wick person?

Impulsive, still fighting everyone's battles for them, said her mother.

Hallie stared at the loom. "How did you learn to shut out the world and weave? Aryn does it with her art. Ramon goes into his music." Through the stone ceiling, she discerned faint beats. He must have succeeded in his jam session.

"Destroying ourselves isn't the answer."

There it was again, the pain she'd felt before. "What did you lose?" Hallie asked.

"Home. Son. Husband." Melody rose, moved her cushion back to the loom, and picked up her shuttle.

Hallie's throat tightened in reaction. What had she expected? She'd seen Melody searching their faces that first night. "I'm sorry," she whispered. She'd done it again, caused Melody pain. It seemed to be all she was good for. Actions had consequences.

When would she learn?

Ran

Ran crept out of bed, wishing that just once he could sleep through the night. He'd done everything he could do for the Wreck without those needed parts. Outside, the wind seemed calmer. He could go outside again. The discard pile had supplied him with another water container, and he had ideas for a pack to haul them in. This time he'd steer farther from the walls and search for that other door. Then back to bed.

Keeping his motions slow and steady, he slid open the door into the hangar and crept through. Once inside, he moved faster, bringing up the lights.

"There you are."

Ran jumped.

Noland sat leaning against the Trilby. For such a big guy, he got to his feet quickly. "You were outside last night. The bullwhips left their mark on your face. What are you up to?"

"Nothing much." Ran's chin stung at the mention of those thorns. "I wanted a look around."

"In the dark?"

"It blew hard all day, didn't it? No chance then. Besides, someone would have stopped me."

"Like I'm doing now. Back to bed, boy. Wick won't approve of your nighttime prowls."

"Have you got a light? You could come with me."

"Nope. You can't tempt me to go out in that."

The wind shook the dome. Noland came closer and leaned in menacingly. "Look, kid, you can go back to bed, or I can hogtie you to it. A ship's on its way. Wick's not going to stand for you escaping before he gets what he wants."

"What does he want then?" Ran's voice rose in frustration. "I don't hold the programming for his tools. He needs the Brain, not me."

"Back to bed."

Ran went back to bed. He lay thinking for a long hour before sleep caught up to him.

He needed a Plan C. He needed a sleep potion to feed to Noland, blast the man! But he also needed to consider that approaching ship. How soon before it arrived?

And where was the *Orpheus*? Had they repaired its damage yet?

DAY SEVEN

Ships?

Ran

"*B-R-I-L-L-L!*"

The loud alarm startled Ran out of bed. That ship again. One thing the base's Brain did well was announcing incoming ship communications. Or was it the *only* thing? The semi-transparent dome overhead suggested it was near dawn. Rapid footsteps announced Wick's arrival at his office.

Ran lay back down. If an AstroMining ship could alert the base, why hadn't they received an announcement of the *Orpheus*'s arrival? And where *was* the *Orpheus*?

At breakfast Wick loudly condemned the food, adding, "During the first break in the wind, I want my team out there finding that B'ite."

That confirmed for Ran that the approaching ship *was* AstroMining. But why didn't they know where the Beijingite was?

He wandered over to his worktable to check the dwindling pile of tools for repair. After sorting them, he carried the discards to the hangar and then jogged under Gooney's eyes.

Breathing hard from his run, he rummaged deeper into the scrap pile. A working hardware fab could have recycled most of the stuff, and put the materials back into use. He unearthed a cleaning bot. That brought a smile, reminding him of his pet on the *Orpheus.* This bot was much larger than the palm-sized one that emerged to clean his tiny cubicle during rest periods. Finding a second cleaning bot, Ran lugged them both to his worktable to take apart.

Capshaw walked past to knock on the office door. Moments later, Wick shouted, "Virile, fly Capshaw in the Mini. I want that B'ite located."

Ran cocked his head. The wind must be down.

Virile leaned into the office. "How much time do we have, Boss?"

"Dunno. At a guess, three, four, five days," Wick speculated.

With Gooney on his tail, Ran followed Virile and Capshaw into the hangar, and listened to the Mini as it exited the hangar. The Mini had the same growl he'd heard in the Trilby.

Gooney closed the hangar doors.

"Too much dust," Ran said.

"What?"

"The engines. They need cleaning. This windblown dirt gets into things. Do you think Wick would let me work on the vehicles?"

Gooney's narrow shoulders shrugged to his ears. "Ask him."

✦ ✦ ✦ ✦ ✦ ✦ ✦ ✦

"No!" shouted Wick.

"Then why am I here?" Ran shouted back. "Everything that *can* be fixed needs your Brain." He was sick of being called *son* and *my boy*. "Send me to the Warrens."

"You're not going anywhere. I need you here."

"For *what*?"

Getting no answer, Ran went back to the cleaning bots; maybe he'd get one working by swapping parts.

About mid-afternoon, Virile and Capshaw returned empty-handed, which set Wick off again. Then all was quiet during a long conference behind the office door.

With a lop-sided smile, Ran set the sole working bot on the floor. He'd turned off its compulsion to clean only at night, admitting to a selfish desire to see one machine actually at work. If the men complained, he could reverse it. Meanwhile, it was a pleasure to watch the track it was leaving on the dusty floor.

Ran looked up when Wick shouted for Noland. A minute later, Noland came out and paused beside him. "Boss wants to see you."

Wick sat at his desk, his lower lip thrust forward. "You want the hardware fab working. We want it working. If you can get the Brain to respond, I want you to repair a couple items for me, asap."

Yes! But cold reason intervened. His machine empathy reached only so far. "If you have problems with your Brain, what can *I* do? I'm not a bioengineer."

Wick got up. "Put on a cleangown." He handed Ran a puffy ball, popped open another to cover himself, and opened the inner door.

Covered from head to toe by a gauzy energy field, Ran entered the sterile room. The Brain, a large pearlescent membrane with a tiny transceiver at its base, pulsed and zinged with life. "What's its name?"

"Just Brain. You've been wanting to see her. There she is."

"So what's the password?"

"Your guess is as good as ours. She does what she does with no directions from us." Wick was finally confessing his difficulty.

"You mean it's functional, but responsive only in certain circumstances?" Ran bent to examine the transceiver. His fingers accidentally brushed the Brain's casing. A spinning vertigo seized him; he knew he was standing in that small room but simultaneously sensing a multitude of virtual worlds, voices, swirling colors, sounds that might have been bits of music or the noise of stars or—

A yell. A slap.

A violent shove finally broke the Brain's hold on him. "Don't touch!" Wick scowled. "You're liable to get executed."

"You mean electrocuted?" Ran's head whirled with that cascade of data. Most particularly, he remembered the Brain's intense reluctance to release him.

The Brain's loneliness? Or his own?

"Whatever. Get out of here."

"What was the point of all that then? I didn't get a chance to talk to it!"

First invited in, then kicked out. More of Wick's craziness. Ran popped his cleangown back into its original puffball. He'd never heard of an organic brain having that effect. It wasn't something he wanted to talk about to *this* crew—but his own thoughts were busy.

Pel

The only thing Pel could say for his and Ramon's job of waste hauling—or shit patrol—was that it conserved more nutrients than say, emptying chamber pots into medieval streets. Finished, Ramon went to his sweeping duty and Pel to the greenhouse.

He bent into the work of thinning beet greens, thinking about the two big gaps in his life: his inability to research and Hallie's distance. She had looked so uncomfortable last night, but like Don Quixote, Hallie was tilting at windmills. Pel wanted Ran back too, but besides a lack of transport, how were they to win against the base's weapons?

On the other hand, Hallie's desire to go to Ran's rescue made her the perfect heroine for his melodrama; a rescue to be won over great odds. What plot to use, *a slow fuse, urgent news, some other ruse?*

He headed back to the kitchen with his basket of beet greens.

"Wash those," said Bork.

Washing completed, he opened his mouth and Bork said, "If you've finished, you're out of here."

Cursing his obedience, Pel left, destined to bounce between Ramon, Gardner, and Bork. When shuttling down from the *Orpheus*, he'd thought it would be so easy to waltz into this group of strangers, ask questions, and write a book.

He slapped his pockets. No noter. Hunched against the wind, he headed back to the greenhouse. The previous evening's recording had only netted a few words, all too cryptic. He'd chosen a seat out of Ed's view, but a sudden move from Ed had caused him to shut off his noter. After listening to it a few times, he'd deleted the words.

[mumble] . . . *going to do?*

Man: *All stashed. What about . . .*

Ed: *Bork's got a collection of missiles.*

Woman: *. . . protect the kids? I wish Del were here.*

Man's voice rising: *. . . fight all the harder.*

They were expecting a fight. But when and why? *What a blow, out of the know.* Pel blew back into the greenhouse and collected his noter from the charging shelf.

Nearby, Amado and Leif bent over a cage. "Hey, Pel, come see this! It's got six legs."

"Six?" A rat-sized creature, the color of planet dust, huddled in a tight ball watching in all directions with three stalked eyes like a crab's. "You've got a furry bug there."

"A whistler," said Leif. "That's what they're called. Gardner says someone trained one once to act as a sentinel."

"Who trained it?"

Leif shrugged. "Some guy who's dead now. Weird looker, isn't it?"

"Gardner won't let us keep it," said Amado. "We have to take it out and release it."

Nice to see *some* teens having fun.

Spotting Hallie and Aryn leaving, Pel patted his pocket to be sure he had his noter and hurried to fall into step with them. Hallie was saying, "Gardner says she can spare some of her hemp crop for our paper since we arrived with that crate of smart cloth."

"Paper?" said Pel. "*Perfect!* That's what I need for making notes."

"Our first batch was way too soft," said Aryn. "Hemp is ideal, but it'll take more time."

"Keep me in mind," said Pel. "I'll write small, or—"

When Aryn laughed, her nose crinkled. "We're working on writing utensils too. Pen and ink so far. Too bad we don't have a fab to produce proper ones."

"I used to enjoy imagining old times," Pel said, "but between shit patrol and no paper or electronics, this life is ridiculous." He wanted the Net. He wanted his data. He wanted people to *talk* to him!

"I do like the old methods for art," Aryn said. "Working with paper and pen or brush, everything around me slows down."

On paper he could write out—*what?* He had nothing. No facts. No stories. He would set his noter up to record again, try to find out what was going on, but meanwhile fantastic words flooded in to shape his melodrama, fed by thoughts of the possible fight to come.

Pel brought his noter to his mouth to record.

Aryn

Pel wanted paper to write on. Hallie wanted to journal. Aryn wondered if others felt the same. She looked back at Pel, who'd halted to stand in the wind, now staring at his electronic device. And without a wind coat.

Hallie's voice was muffled by her hood held close around her face. "I shouldn't have interrupted Pel's meeting last night," she said, "but don't you agree we need to rescue Ran?" She sounded more doubtful as she added, "*If* we can find a way."

"Why do you want to?" Aryn distrusted Hallie's rush to action without weighing all the angles.

"Don't you want him back with us?" Hallie sounded disbelieving.

They pressed through the slats into the welcome calm of the Warrens.

Aryn lowered her voice. "Yes, of course I do. But no matter how much I wish it—and I think about him all the time—I can't find a . . . an answer that feels right." She dropped her wind coat on the pile and headed down the ramp into the gathering room, Hallie beside her.

Her voice still low, Aryn added, "I keep wondering if there's a purpose behind Ran's being there that we don't know anything about."

Hallie sighed. "I don't buy it. You seem so unworried. Is it your art that gives you such serenity?"

"Serene? I'm not! I'm one huge question mark inside." Cooking smells as they neared the kitchen reminded Aryn that Sam was joining her for lunch.

"I hate that no one will tell us what's going on," said Hallie.

"Wait." Aryn grabbed Hallie's arm, stopping her to whisper, "The night when Ran reached the top of the ridge, Wick showed up. Wick was expecting to find someone—or something. And when Ran and Perk came for me, Perk said someone keeps the base informed of what's going on here."

Hallie's hand flew to her mouth. "Spying? Is that why nobody talks? When we first got to the Warrens, there was such a fuss because we'd interrupted plans—for a raid or something."

Aryn nodded.

"And I announced my intentions loud and clear last night! Thanks for the warning." Hallie ran down the steps.

Aryn followed to collect her sketch pad.

"The base. Right there." Sam pointed at Aryn's sketch made so many months ago.

Aryn stared at the hilly landscape so like—yet unlike—the area around the Warrens, and at the double-domed structure that she had taken for more hills.

"It's slightly protected from the winds, but as soon as you move out here," Sam's finger traced a curved path around one of the hills, "it hits you."

Ran was there.

"When did you see that?" Sam asked.

"I didn't. I drew it before leaving Earth."

"You *are* your mother all over again, aren't you?"

"Was— Did she draw?"

"No, she simply *knew* things." He closed his eyes. When he reopened them, his expression held the warmth of a good memory. "Before you were born, she told me you would be the perfect blend of us, my eyes and her sight." He smiled and patted her shoulder, saying, "See you later," and left to return to whatever his job was.

Aryn smiled in turn, thinking of her mother. Her finger traced the domed roof. Was Hallie right? Did Ran need rescue? Was that why she'd drawn this landscape so long ago?

No answer came, neither yes nor no. *Not now then.* She sighed and pulled out the sheet of overly soft, lumpy paper, her share of their first paper run. The native plant sprig had grown limp after her many attempts to draw it. Rendering it with charcoal would be a challenge.

Lodestone flared with the heat of molten rock in the passing of—

Aryn blinked. In one corner of the sketch, a shriveled plant frond seemed to cry for help. The wake from the object's passage had created the same black line seen from the lander—the Rift—except her lines revealed only a blackened strip of almost flat ground, not the deep trench it was now. The gathering room came back into view. She'd been somewhere else, feeling the heat of that huge body. What was it? A meteor?

"That's the Rift." Aryn started at Pel's voice. He indicated the edge of the sheet where a huge *something* entered the sea with a hint of steam rising from the waters. "We saw it while descending in the lander. The Rift ends in the sea just like your object does. And here I thought my melodramatic villains were going to be the men from the base," said Pel. "What if the villains are aliens?"

Aliens? "Are you saying it's a *ship?*" Aryn asked. Of course. It had to be a ship of some sort. While she was hobbling down from the ridge with Perk and Ran, Ran had asked what they mined. Perk said, *Beijingite,* and Ran said, *"That's impossible."* Of course, a ship.

Drawn to the discussion, the other teens on their afternoon break surrounded her. "Shipwreck?" Nick picked up the sketch and passed it to Manuelo.

"It makes sense," said Reba. "Just think what they're mining!"

"The Beijingite *has* to be from a shipwreck." Manuelo stated it as fact.

"Alien or one of ours?" said Dacey.

Pel reached for Aryn's sketchbook. "Did you ask your father about your landscape?" He opened it to the page.

"Yes. He says it's the base. That"—Aryn's finger touched the double dome again—"is the building."

Whatever did it all mean?

Hallie

Sitting beside Melody at supper, Hallie's eyes kept finding Pel slouching on the wall bench in the far corner. For a change, he wasn't with Aryn. Remembering Aryn's caution, she wished she'd exercised some of her own. An apology was called for.

She ate quickly, cleared her dishes, and squeezed past Ramon's musicians to reach Pel, who was speaking into his little dumb device.

His face brightened at her approach, a reassuring sign, and he straightened to make space for her.

"I'm sorry about last night," she said. "I was out of line."

"It was Ed who was out of line," Pel said. "It was an open meeting. You had every right to say what you felt."

He waved the maroon device he'd been speaking into. "What do you think? Ramon and I are going to put on a musical about orphans cast into the void. To the mixed-up tunes and refurbished lyrics of Gilbert and Sullivan. I'm making you my heroine."

Heroine? He was crazy!

"Listen to this." Pel sang:

I've got a great big list of potential reasons missed.

Of arch evil creatures taking charge and—

He was singing about lists—parodying the Lord High Executioner's list of people to put to death from *The Mikado*. His words were *way* too convoluted, just like those operettas. Now Pel was distracting her from her purpose.

Hallie scowled. "That's how everyone gets complacent and lets years go by without even trying to get home."

"You have a better idea?"

"I'm not about to settle for musical plays."

"But you're my heroine," said Pel. "You and your rescue idea."

"What? A plan no one will listen to? A musical would take months."

"No, no. I'm going for brief. A musical melodramatic skit. Something to stay busy with, to soothe, to entertain."

"Besides, I don't sing."

"Yes, you do. I've heard you."

"When did you ever hear me sing?"

"At that fateful picnic."

Her mouth opened. Then closed. She got up and walked away. Her lost day again! She had sung to Pel? None of her dreams or nightmares had included singing. Even her part in last year's production of *Iolanthe* held next to no singing.

Ramon's group broke into a loud rendition of the pop song "End Times." Tesia and Dacey belted out the words, while Luisa played her flute an octave above. "End Times" was a fitting title for this place. Pel should make *that* his melodrama title.

"Stop that noise!" howled a man from a table.

Ed got up from his own table to approach the card players. "They have to be somewhere," he told them. "Take your game downstairs."

So sometimes the man was fair. Hallie shook off her grouch. *She* was too often unfair herself. She had almost reached the stairs when Rumbo blocked her way, smiling down.

"Miss Hallie. I'm on duty, just stopped to collect some food. How about a brief tour of the mine office? The wind's down slightly."

Rumbo was her one source of information. She looked around at Ed still talking to the card players, his back to them. To a black hole with Ed's rules about going off with strangers. Rumbo had been far more helpful to her than bossy Ed.

"All right." She followed Rumbo up the ramp and pulled on a wind coat. Only too aware of his hand firm against her back, she said, "Where do you house your vehicles? They brought us in a truck that I haven't seen since."

"There's a shelter for them, out the other side of the greenhouse." He waved a hand. His wave indicated a point beyond and behind both greenhouse and Warrens. Farther than she'd gone or cared to go in all this wind.

Quit being a wimp! So then. On her next afternoon break, she'd explore.

Their path curved around a hill to a structure built into another hill. Rumbo pushed the door open. "I'm back," he announced, placing his supper on the desk.

The man watching monitors grunted and frowned at Hallie. "After Virile's visit, now you're bringing a *girl* out here?" The man didn't wait for an answer. Wind slats clattered behind him.

"What visit?" Hallie asked. "Who's Virile?"

"Just a couple of guys from the base today, checking up on progress," Rumbo said easily, but his answer didn't match the other man's attitude of danger. To her? Who was Virile?

The stark room contained only a chair and a desk, with monitors affixed along one wall. "You seem to have plenty of energy here," she said. Another structure grown like the Shed, with built-in solar and wind collection. "I wish we had energy at the Warrens. Everybody who brought devices is complaining."

"Problem with the Warrens is it's all underground. No good way to transmit, although we managed to get enough energy for lights through the airshafts."

Hallie approached one monitor. A bot with a rounded back, a scraper on its front end, moved out of daylight into a tunnel.

"We call them turtles," said Rumbo. "That's Turtle 4 there. They load their scrapings into bins at the upper end of each tunnel. Over here, you can see a mole." The mole bots were more bullet shaped, with extendable arms.

"They're mining out in the open? I pictured mine shafts underground."

"We can't go into the Rift ourselves so we tunnel to it. Now, beautiful lady, you've seen the mining office. We'll brace the wind back to the Warrens."

"What about your job here? Doesn't someone have to be on duty?"

"Several are working as we speak." He tapped the first monitor. "I need someone at first base for a few minutes."

"On my way," came a crackling reply.

Hallie looked around. "Where *are* the other workers?"

"Different trouble spots. As each ore bin fills, it has to be moved. Takes several men, since we're short a hauler. I understand your friend who's now at base managed to wreck the one stored at the Shed. We're going to need it when we start moving this stuff for pickup."

He was blaming Ran?

"Where were you all when we got here? Why didn't you know of the ship's arrival? If you want nothing broken, you ought to pay attention."

Rumbo grinned. "Feisty lady."

"And if your next ship is so overdue," Hallie said, "why didn't we see stuff waiting for pickup when we arrived? I'd think it would be there waiting."

"It's there. In a cache. We want to get on the ship ourselves, and if we make it too easy, they might not wait for passengers."

She blinked. They *were* calculating ways to get off the planet then. But whose side was Rumbo on? Was he the base's informant? Had it been wise to come out with him?

She pointed to a device over the door. "That looks like a small scanner."

"Vid-cam only."

"Like the ones watching inside the mine?"

"Yep. This one's courtesy of Wick. Someone delivers the data to him periodically."

"You?" She wondered again why he'd brought her here.

"I do my job and I pass on any mine information, that's all."

"Why not just transmit the data?"

"Our lone satellite is too intermittent, due to solar storms, and besides . . ." Rumbo shrugged one shoulder. "I understand their Brain isn't exactly working right now."

Was *that* why no one had known about their arrival?

Rumbo's replacement appeared. Hallie didn't know his name; she'd seen him at meals. "When you've finished philandering, I'm needed at loading," the new guy grouched.

He made Rumbo sound like a womanizer.

"Be right back," Rumbo told the man. He gave her a gentle push toward the wind barrier slats.

Back out in the wind, his leg brushed against hers. He was walking too close, closer than he had on the way out. She edged away, unwilling to challenge him. She still needed to see his maps.

Hallie sat on her bed watching Melody weave while she stroked the paper booklet Melody had helped sew together. Now that she had it, she hesitated to write down her thoughts—even if people *had* written journals by hand once upon a time.

"What are people worried about?" she asked Melody. Not that she couldn't think of lots of things, but why wouldn't they talk? "Is it Wick?" She only knew the name, not what threat he posed.

"They say time's running out," Melody answered slowly, "but they don't tell me what they mean, so I just keep on weaving."

Hallie hesitated. Melody probably knew nothing about Brains. "Rumbo told me something. He said, 'I understand their Brain isn't exactly working right now.' What did he mean?"

Melody swung around on her cushion, her eyes alert. After a long pause, she said, "That's very interesting."

"I wondered if that was why no one knew our ship had arrived."

"I don't know." Melody returned to her weaving.

Hallie pulled over the basket of silk plant strands that she was learning to spin. The slightly sticky fibers held together as she wound them on the spindle. She hummed the tune Ramon had been playing upstairs in the gathering room, then broke into the refrain,

"*Watching waters ebb and flood,*
Floating on this ark called Earth."

"That's pretty," said Melody.

"Pretty" was what her mother would have said. But pretty didn't get them back to Earth! Too weird. What song had she sung to Pel on the picnic? *Just tell me what I did!*

"You're almost out of fibers," Hallie said, fingering the last remnants.

"Yes, I need to go collecting soon. The plants hold their seedpods tight during wind season. Once they can control the direction, they throw them. I'll have only a short time to capture any."

"What were you looking for, that time you discovered your silk plants?" Hallie clapped her hand over her mouth, remembering Melody's ominous silence the last time she asked.

Melody released a deep sigh. "They said I was sleepwalking. They stole our baby."

Hallie's eyes prickled. Sleepwalking on *this* planet. Dreaming of a baby left on Earth. Looking for her baby—*here.* The adults had been ripped from children and lives.

And when Pel asked his question about *disappeareds*, the NODE had shipped them into space, treating the teens as unfeelingly as AstroMining had treated the teens' parents. Unfeeling. That was how the universe acted, stars exploding, swallowing planets. Humans stepping on ants with no thought of lives underfoot.

Get over it. Take charge of yourself.

All right, she would. Her first mission was to rescue Ran. She was *right* to do this.

She settled on her bed. Might as well practice writing.

My name is Haldis Pollard.

Her printing was big and blotchy on the rough surface.

My mother had two children so I am one of the few with a sibling. My aunt and uncle signed the papers that made them my second parents, since Aunt Bet had no child of her own.

She still had no memory. Only those odd nightmares of being chased. She started a new line.

Dream image of a cotoneaster. I'm lying under it, looking up.

Her pen dug into a slub, leaving a splotch of ink. Was that a memory? She remembered those gray-green plants with their red berries and angular branches at the park. At least they didn't have thorns and prickers. Dead-end line of thought.

Her rescue mission—make a list of steps. Be cryptic.

• Tomorrow, locate vehicles.
• Asap, see maps.
• Find out about base.

Her shoulders sagged. At lunch, she'd asked Bork how many were at the base. His answer was, "Seven or eight." No good. Any vehicle she flew there would be seized. She'd be walking into a trap. Then there was that man's comment in the mining office: *After Virile's visit today, you're bringing a girl out here?* One worry at a time. First find the transport.

Hallie tucked the journal into the bottom of her orange case and carefully set the ink where it wouldn't spill.

Interesting, Hallie thought, Melody's reaction to her comment about the base's Brain. What did Melody know that she wasn't saying?

Pel

Into his charged noter recorder, Pel said:

You tell us, don't ask. To stick to our tasks.
You make such a fuss. Don't underrate us.

He sat in the corner behind the musicians, disgruntled. His rhymes went nowhere; neither did his attempts to record the adults. At supper Ed had seated himself with his evil eye focused on Pel, who hadn't dared eavesdrop. The adults were preparing for some fight, and they weren't warning the teens.

"*They treat us like babies. Our only info full of maybes . . .*"

What about *alien* enemies? Strange how Aryn's sketch had shown a flattish scar, as if the ship had barely scraped the planet surface. But then something had eaten down into the planet. Would erosion do that? He should ask Perk, the planetary geologist—*if* the man ever came back and *if* he'd be willing to talk.

He missed Ran, wanting Ran's opinion on what was going on, wanting an open discussion of whatever danger the Warrens faced. Maybe the Warrens adults had reason to not blab to their kids if there was an informer, but Pel didn't feel like being reasonable.

Amado settled beside him, listening to the musicians. Amado and Leif both had rough, chapped faces from all the time they spent outside in the wind.

Pel asked, "Did you and Leif find anyone knowledgeable about Lodestone's fauna?"

Amado scrunched his mouth. "Not much. Nobody spends any more time outside than they can help, and no one's bothered to keep records. Except Nick's parents told him that someone had made a delicious drink from one of the native plants, and he's determined to find it, even though they told him there aren't any around here."

"*Uh-oh*," said Pel.

"Yeah. Nick is out to poison himself again." Amado brightened, saying, "Leif and I are planning an overnight. Those whistlers seem to be crepuscular, like deer. There's nothing big enough out there to threaten us, but we have to convince the parents. They say wind season lasts only a short while. As soon as there's a lull, we're out of here."

"I don't think it's the planet people are worried about," said Pel. "There's some human threat, but I'm not sure what."

"Oh, yeah?" Amado's eyes widened. "We spotted an aircar when we were out today."

"From the base, do you think?" Pel asked. Ramon's musicians filled the room with sound and he wanted no more meetings under Ed's eye. "Tomorrow, let's all meet on our afternoon break when not many adults are around. Pass the word. We can share what we know. Maybe someone's picked up other hints about what's going on."

Motion brought his eyes to the ramp. Hallie came inside, looking thoughtful. She'd gone out with that big guy again. If she was anywhere in the room, he always knew where she was. Like a thirsty man in the middle of a drought, Hallie was water to him. She deposited her wind coat on the pile and crossed the room to the stairs.

Aryn joined Pel. He said, "Will you take part in our musical production?"

"I can't sing. I'll do your scenery instead."

The melodrama was a distraction. He knew that. It kept him from thinking about Hallie—even though writing the play was a constant reminder. The singers finished their final refrain:

"*Fly times. Spiral times. My times. Wanting you.*"

Wanting Hallie. Yes, he did.

Ran

an crept out of bed, accompanied by Gooney's snores. He kept his movements easy and slow while crossing the big room. After accidentally touching the Brain earlier, he had no desire to experience that vertigo of sensations and input again. Tonight his sole purpose was to find out if it remembered him. Heart beating fast, he touched his palm to Wick's office door.

The door slid open. *Yes!*

Triggering a cleangown, he entered the inner chamber. The door slid closed behind him.

"Brain."

The Brain remained silent.

Ran considered it. All organic brains were clones of Atlas Corporation's original one, which, after two conflicts—or wars—for its control, had become the NODE. The NODE had blocked Pel's Net searching, but had then provided subliminal clues to the passwords needed to access the information Pel wanted. Would those same words hold any sway over this Brain?

"Rosemary."

No response.

"Whistlestop."

Again, nothing.

"ThymeSage."

Nothing. So much for that idea. There had been one more. Something about falling down? An earthquake? *Crumbling!*

"Crumbling Pyramid."

"What are you doing here?" Wick!

Ran hadn't heard the door slide open behind him. "*Blast!*" He swung around.

Wick's stocky frame filled the doorway, with Virile looking over his shoulder.

"I woke up hungry" Ran said. "Supper was awful"—*no lie!*—"and I thought I'd try the Brain again."

"Get him out of here," Wick growled.

Not bothering with a cleangown, Virile slipped inside. Ran stepped away from the Brain, wanting to protect it. Virile grabbed his nearer arm, twisting it behind his back, and forced him through the doorway. Ran's ribs shrieked. He moved farther into the twist, which put him even more off balance.

"COMMAND?" A toneless voice sounded from the Brain's transceiver.

Ran was surprised the Brain's vocoder revealed so little personality. Not that it mattered.

From his pretzeled stance, Ran yelled, "Enable hardware fabricator to my voice." He was going to escape this madhouse *asap.*

"I told you to stay out of there!" Wick, purple with rage, smashed his fist into Ran's cheek. Virile propelled Ran toward the office exit.

Tasting blood, clutching his ribs with his free arm, Ran reeled into the doorframe, smashing his nose. Somehow his crash triggered his clean-gown control. The puffball bounced across the floor.

Ran caught a glimpse of Virile's smirk of pleasure right before the pale man jabbed a knee into Ran's kidneys. Releasing his twisted arm, Virile shoved him out of the office onto the main room floor. Ran fell sideways, unable to control a yowl of pain.

Red droplets sprayed on the dusty floor. His ribs spasmed, refusing to expand. Blood blocked his nose, his mouth gaped open, every cell in his body demanded breath—which wouldn't come. All those hours spent in virtual exercise on the ship, and hardly any of them on self-defense. Just wait—he was going to master them all! He'd had enough.

Gasping, Ran rolled over onto hands and knees, this time splattering drops of sweat as well as blood. He was going to smash in Virile's grinning, sadistic face.

He saw feet.

Lots of feet. Mostly bare. He was surrounded.

Spread-eagled, wrists and ankles tied to the corners of his bed, Ran could only scowl his defiance at Wick and his men. If they were on Earth, Wick and Virile might already be zombies, their impulses to violence eradicated. Instead, they'd succeeded in triggering his own desire to pound them both into fodder for a food fab.

All through school, he'd had nonviolence drummed into him.

Self-defense was permitted, but the basics were all taught virtually. No martial-arts master would take on a student without the basics. If he ever got near a VR again, he intended to master self-defense—*asap*.

"Now that you got the Brain's attention, you can fix the analyzer. If you do, we feed you. Simple as that," said Wick.

"Not simple." Ran's voice came out nasal, due to his bloodied nose. "You tell me to visit the Brain. You order me away from the Brain. Why should I take your word for anything? I'm doing nothing more for you till the food fab's reprogrammed and I've had a decent meal."

He was going to need to empty his bladder soon. "And I want—"

A clicking noise caused the men to turn. The hardware fab rolled into the sleeping room. As ordered, it had responded to his voice. Ran gasped out a laugh, as much as his miserable ribs allowed. "I'm going to call you Roly. My new pet."

"Regular Pied Piper," Wick snarled and turned to leave.

"Catch more flies with honey . . ." Einstein followed him. "I told you, Boss. He's a straightforward thinker. He doesn't think twisty like you."

"Starving the Warrens never worked," Noland said. "Let him get the food fab operational for all of us."

"I wouldn't put it past him to have gotten the food this bad on purpose," said Saxon.

Ran's mouth twitched. The fab's food hadn't been any good to begin with.

"Cooperate with him, Boss. Let the kid fix my analyzer," said Capshaw. "I've got to have it working if we're to locate that B'ite."

"Later," said Wick from the doorway. "Almost morning. I want to look for myself. We'll all go, leave Gooney behind to babysit. The kid can starve a little longer, soften him up for some real work. Soon as the wind's down, we'll take the Trilby out."

Why didn't the mining boss know where the stuff was? Ran wondered, not for the first time. Something was going on between base and Warrens. He knew which side he wanted to be on.

In spite of the pain in his chest, Ran's eyelids grew heavy.

A hand tugging at the knots on his wrist brought Ran's eyes open. "I'll deal with you when we get back." Wick, making extra sure he was held fast. "And get that fab out of here!" he said to Gooney.

DAY EIGHT

Power Plays

Ran

Very early morning. The dome revealed a slight grayness to the sky.

Ran blinked at this sign of approaching day. He didn't know if he ached more from Virile's brutal handling or from his inability to move. His lower half was soggy after giving up on holding his bladder.

Footsteps brought Ran's head around.

Wick stood in the doorway, with Black-bearded Noland looking over his shoulder.

"Stinks in here. Fix the analyzer and we'll feed you," Wick said from the doorway.

"Why should I?" Ran had never felt less like cooperating. "I could have done it already, but you had to push me around." Talking caused his teeth to rub against his sore cheek, reminding him how dry his mouth was.

"Leave the door open," Wick ordered. "Let him know what he's missing," but from the main room Capshaw's outraged voice howled, "What *is* this shit?"

"You'll never make him hungry with talk like that, Cap," Noland said with a snarky laugh. "Try praising it instead."

Ran's lips curled in a lopsided smile. What a huge difference that tiny change in the insert contents could make—though he hadn't expected such a foul smell.

"Boss, I have to have that analyzer," Capshaw pleaded. "The kid's proved he can deal with the Brain. Let him fix it before it's too late. And we can't eat this crap!"

Ran's eyelids grew heavy. If they wouldn't untie him, maybe they'd leave him alone long enough to get some sleep.

"B *R-I-L-L-L.*"

Ran woke. The ship again. The hardware fab waited beside his cot. His lips cracked from dryness as he smiled. Nice to have a friend nearby.

<<"This is AstroTwo . . . [crackle crackle]">>

"What's the com lag, Boss?" Capshaw yelled.

Wick shouted, "This is base. What's your ETA, *AstroTwo?*" Both doors—Wick's office plus the inner one—must be open for Ran to hear so much.

<<"ETA uncertain, base . . . [crackle] We'll inform you when closer.">>

"Still need a line on the Beijingite, Boss," reminded Gooney, and Capshaw demanded his analyzer again.

"Be nice to the kid and he might fix it for you." Noland's advice made sense to Ran.

"I don't trust him any farther than I can throw him," said Wick.

What had he ever done to make Wick so mad? Ran rolled his head back and forth seeking some ease for his body.

"I'll leave him to soften up while we go to the Warrens," said Wick. "He's my hostage in case we have to twist arms, and he'd better be ready to work when we get back—or else."

Ran shifted uneasily against his bindings. He'd never been any good at understanding people. Wick was at least half crazy, and unpredictable.

His eyes rested on the hardware fab. "Hardware fab," he said softly, "your name is Roly."

Roly rolled nearer to the cot, bringing a choking sensation to his throat. Machines he *could* understand. They'd always made up for his lack of friends.

No lie, he *was* lonely. He'd always been lonely. If only the men would leave . . .

The long hours tied to his bed had honed some understanding of the Brain. It—she?—received no stimulation other than Wick's rants and the rare ship contacts. Maybe the Brain wasn't crazy—*yet*. More like a kid's trick of gaining attention. He knew that one.

Teachers had accused him of using his VR phobia for attention. As if he'd *choose* to be isolated from all his classmates. He'd *wanted* to belong. Then came that day—he was six—when his teacher and the principal announced upgrades to the VR education system. A new approach.

"The Durant Effect, it's called," his teacher said. "We think it might work better for you than the old system. We want you to try it." They were tired of teaching him using old methods, and Ran was sick of being set apart. He agreed to try.

Major disaster. A full week passed before the school's system was restored. The techs couldn't figure out what had gone wrong. That was the last time anyone tried to cure his phobia or accused him of wanting attention.

His eyelids grew heavy again. A machine needed to be needed. What had the Brain intended by deprogramming the other machines? How *aware* was the Brain?

Hallie

Hallie's dreams woke her over and over, each time with her heart racing. Always running. Always panicking.

She portioned out yeast crackers and a mushy dip for the breakfast line. A good thing her fingers knew what they were doing; her head felt disconnected.

Rumbo accepted his serving and smiled as if she were the most gorgeous female in the room. When he did that, she forgot restless nights and impossible hair.

"Beautiful miss, I apologize," Rumbo said. "I've been told I shouldn't have given you that tour. People are concerned for your health. The mines are dangerous."

"But I wasn't in the mines," Hallie said. "Why should anyone care if I saw your office?"

"No, no, they're right. The mine is too close."

"You're still going to show me those maps?"

"That I can do! See you later."

Next in line, Reba looked at her plate doubtfully. "It's not too bad," Hallie told her.

In the far corner, Pel was eating and talking with Aryn. The line dwindled, and Hallie joined Melody with her own plate. Maybe Pel would ask Aryn to be his lead singer instead of her. *Miss Perfect* could do everything.

All a waste of time. *Go home now!*—as if they could.

After eating, Hallie and Melody proceeded to the greenhouse, where Gardner told them, "I have to consolidate. Harvest those beets, and then you can set out these sprouts in the same container."

Melody's thoughts always seemed to be elsewhere, yet she fulfilled any duties with surprising competence: food prep, greenhouse tasks, cleanup, weaving. Melody began the planting while Hallie carried the beets and greens to the kitchen.

Bork ordered her to wash the greens while he rinsed the beets and threw them in the oven. Hallie worked carefully, enjoying the deep, glossy greens and hints of red in the mound of leaves. Unfortunately, they would cook down to barely a mouthful or two for each person. Everyone was hungry, so hungry that even with their work breaks, the teens collapsed by mid-afternoon, all energy expended.

She finished the greens, wiped the food-service counter, and moved on to clean the table in the center of the kitchen.

"You're going to wear the stone down to nothing," Bork said.

Startled, she looked at him, then at the cloth she was scrubbing with. "You're more afraid I'll wear out this rag."

He jerked his head. "Go on out and join the others till lunch. You've done your share."

She should go back and help Melody, Hallie thought. But it was almost lunchtime.

On the far side of the room, Reba and Tesia had their heads together over something. Good. First, she'd ask them to join her in exploring. As she crossed the room, Ramon started up his music device, and she recognized the soaring tones of the popular Cepheid Variables singers and—on the flickering hologram—their trademark halo of airboard acrobatic dancers, the Pulsators. Ramon's charge wouldn't last long with that display, but its bittersweet reminder of home was irresistible.

A hand on her shoulder brought her whirling around with a gasp.

"Pretty lady, didn't mean to startle you."

Only Rumbo. She sighed. His touch had triggered the memory of dream terrors.

"My lucky day," he said. "I got off a little early. Since I have to go right back after eating, maybe you'd like to see my maps now."

"The maps." She took a breath. "Yes, I'd like that. And thank you for all the help with our paper project." Rumbo had provided screening and a press.

"*De nada*. It's a pleasure to have a new challenge."

She followed him down the stairwell, her fingers trailing along the stone wall. This dwelling place still amazed her. The one who drilled it out must have been a master designer. Earth could use more underground construction to escape heat and pests. And carving into rock prevented the tunneling creatures Gardner complained about.

"Who designed this place?"

"Someone dead," Rumbo said.

He led her past Melody's doorway and stopped at the far end, near the steps descending to the third level where Hallie had never ventured. She wondered why. Too tired, came the answer.

"After you."

"Your room's smaller." The single room contained a bed in one corner and a few cushions.

"I'm only one guy." His wall nook was messy with clothes and stacks of plastic sheets. He rummaged through the flimsies and pulled out a couple, but turning away, dislodged them all. "Sit, sit."

She sank cross-legged on a cushion, reaching to gather up loose flimsies. The markings on them were indecipherable. "I thought they'd be holographs. How can you read these?"

Rumbo handed her a foot-long sheet and settled close enough for her to feel his warmth.

"You need to train your eyes is all. A lot of history was built using this flat method. Here's the Warrens' upper level." With his guidance, the gathering room was easy to pick out. Angled lines indicated the sloping ramp. "You see the tracks of the pipes and how they lead down to the next level."

Her eye followed the movement of his thick index finger as he nipped the next semitransparent sheet and placed it below the first. "See how they match?"

Each level included impressive stonework plumbing. And Rumbo wasn't the only one to have a single room.

"Here's the third level down. It's still unfinished." Rumbo produced another flimsy.

He leaned closer, his shoulder touching hers. Hallie flinched away while studying the rooms that ran along one side of the third-level hallway. Midway on the other side, a dotted line indicated a door and a planned corridor.

She pointed. "What's this?"

"Never was built."

Her eye snagged on the top flimsy of the stack she'd picked up, showing the terrain and the long Rift. "Where are we, and where is the base?"

"We're here." Rumbo pointed to a smudge. "Near the Rift but not too near. Here's the Shed, where you landed." That angled farther from the Rift. "And over here's the base." The three points made a long oblique triangle with the base farthest away, and even closer to the Rift than the Warrens.

"What caused it?" she asked, her finger tracing the scar.

"Perk says . . ." He stopped. "Actually, we still don't know. Originally thought to be plates pulling apart, but that break cuts across the continental plate we're resting on."

Didn't he know? He *had* to know. It seemed so obvious to her since Aryn's sketch.

"Why must you have so many secrets?" Her impatience with Ed now encompassed Rumbo and every adult. "If a ship crashed—probably an alien ship—and you've been mining the Beijingite scraped from its hull, why can't you just say so?"

Rumbo tossed the flimsies toward the messy wall niche. "Beautiful Miss Hallie." His face was inches from her own, smelling of sweat and windblown dust.

Hallie's thoughts scattered as Rumbo's lips neared hers. She'd never kissed a man.

He hadn't answered her question!

She ducked. His lips grazed her nose. "No! I'm not of age."

Rumbo grasped both her shoulders. "That's not what the scuttlebutt says."

"What do you mean?" She turned her head away from his mouth. "What are you talking about? What *scuttlebutt*?"

"Word is out that you and your pal were regened to appear like teens in order to infiltrate this place. And that's good enough for me. You'll do."

You'll do.

"You're crazy!" Hallie twisted out of his grasp. "I'm only sixteen."

You'll do. That sounded so sinister. Rumbo loomed over her.

You'll do. As if she were just anybody. The words morphed. *She'll* do.

That was what *they* said. On that picnic. She'd gone walking while Pel napped and Ran sailed his boat. The park trail. Those two men. "*She'll do.*"

Her heart thundered, about to explode.

Rumbo pulled her closer.

Hallie rolled away from him off the cushion, arms flailing, landed on hands and knees, the stone floor cold and hard beneath her. She stood so quickly that her head banged Rumbo's jaw.

He recoiled and she reached the door, gasping for breath.

Those two men at the park. They'd said, "*I can't spot him anywhere.*" They had been scanning for someone male, and she had walked right past them. "*She's one of them. She'll do.*"

One of *them.* Ran. Or Pel. Or *her.* She hadn't caused this exile. She'd disobeyed Liz, but it was *them*! Those men. Maybe they'd also bombed that woman on the airboard.

The little room pressed around her. She brought shaking fingers to her face.

"What's wrong?" Rumbo asked.

She clung to the door to stay upright and turned. Rumbo stood where she'd left him, no longer a threat. His hands had fallen to his sides, concern on his face, a gray tinge to his complexion. He was just a man thinking—

What *had* he been thinking? She had to find Pel. Tell him she had her memory back. But first— "What did you mean, *scuttlebutt*? Who said that about regening?"

"This place is a hive of gossip. It's what I've heard from several people."

"It's a lie! I just started tertiary. I'm not even seventeen. And Pel is the same age. You said '*infiltrate*.' You mean *spies*? Spies for who?"

Rumbo lifted both hands in unknowing.

Hallie puffed out a breath. *Modified to be younger?* She'd rather be older, thank you!

"I've got to go." She burst out of Rumbo's room and rushed toward the stairs. Ahead of her in the hallway, Melody slipped out of their rooms and headed up the steps, one hand on the wall, a wind coat on her arm, her shoulders slumping.

Something was wrong.

"Melody!" Hallie called. She caught up where the steps curved. "Are you going up for lunch?" A basket hung from Melody's arm, half hidden beneath her wind coat.

"I have to go to the silk plants," Melody answered without turning.

They reached the top of the stairs. "But what about lunch?"

"It's the calm. I have to go now."

"All right. I'll go with you." Her memory was secure enough. Finding Pel would have to wait. Melody ignored the food, but Hallie's stomach rumbled.

Aryn, standing in line, looked at them. "Are you going to the silk plants?"

Hallie nodded. "She insists on going now."

"I'll come too." Aryn turned to Luisa who was dishing out servings. "Save three portions, please."

Shrugging on wind coats, they followed Melody into gusts that made Hallie gasp. This was a *calm*? Melody walked quickly, hugging her basket and leading them toward the greenhouse, then veering right to circle the base of the same hill the mining office sat against.

Hallie's stomach screamed about its missed meal, but the other two didn't complain. And where was Pel? She hadn't spotted him in the gathering room.

Past and present jostled for attention in her head: the trail she'd followed the day of the picnic; the trail the three of them were following to reach the silk plants; Rumbo's attempt to kiss her; the regening lie that was circulating. She longed to share her thoughts with Aryn but couldn't speak with Melody so near. Protect Melody. Protect her from what? Hallie couldn't say. Just—she didn't want to increase the woman's pain.

The way toward the mining office was well trampled with no threatening prickles. Then Melody turned off onto a narrower path.

They arrived at a flat space sheltered by the surrounding hills. The straight rows of plants reminded Hallie of ancient telephone poles stretching across the prairie—back when phones and homes used electrical wires. Or maybe like a row of toy soldiers standing at attention, short arms angled out from their sides. Stalks held branches at right angles, covered with sharp stickers. Each branch held a blob, no doubt equally prickly. The silk plants were staggered as if planted deliberately to not block the light from other rows. Beyond and among them, dead-gray plant skeletons crumbled.

"Why do you suppose plants feel so much need of protection on this planet?" Aryn asked.

"We all wonder that." Melody sounded as if she was only half present. She walked up to the nearest plant and held out her hand. Wind muttered against her coat. "Thank you," Melody murmured. In her hand rested a blob. The husk remained on the plant, spread wide and empty.

"How did you do that?" Aryn asked.

"I thank them. I promise to plant their seeds."

"I'd like to try," said Aryn. "How do you choose? Are they all ready to release?"

"I'm not sure. Maybe a sense of fullness. What I don't harvest, they'll cast off soon now."

I've got to find a better name than blobs, thought Hallie. Cotton has bolls. Silk bolls, then. She shivered, her stomach hollow and complaining. Might as well give it a try. She moved to the left of Aryn and studied a plant her equal in height. *I'll plant your seeds*, she thought at it. *Thank you for the gift of your fibers*. But being so close made her cringe. For visible and less visible prickers she was *not* thankful. And she wanted her lunch.

Crack! Something shot past.

"Oh!" Hallie ducked. The plant had flung its seed packet over her shoulder.

"Ah," said Aryn. "How lovely. Thank you." She dropped a boll into Melody's basket, which now held three, and placed her hands beneath the next limb.

The contents of Hallie's boll had blown due west. "Can the thread be gathered up?"

"Yes," Melody said. "It will have to be washed before spinning."

Just her luck. The strand was going to end up tangled. Hallie bent to collect the fiber as another boll burst from the same plant.

"*Ouch!*" Stray prickers embedded in the sands clung to her fingers along with the fiber. By the time she'd collected those threads, Melody's basket was full and Hallie felt as prickly as the surrounding plants.

"We should have brought more baskets," said Aryn. "Can we come back? I'd like to spend more time here."

Of course Aryn wanted to. Hallie rubbed her stinging fingers and added her tangled mass to Melody's basket. On their return, she paid particular attention to the waving fronds that threatened to slash or scratch or in some way leap out at her. They reminded her of playful kittens, but without the cuteness or logic of a kitten's pounces.

Ahead of the other two, she rounded the base of the hill and came out on the trail to the mining office. A Trilby passed overhead, reminding Hallie of her need to locate the Warrens' vehicles. She turned to look for the greenhouse and almost stumbled over a shape in the path. "*Wh—?*"

A wind coat. But not merely a wind coat. She knelt. Beneath the head covering she felt a cool cheek with short stubble. A man. *Rumbo?* But she'd been with him—an hour ago?—longer now.

Melody set down her basket to crouch on the other side and reached for a wrist.

"Is he . . . alive?" Hallie asked.

"I don't feel a pulse. Go get help."

Hallie scrambled to her feet and ran.

Pel

Following his morning duties, Pel discovered he was one of the last to collect his lunch. He wondered where Hallie was. Some of the teens had gathered at "their" table. Hallie, Aryn, Nick, and Manuelo were missing. Should he wait or begin the meeting he'd called?

A tense group of adults stood in a tight group at the far side of the room, paying no attention to the teens. That decided Pel. He called the meeting to order, speaking softly.

"Listen, everyone. I overheard something, and I think you need to know. I didn't catch any details, but the adults are preparing for some threat. I'm guessing they're worried about Wick and the base. Plus, Aryn learned someone is passing information to the base. The reason adults won't talk to us may be because of that informer."

"This morning Leif and I spotted a Trilby," said Amado. "It seemed to be looking for something."

"Maybe that's what's concerning them." Pel glanced at the adults, then returned to the wide-eyed teens. "Just keep alert and aware. And don't say anything to anyone."

The wind slats rattled.

"*B-l-a-r-g-h-h!*" The sound of retching.

"It's Nick!"

Descending the ramp, Nick looked green in spite of his red, wind-scoured face. Manuelo followed him inside. Adults rushed over, his mother grasping Nick's elbow.

"It tasted good," Nick said, "so I took a real bite."

Pel groaned. Nick, looking for something, *anything*, edible on the planet. Leif and Amado had the right idea: Study animal life. Leave the plants alone.

"We'll eat what food we're given," said Reba, "with no complaints."

Agreed, Pel thought. After eating, he went to collect his noter from the greenhouse.

It wasn't there. He had put it on the shelf—hadn't he?

Pel rushed to check his sleeping space—knowing it wouldn't be there.

Back in the greenhouse, coatless, he looked around all the plants near the shelf, patted the ground, felt into crevices. Nothing. *Not there, the shelf bare*—of the noter, anyway. Ramon's music collection was charging.—*Lost. At what cost? Must exhaust all possibilities.*

Taken. By someone objecting to being spied on.

Their own fault! They might have tried talking to him. Recording them was an intrusion, but still—

The noter didn't even require a password to replay. "*Aargh! Dung. Feces. Frass. Turds. Spam. Crud!*" Shivering he let the wind push him back toward the warmth of the Warrens. Who had his noter? He was so cooked. And where was Hallie? She hadn't been at lunch. Come to think of it, he hadn't seen Aryn either.

Pel tried to ignore his anxiety, wishing for some of that paper-making project so he could work out lyrics that didn't include Hallie as heroine. He'd gotten the orphans *stranded, bare handed . . .*

But what was the threat?

Creeping, sneaking, on parents we are spying.

We're lost, we're lonely, you haven't let us in.

You saved us, you love us, but where do we fit in?

Rhyming *in* and *in*? He was wasting his time.

The island shakes, nothing fakes the deaths that we're defying.

Island or planet? What kind of ship was needed?

"Help!" Hallie's voice. His heroine, exactly what she might say. "Outside. Rumbo. On the trail. We think he's . . . dead."

Hallie stood at the foot of the ramp. Several men dashed past her. Another went into the infirmary and emerged with an expandable stretcher. Pel crossed the room to join Hallie. Moments later, Melody entered with Aryn, crossed the room with her basket, and headed down the stairs.

The men returned, two of them carrying the stretcher, with a body wrapped tightly in a wind coat. Hallie bit her lip as they entered the infirmary. Pel took her hand, wanting to give comfort. Melody returned without her basket and went into the infirmary as well.

From the top of the ramp, Ed announced, "It's Rumbo." He waved a palm-sized maroon gadget.

"My noter!" Pel squawked. "Where did you find that?"

Ed glanced at him, then away as he walked down the ramp and took his place at the head of the room. "Attention. Everyone sit. Meeting is called."

Bork rang his gong. People poured in from seemingly every direction, though there were only two directions—from outside or below stairs.

Ed waved Pel's noter, his *lost* noter. "This was found by Rumbo's body. The killer dropped it there. And who does it belong to? Him." Ed's pointing finger snared Pel's eyes.

Killer? Ed was accusing him of murder? Shades of his ancestors! This felt like a lynching for sure. Forget the melodrama. This was reality, *a mob on the loose, waiting with a noose, lies and abuse . . .*

With an effort Pel shook off rhymes. "It belongs to me. As for Rumbo, I don't know what you're talking about."

But it was Ed and whatever underlay Ed's accusation that explained why no one would talk. And he was sunk. The NODE had shipped him lightyears from Earth, away from a trial where he would have faced the *zombie judge,* defended by an incompetent court-appointed defense counsel. He might have lost his case, but at least he'd have had truth on his side. Where was he to find any truth here?

The rattle of wind slats brought all eyes back to the ramp where four men entered.

"Where's the B'ite?" A burly man armed with a Snub stomped down toward them, flanked by a pale, thin man whose hand rested on his own holstered weapon. Two taller men followed, their height accentuated by the ramp's elevation.

In slow motion, Ed turned. "Hello, Wick. What's up?"

"I've come to collect the B'ite."

Ursa said, "No more. You got last season's. We're hanging on to the little we've collected until you pay what's owed us."

"You want food? I'll get you food. Where's the B'ite?"

"Where's the food?" she snapped back. "We've got kids to feed. And we want passage back to Earth. Are you going to negotiate that for us or not?"

Beside Pel, Hallie stiffened and stepped forward. "And where's Ran? Why didn't you bring *him* with you? He belongs *here*!"

Wick shot her a look and scowled. "Where's Rumbo? I might get some sense out of him."

"Dead," several chorused.

"What d'you mean, dead?" Wick waved his Snub.

"Orenda's looking into that as we speak," Ursa said. "We don't know yet."

From beside her, Satch said, "Come on, Wick. You can't shoot us all. Put that away."

Pel noticed that parents and stepparents had sandwiched their offspring between or behind them, like mother hens. Only he and Hallie had no protectors.

Wick turned to his men. "You two stay here. Come on, Virile." He holstered his Snub and pushed through the crowd to the infirmary, followed by the smaller man.

Orenda blocked Wick's entry. "We all want to know what caused his death. You'll have to wait till I'm through, like everyone else."

Wick looked past her into the infirmary, then stomped back up the ramp. One of his men said something in a low voice, and Wick gave a curt nod. "Let's go. We'll find the B'ite for ourselves."

"A ship must be in contact if he's looking so hard," said a man.

"What happens when a ship comes in?" Hallie asked.

"Nothing, if we give them the goods," said Ursa. "They take the Beijingite and leave. This time, we're not so willing."

The Warrens *had* been working on their escape even before their kids came, Pel realized. *That* was what their arrival had interrupted.

"All right!" Ed yelled, bringing an end to the hubbub. "Back to the subject at hand. The B'ite can wait."

Pel groaned. Ed was going to accuse him of spying and murder.

Hallie

Hallie stared at Wick's retreating back. What horrible timing. If she'd known he'd be here with half his men, she could've staged her raid on the base to rescue Ran—except she still hadn't found the vehicles or a pilot or . . .

And Rumbo was dead. And . . .

"Back to the subject at hand." Ed sounded angry.

She couldn't blame him—until his gaze fixed on Pel, who looked pale—if that was possible. Sort of gray-brown. Why was Ed mad at Pel? Ed again waved Pel's noter.

Murder? Pel? Furious, Hallie moved back to his side, her arm brushing his. "You don't even know how Rumbo died, Ed. Why don't you wait to hear from Orenda before you make accusations?"

"You think I don't know why the two of you are here?" said Ed. "Acting as spies!"

Pel's start bumped her shoulder. "Spying for who?" Hallie demanded. "For what?"

"How do *we* know? You were genetically modified to resemble teen-agers just so you could slip in with our kids."

"That's a lie!" said Hallie. "Rumbo told me that rumor. He said he'd heard it from a number of people. Who started it? *You?*"

"That's not the issue. We have a dead body and this"—the maroon stripes glinted in Ed's hand as he waved Pel's device—"belongs to *him.*"

"I've been looking for that." Pel's feeble response increased Hallie's fury.

She raised her chin and her voice. "Of course Pel didn't kill Rumbo. You don't even know how Rumbo died. You're looking for a murderer before you have proof of a murder. Is *that* how you all ended up on this planet?"

"Follow the rules, Ed," someone shouted. "If you don't, we'll elect a new leader."

Ed waved the noter again. "All right. Everybody come to order. Maybe I was hasty. But I *do* know he was recording with this device. And I don't understand what feeble excuse could justify shipping you two here."

"Neither do we," said Pel, sounding more like himself. "As for my noter, I live for research. No one would talk to me. Maybe I was wrong—but this *is* a public room. Back home, recording in public is automatic and perfectly legal. I never recorded any private conversations."

Hallie took a step nearer to Ed. "As for feeble excuses, if you hadn't imposed silence on everyone, they might have talked to us and come to a better understanding of who we are days ago. No one told us why we were sent, but we can make some guesses."

"Let's hear what they have to say," called a woman from the back. It sounded like Leif's stepmother.

"All right then." Ed set down Pel's noter on the nearest stone table and folded his arms. "Tell us. I didn't trust you because you knew more than you should have from the beginning."

"You people disappeared from Earth," Hallie said. "Pel researched you. He told you as much that first night."

Overwhelmed by the enormity of their story, she looked at Pel. "Where do we start?" Then she remembered her rush to find him. "I've got my memory back!"

Pel's eyes lit up and she wanted to hug him. "You've got the ball," he said. "Throw yourself through the hoop." His grin was weak but conveyed confidence in her.

She flashed him a return smile and turned to face the forest of watchers.

"There were three of us, sent here without explanation. Ran was a fosterling who came to work for my uncle, and I met Pel through him. Pel spent years researching disappearances—ever since his childhood friend disappeared. He got a chance to ask the NODE a question directly, and that same day the three of us celebrated with a picnic before Pel went back to his village. But he never got there. It was at that picnic that two men grabbed me and sprayed me with an amnesiac spray."

She had turned to include the room. Several women visibly recoiled at her words, and she rushed to reassure them. "Ran came to my rescue, and there was an accident that killed the two kidnappers."

Pel took over. "I still think Ran is one of your offspring. Back on Earth, there was at least one attempt on his life. Hallie is right. We need to get him out of the base. I've considered two possible triggers to why Hallie and I were sent here.

"First, in my question of the NODE, I asked for information about the few of you I *had* identified, *and* any offspring.

"Second, because that fatal accident got the three of us in trouble, we may have been shipped here for our own safety."

Hallie lifted her chin. "The picnic was my idea. Right after Pel asked his question of the NODE, we walked to a park. Ran had built a model boat he wanted to sail. We ate, Ran went to the pond, Pel fell asleep, and I took a walk. Halfway around the perimeter trail, I overheard two men talking. One said, 'I don't see him anywhere.' The other said, 'We know he's here. Something's masking his chip.'"

Her voice shook. "I was scared, but they'd said *he* and so I went on. I almost reached the bend in the trail when one of them said, '*She's* with them. She'll do.' I ran, but they caught me and sprayed me. I woke in the hospital with no memory. It's finally come back."

Pel again took up the story. "Ran heard Hallie scream and went after her. He cut the fuel line in their aircar—the same make and color of the one that had attempted a hit-and-run on him. The men dropped Hallie and took off before the fuel could dissipate. Their car exploded. Ran got badly burnt protecting Hallie. I was farther away. All three of us ended up implicated in those deaths, and the dead guys had influential parents who wouldn't allow the truth to come out."

Hallie broke in. "Those kidnappers wanted Pel or Ran."

Pel reached into his pocket and held up his gold databank. "Proof of all that is supposed to be here, but so far I haven't been able to access it. This databank holds the writ of supersedeas that sent us here, the inadmissible testimony of a nonchipped boy who witnessed the accident and—so I'm told—also contains the NODE's answer to my question, on a time lock. Maybe it simply needs a thorough charging, but I haven't dared let it out of my hands."

"Let's get it charged and hear what's on it then," someone called.

Hallie relaxed. The adults were going to be reasonable.

The infirmary door opened. Orenda faced the room. "There are no visible signs of injury on Rumbo. It will take an autopsy to determine exact cause, but I believe it to have been a natural death, possibly a stroke. A few weeks ago, he complained of an excruciating headache, but refused to allow me to monitor him. He insisted on going back to work."

"Why was my noter found with him?" Pel asked.

Hallie wanted an answer to that too.

Several adults converged on Pel while Aryn pulled Hallie away to hand her a plate of food. "You must be starving. Here's your lunch, plus the first serving of supper. Bork likes you. He says you're a straight shooter."

"I had to defend Pel." Hallie forced a weak smile at Aryn. "Thanks."

She found space at the back of the room and collapsed. She'd let her anger take charge—again. How many times had her mother said, *You've got to learn not to be so impulsive?* But she never *had* learned. Anything unfair might set her off. Like that day she came home with torn pants and bloodied nose. *But Mom,* she always began. "But Mom, Cass needed me to stand with her against that bossy Teresa." And the time she came home scratched and her mother rushed her to the clinic to test for pathogens, saying, *In a world full of lethal infections, you go and rescue stray animals.* "But Mom, the cat was lost. It shouldn't have been on the streets."

She'd done the same for that dog the day she met Pel. *I had to,* she thought. It always came down to that. Was that who she was? Her *real* self? She never felt muddled at those times, as if she were two people: one fearlessly going to anyone's defense; the other, her ordinary self, desperately trying to prove she deserved to be alive.

Maybe she was the very thing her mother deplored. Maybe that was why she'd liked Rumbo. He'd encouraged her to be feisty. He made her feel attractive, even with her bad hair. And he *had* backed off when she made it clear she didn't want to be kissed.

Or—remembering how ill he'd looked—was that the beginnings of his stroke?

What did it matter? She pushed away her plate, heaving a deep breath. Tears of shock prickled her eyes. *Filthy spamguts.* Rumbo was dead.

Pel

Pel sank onto a bench, exhaustion warring with exhilaration. He'd seen Hallie in action before, ready to rescue any creature with no thought to her safety. This time she'd fought for him. He wished . . .

A purposeful group approached, and Pel pushed himself back to his feet. Geraldine Ramirez said, "Well, young man, you've done your research. I was gratified to learn through my son that I was remembered for honesty and not for the calumnies I was accused of." She glanced at those with her. "We believed DeWarg's lies, long after he was dead."

"DeWarg?" Pel said. "I've heard that name."

"He was in charge when we arrived. Died in the mines."

Pel gave a nod but knew there was something more. He *needed* his data.

Another small group huddled with Bork at his counter. What were they planning? Probably talking about Wick's visit and a future attack.

"Isn't it time to tell our stories?" Geraldine's question brought Pel back to those surrounding him. "Delver always insisted we had nothing to be ashamed of. I believe he was absolutely right."

"My daughter has spoken of your disappearances research," Sam

Suzuki said. "I never knew why they grabbed me. I was flying to record an interview when my flight went down. Then I was here, and going out of my mind with shock and worry for my wife and new-born daughter. I've always wondered if I interviewed someone with a secret or if I was intercepted before I could learn it."

"But why not remove your last interviewee instead, if that was the case?" asked Pel.

"We were *both* removed. Milt was the last man I interviewed, but he died shortly after we arrived here."

"Tell us what you know," said someone Pel couldn't put a name to.

"I'll do the best I can," Pel began, "but you realize my data are all stored, and I may make mistakes of memory. There are some names I haven't found here, and since no one would talk, I haven't been able to discover if they were ever here at all."

"Name them, and we'll tell you," said Reba's mother.

"The names I asked about were Sam Suzuki, Geraldine Ramirez, Father Dominic Rivera, Taylor Layton, and Gabe Fletcher."

Tesia and her mother pushed closer. "Dominic was here," said Tesia's mother. "He was my husband."

Ooops. He *knew* Tesia's last name was Rivera. A married priest.

"What I know," said Pel, "is that Father Dominic fought for more arcologies as a solution to refugee relief. Some hints I came across suggested that, although it wasn't his field, he was aware of certain 'peculations'—embezzled monies meant for arcologies—but it was never clear to me why he was among the disappeareds. Unless someone just wanted him out of the way."

"That's not why," said Tesia's mother. "You seem to have a leaning toward male victims."

Pel closed his mouth.

She continued. "I was the cause of our removal. My name is Topaz Galliard-Rivera, and I always felt bad that Dominic was prevented from continuing his work. I was tracking the movement of goods slated for arcology development because half of what the quarry shipped was not arriving. My husband was aware of those peculations, though how you found that out, I don't know. That was confidential. I never did know who grabbed me that last day."

Pel's heart thumped. *Finally!* "What company were you investigating?"

She shook her head. "Some subcontractor. I didn't have time to find out who held their contract."

The gong rang. "Attention everyone," Ed said from his position at Bork's counter. "Bork says supper will be ready shortly. Meantime, it's been decided that tomorrow Pel will be assigned to the mining office in order to charge his databank."

Pel blew out his breath. So. He might finally discover what the databank held.

Ran

Ran jerked awake with a groan. *Aryn had called out to him and he'd climbed on Pel's bike, but the wheels spun round and round without going anywhere. While he pedaled madly, Wick said over and over, "You can't leave. You're my son."*

His body ached to move, to stretch, to flex. He hadn't meant to fall asleep. Gooney snored on the next cot over. The dome was bright with light. Midday? Later? The door stood open, but all he heard was Gooney's loud breathing.

"Roly, anti-grav on," Ran said softly. The boxy shape of the hardware fab slowly rose.

"Hover." He tried to gauge the distance between the fab and his fastened wrist. An awkward business, since he couldn't raise his head very far to see.

"Extrude blade." Pure energy, it could cut his hand off if he wasn't careful.

"Move three centimeters to the left . . ."

"Move two centimeters forward." He stretched his wrist as far as the cord allowed, which wasn't much. He could feel the heat from the blade's operations. "Extend one centimeter."

Gooney gave a snort.

Ran jerked. He hissed as the blade contacted his flesh, but the cord was severed. He pulled his arm back and lay still.

Gooney rolled over onto his side and his breathing quieted.

Ran tried to reach the cord that held his left wrist, but the twist of his torso made his ribs scream, and his spread-eagled legs wouldn't allow access. All right then.

"Roly," he whispered.

The hardware fab moved forward.

He raised his head and propped himself on his elbow, bleeding wrist pressed into the blanket, and directed the fab to his right ankle, with pauses to be sure Gooney still slept.

His ankle released, he rolled onto his side, pulled his little knife from his pocket, and cut his left wrist free, then his left ankle. He crept out of his clammy bed and floated Roly away from sleeping Gooney.

The returning Trilby sounded overhead.

"*Blast!*" Ran talked fast, giving Roly instructions.

Wick's voice preceded him into the main room. "Noland, go check on the kid."

Gooney grunted and rolled over. Seeing Ran, he got up. "What's going on?"

"He's bleeding," Noland said from the doorway, addressing Wick. "He got himself free while Gooney slept."

"Some guard you are, Gooney! I'm fed up!" Wick said. "Rumbo dead. No B'ite. And the kid thinks to run out on me." He peered into the room. "You're not going anywhere until that analyzer's working."

"I don't do anything until I've had a good meal." Ran's tongue felt thick, making it hard to talk.

They were going to tie him up again. It took three days for a man to die of thirst. He wished he could've grabbed a drink, but first things first.

DAY NINE

Preparations

Ran

Gooney complained of the stink. He pulled the coverings from Ran's former cot and hauled them off. Tied, thankfully to a different cot, Ran dozed.

He woke, listening to an argument in the main room bouncing between Capshaw's "My analyzer . . ." to Wick's "I don't trust him . . ." to Noland's "He's only a kid . . ." Were they going to argue all night?

His tongue felt glued to all parts of his mouth; he was thirstier than when he'd climbed to the ridge, his ribs throbbed, his back ached.

Ran's only comfort was Roly's presence. The men had paid no attention to the hardware fab in the corner where he'd told it to stay. Like a well-behaved pet, Roly made small clinks and clanks as it processed the replacement anti-grav regulator for the Wreck, Ran's only accomplishment. He wished he'd risked waking Gooney and ordered it sooner. Printing out parts took so long!

With silence in the main room, Ran's eyes closed. *A drop of rain hit his face. He raised his chin to look at the sky.* "Wake up, kid," said Wick.

Ran opened his eyes. Instead of his dream rain, Gooney held a wet cloth over his head.

Wick glared down at him. "Last chance," he growled. "You do the work, you can have water."

"No, *your* last chance, Wick," Ran slurred. After all this misery, *he* was going to call the shots. "I'm going to the Warrens. I don't fix any tools until the Wreck is ready to fly."

"Better give in, Boss," said Capshaw from behind Wick. "We don't have any time left."

"They know he's here," added Einstein. "That girl— If he turns up dead *no* one's going to deal with us."

What girl? What had the men been up to at the Warrens? How long had their argument gone on? The dome was the deep gray of early morning.

"What do I care?" Wick stomped to the door, then threw up his hands. "All right! We need that analyzer. Let him up. Give him everything he wants. But he doesn't leave until the analyzer works."

"What d'you want first?" asked Gooney, as he freed Ran.

Duh! "Water." Ran rolled over carefully to ease the twist on his torso. "A gallon at least. Then a shower. Then the food fab."

When the shower timed out he waited, ignoring hunger, for the unit to recharge. He showered again, letting the heat sink into his aches, but thoughts of food overpowered any temptation for a third shower cycle.

In a clean coverall, Ran ordered Roly to follow him into the big room where, on shaky legs, he removed the inserts from the food fab. With Roly rolling along behind, he then went to the hangar to collect fresh inserts from the crate brought from the Shed.

While there, he wondered if Roly needed to be resupplied. "Roly, display requirements."

Ran whistled in surprise at the holograph readout. Low on nanites. Not *that* many tools required them. Had someone already ordered an analyzer from Roly?

"Roly, display previous requests." The holograph listed his anti-grav regulator on top; the previous request appeared as a diagram only.

Gooney cleared his throat.

Ran's stomach rumbled. "Roly, stay here." With Gooney's help, he carried in the replacement inserts and installed them in the food fab.

Next, he had to visit the Brain. Wick scowled as Ran entered his office. Ran requested the Brain to reprogram the food fab and returned to wait for the fab to display settings. His first order was for spicy crisps, hoping they'd process fast. All but Wick gathered around to watch him work, discussing what to order next.

"Steak," said Saxon.

"Nah, stringy meat takes too long. Spaghetti and meatballs," said Capshaw.

"Burritos." "Cheese fries." "Sweet-and-sour chicken." "Sweet-and-sour pork's better." "Milkshake." "Beer."

So long as Ran got something *soon*, it all sounded delicious, especially that milkshake. He was starving! Too restless to stand around, he returned to the hangar, where he made sure Roly was fully stocked, and queued up a new fuel cell for the Wreck. Minis needed two fuel cells—to pull in continuous hydrogen from the air to store as fuel—and he wasn't going to chance flying with only one. Bad enough he had to fly without a fully operational computer and guidance system.

He foresaw a very long, slow day before all parts were finished.

By the time he got back to the main room, the spicy crisps were ready. The men had already started eating them. Ran looked at the fab's orders—a pizza was next in line—and added a mocha shake to the food fab's queue. Calories and caffeine. Perfect.

Munching crisps, he wondered about that diagram on Roly's display. It almost made sense to him.

Hallie

Again and again in her dreams, Hallie stumbled over Rumbo's body on the trail. Each time she woke, she longed to record all that had happened. At home, she could have used her journal function to speak her thoughts, even in the dark. But here the laborious effort of writing on lumpy paper felt far too difficult.

Melody's movements told her it was morning. Hallie sat up, pushing hair out of her eyes.

Her hostess handed her a narrow strip of silk weaving. "This might hold your hair back."

Hallie fingered the silken band. "It's beautiful." She glanced at yesterday's collection of silk bolls and said, "You're going to need more silks." If only she could learn to capture those bolls intact.

"Maybe." Melody sighed.

Hallie dressed and tied the band around her head, wishing for a mirror. "I'll treasure this! How does it look?"

Melody smiled and tucked in a few hairs. "Quite nice. Let's go."

While they waited in line for breakfast, Ed yelled, "Listen up. We've gone to around-the-clock scheduling." As if to underscore his statement, three men trudged inside with tired faces. "Everybody, expect to work double time, double fast today."

Did that mean no more afternoon breaks? Sure enough, Hallie's assignment placed her in the greenhouse for the entire day, aside from *Take lunch to mine office.* Deliver Pel his lunch? All right!

As Hallie entered the greenhouse with Melody, a harassed Gardner waved Aryn off with "Continue pollinating" before she turned to them. "Melody, you and Hallie can harvest algae."

"Gardner," Hallie said, "did you notice Rumbo in the greenhouse yesterday?"

The woman's lips tightened with impatience. "Rumbo? No. A couple of the kids retrieved their charged items. Ed stopped by looking for Marney." She sniffed. "He didn't bother to read the schedule. Who else? Your young man came—twice, I think—searching for his device. And Bork stopped by to see what he could expect to cook."

"Thanks." *Your young man.* Hallie wished. Harvest algae—*yuck.* She followed Melody to learn how, hoping Bork was good at disguising *that* taste.

On her way back to the Warrens for lunch, Hallie found Aryn beside her. Aryn leaned closer as wind tried to blow her words away.

"I need to ask you something."

Wary, Hallie nodded, but Aryn said no more. They entered the Warrens with a clatter and *whoosh* of dust-filled air.

"Wait for me," Aryn said. "I have to grab my sketchbook."

Hallie had collected Pel's lunch and one for herself by the time Aryn rushed back. "Here." She opened her pad to the last page.

"That's Ran," said Hallie, "but I never saw that expression before." She glanced at Aryn and back down at Ran. "He must like you."

"I like *him.*" Aryn's cheeks brightened.

"Then you and Pel aren't . . ."

"Of course not! Pel only looks at you."

"Good." Hallie took a quick breath. "Sorry. What was your question?"

"Look at Melody, her eyes. And at Ran's. Dad saw the resemblance first. I should have seen it. Same color. Same shape."

"Melody is *Ran*'s mom? Oh, *nova*! I had wondered about her baby . . . But—"

Aryn nodded. "That's the question. Do we tell her?"

"She gets so quiet sometimes," Hallie said slowly. "It'll make her so happy. But with her husband gone, and then to have to go on waiting . . . We've got to get Ran back!"

"Yes, but I think he's made his own plans." Aryn touched his face again before closing the cover of her pad.

Maybe he had. Or maybe he needed help. There was still something Hallie had to know.

Pel

Yancy, a thin, balding man, accompanied Pel to the mine office, moving with a limp that caused him to list slightly to the right. Once out of the wind, Yancy said, "I'll be in and out of here this morning. They meant it when they said double duty. Your job is to watch the monitors."

The monitors along one wall displayed views of tunnels opening out onto the Rift floor. Clearly, the monitors and moving bots received enough ambient energy.

Pel set his databank on the monitor shelf and said, "So what's happening? A ship is coming in, and Wick wanted to talk to Rumbo? Would Rumbo have told him where you've stashed the Beijingite?"

"Nah. He was on our side. He'd have given them a song and dance."

"Wick didn't think so."

"Wick has never understood. Some of the others—both sides—don't get it either. It's what Delver said all along: we're in this together. Wick pretends to be boss, but no one can boss the unwilling."

"Do you have time to tell me how you were shipped out here?" Last night had only whetted Pel's appetite for information.

Yancy checked the end monitor and gave a nod. "First though, that red button's the alarm. If any of the bots stop"—he motioned with his chin at the monitors—"hit the alarm and announce which tunnel. We'll take it from there. The diggers we call moles. Those that scrape up the B'ite are called turtles."

Pel nodded. "If a robot stops, I hit the red alarm button and announce the tunnel number."

"That's it. Okay. I listened to you and your friend last night and sure am curious about what your data say. I never did know why they hauled me out here."

"What's the last you remember of Earth? Do you mind if I record?" Pel waved his noter. At Yancy's headshake, Pel said, "Yancy," into the noter and set it down. The noter flickered, actually charging as it worked. At last, a place with an ongoing energy feed!

"My first name's Yale. I have—or had—a twin brother, Yorick. He went into accounting while I preferred teaching. He is—or was—more of a loner than me, and the only theory that ever made any sense was they wanted Yorick out of the way due to something he uncovered. He was an accountant for a fairly new start-up doing contractual jobs. That last day after school, I got a message to meet him. I called to tell my girlfriend I'd be a little late coming home and went off to the designated park. He liked to take a walk after a day of figures. I arrived and saw no sign of him, but two toughs nabbed me before I could enter the greenspace. The next thing I knew, I was out for the count on a trip to the stars."

Pel was sure he'd never researched any Yancys. He'd have remembered those names. "Did you ever suggest to your kidnappers they'd made a mistake?"

"*Ha.* That's a laugh. When I landed here, DeWarg made it clear our pasts were gone. He claimed we'd all broken the law, and they'd rescued us from some terrible fate. If they'd gotten the wrong brother, I didn't want them going back and nabbing Yorick too."

"Didn't anyone notice your ID chip spelled the wrong man?" Pel couldn't imagine making a positive ID without a scanner.

Yancy shook his head. "They thought they knew. No one asked me who I was."

"Any thought or suspicion that your brother set you up?"

"Only in my crazier moments. A man can imagine anything in the middle of a miserable night—stealing my girlfriend and all—but no, not possible."

"So he has no idea where you disappeared to?"

"Probably not. I've always hoped he saw this coming. I think he knew he was in trouble and was about to run. I hope he managed it."

"Why are you willing to talk now?"

Yancy rubbed his nose. "A lot of years have passed. Water under the bridge. Either he got away or he didn't; either he acted on what he knew or he didn't. Telling you isn't likely to change anything. Anyway, that's why I'm breaking DeWarg's rule of silence."

"DeWarg. What was he like? There's something about that name that bothers me."

"He's long gone, eaten up in that first mine disaster . . . What was he like? Acted like he'd been raised rich, with all the privileges. Why would he have settled for bossing this place?"

Pel shook his head, his pulse quickened. As an accountant, maybe Yale's brother had traced Atlas's various secretive subsidiaries—that spiderweb of links. Follow the money.

"Thanks! You've helped a lot."

"Gotta go. Watch those monitors."

Pel checked all the monitors and considered his gold databank on the shelf. Ran had said the databank was performing some other duty. A lot of power could be stored inside that small container. Was he charging a time bomb? He shivered. If Ran were here, maybe he'd know.

Pel watched the monitors.

Hours later, Hallie blew in. "No escort?" Pel asked.

"I told Melody I knew the way, and she let me come alone. How's the charging?" She set two lunches on the table and pulled off her wind coat. The gleaming band around her head resembled a halo. Angelic—or not—she definitely glowed.

Pel picked up the databank. "We can check. Turner gave me this on the way to the shuttleport. He's head of your sister's Info Tech Department. They released me into his custody, but he wouldn't say where he was taking me." Pel made a face. "Later on, when I *did* find out, I freaked. That's when he made me call my parents. Telling them was even harder than getting on that ship." He could tell from Hallie's nod that she understood. "But before all that, he handed me the databank and had me say 'Affidavit.' I suppose he wanted to delay telling me where we were going, and also to assure me we had a witness to what happened at the park. Anyway let's try."

Hallie moved closer and gave a surprised breath when Typhus flickered into view against an alleyway wall. Yancy arrived just then and came over to watch.

"It were a chance to see Fixer again. UncLum be training me to tail. We both sees it happen." Pel was more conscious of Hallie's presence than of Ty's affidavit, which he'd heard before. The hologram faded halfway through. "Still not enough charge. I don't understand why it requires so much energy."

Pel replaced the databank on the shelf while Yancy checked all the monitors.

"That boy, the no-ID kid Typhus," Hallie said, "you mentioned him the first time you came to my aunt and uncle's. Aunt Bet worried about noids, but I never gave them much thought before now. Why do they live in hiding?"

"You want to go to their rescue?" A Hallie impulse for sure. "Whenever I saw him, I was rushing back to Workless and never had time to find out much. I'd love to research them for you."

She smiled. "You can when we get back. I'm going to study law. I can't believe I never thought of that before yesterday. Mom was always complaining about how impulsive I am. She was right, of course, but my impulse is always to defend—so I'm going to learn how."

She sat down on the short bench and scooted over to make room for him. "Let's eat. I'm due in the greenhouse for the afternoon."

Eating took hardly any time. He wished she could stay.

"Listen, Pel." Hallie gave him a sideways glance. "I want to check on something tonight. Will you go with me? After everyone goes to their rooms?" His fierce-as-a-tiger girl seemed almost shy asking him.

"Sure." What else could he say? Ah, well, he'd rather face trouble with Hallie than with anyone else.

Ran

By midday, most of the men had disappeared, probably napping on their full stomachs. Only Capshaw waited, keeping an eye on his tool resting in the middle of Ran's worktable.

Ran grabbed a slice from the still-steaming pizza and returned to the hangar. Probably a good thing the food fab produced as slowly as it did or he'd eat faster than his stomach could process, but it seemed like he was never going to feel satisfied.

He collected the fragile, cylindrical anti-grav regulator from Roly and carefully stored it before ordering Roly to produce a housing. Hurry up and wait. The Wreck's damaged computer meant he'd have a problem navigating, but at least he knew the Warrens' general direction.

Back in the main room, the food fab was working on the next item in its queue. With nothing to do until Roly finished, Ran picked up Capshaw's analyzer. His first attempt at testing with his smart tool had resulted in nothing. This time, the tool brought up a holograph.

That Brain! Controlling any and all smart tools in the place; the way it messed with the fabricators made it a trickster character, something he remembered from a lit class. What did the Brain really want?

"So what's it need?" snapped Capshaw. He got up and came over to the table.

Ran turned to the display. "It's low in nanite levels. And it needs a new powerpack. I'll get that queued up on the hardware fab."

Roly's jobs kept increasing. It was going to be a long day.

Hallie

Hallie's shoulders sagged as she waited in line for supper. It had been a long afternoon in the greenhouse. The other teens looked equally exhausted.

Ed shouted for order. "Eat quietly, everyone. We have lots to do and not much time for our meeting."

Melody sat alone, so Hallie slipped into the empty seat beside her instead of joining Pel at the teens' table. Ed's meeting concerned the incoming ship threat, but in her opinion the discussion wasn't achieving anything.

Nick's mother said, "We've got to get them back to Earth. Can't we pay our way with the B'ite we've got in hand?"

"You expect them to let each of us carry a bit on board for our fare?" scoffed Dacey's mother.

"That's an unfair fare!" Leif's stepmother's interruption got both chuckles and scowls.

"We can't trust them. They brought us here," Dacey's mother continued. "If we manage to get aboard, they'll likely dump us in space."

"What about the *Orpheus*?" Ramon called out. "They brought us. Where's that ship now?"

Pel stood. "Ran told me the *Orpheus* had some survey work to do. Maybe they planned to swing back around for us."

Wishful thinking, thought Hallie, and the next speaker said exactly that.

Beside her, Melody said, "I won't leave without Del."

"But he's dead, isn't he?" Hallie said, startled.

"He's not dead." Melody sounded sure. But then, where was he? And—

Hallie got to her feet. "We can't leave without Ran. He belongs *here*, not at the base."

"All right!" Ed clanged his metal cup against the stone table. "We've aired opinions but no useful ideas. Meeting to resume tomorrow. Meanwhile, there's work for some of us."

Ed *did* look tired. She almost felt sorry for the man. Too bad he wasted so much time keeping secrets.

Melody went down to her loom. Ramon's musicians began warming up as Hallie hurried across to Pel where he sat on the corner seat looking reflective. In spite of the trouble hanging over them, she felt lighter than she had in days. Pel's eyes went to her. Aryn said so.

She sat down beside him. "What's your musical about?"

"It was an exercise in not feeling hopeless. I pictured us as castaways and was playing with crazy solutions to our dilemma. You're still my heroine, you know. More than ever now. I pictured you in a dramatic rescue, flying an alien ship or . . ." He gave a shrug. "Now people are talking to me, and everything's changed, even though nothing has changed."

"I'm sorry I refused when you asked before. My mother always pushed me toward the stage, and I resisted, because it got in the way of figuring out what I wanted to be. Now that I know, I'll sing if you want me."

When Pel said nothing, Hallie continued. "Rumbo was the only adult who'd talk to me. He told me he had maps of this place and the planet, and I thought I might find out more alone. Then whenever I looked, you were talking to Aryn, so I thought you liked her better."

There. She'd said it.

"No!" Pel sat straight. "Of course not."

Hallie felt a smile begin in her heart, warming her like a sunbeam. "That's good," she said. "Have you thought of ways to rescue Ran?"

"Nothing workable. How about you?"

"I want to find out where they store their vehicles. And there's another mystery—which may or may not be related." She moved closer to talk under the cover of the musicians.

"Yesterday—" She gulped. It was only yesterday she'd seen Rumbo, alive. "I can't believe how much has happened in such a short time. Listen, Pel. Yesterday Rumbo showed me the building plans of the Warrens. When I asked about a door off the hallway down on the third level, he said it had never been built and tossed the flimsy away. Then I asked about what caused the Rift, and he tried to kiss me."

Pel growled, and looked ready to hit the dead man.

She hurried on. "When I resisted, something Rumbo said connected with my lost memory. Suddenly, there I was, remembering the two men in the park. Later though, I wondered if, in grabbing me, Rumbo was trying to distract me. But from what? From the Rift? Or from that hallway? They have so many secrets here."

She put her head in her hands. "What if I was the one to cause his death?"

"How could you be? If he died of a stroke, the problem was inside him, waiting."

"Tonight I want to check that hallway marked on the plans that he said hadn't been built. Don't try to stop me."

"I won't let you go alone."

She smiled at his protective attitude. "Good."

They sat in a comfortable silence, Hallie listening to Ramon's music, Pel occasionally saying something to his noter.

Lights blinked, signaling everyone to go to their rooms. The teens gathered up their musical gear and disbanded. Hallie sat unmoving. Maybe she should reconsider. No! Just do it.

The Warrens grew quiet and lights dimmed. "Do you think we've waited long enough?"

"Seems pretty quiet," said Pel, speaking not nearly soft enough. "'Tis better 'twere done when 'tis done'" Quoting from *Hamlet*—or was that Lady MacBeth speaking?

"*Shh!*" They crept down the second-level hallway. Pel's footsteps made a scuffling noise and she looked pointedly at his feet. He lifted them higher, invariably scuffling as he put them down.

"Slippers," he murmured, "or socks, quieter than shoes."

A door closed, causing them both to look back. She was sure someone had peeked out. At the far end, they descended to the third level. The same arrangement of bathrooms at the end of the hall with vertical piping from the kitchen running through the other two floors. Doors opened off the corridor along one side. The other side was smooth rock, though marked for future excavations. And no access.

"It was about here," Hallie whispered. Her fingers detected a rough vertical line. "I can feel the seam. It's disguised."

She darted a look up and down the hall checking for movement. If this was a hidden door, there had to be a way in. She pressed and pulled at protrusions. One of them moved!

The door slid open one centimeter and no more.

Footsteps. They were going to be caught.

Pel

Give him data any time to pry into, but Hallie was searching for hidden doors. Footsteps sounded on the steps, stretching Pel's already taut nerves. Well, he'd agreed to help.

He grabbed at the edge Hallie had exposed and pulled.

"What are you kids doing down here?" Ed made no effort to keep his voice low. Windblown and dirty, he must have been doing hard labor somewhere.

Pel swallowed a groan. "We were . . ."

What *were* they doing? He didn't know.

Doors opened. Zane. Gabe. Others he knew by sight. None of the teens.

Hallie said, "Rumbo was hiding something, and I wanted to know what."

At least she had the guts to speak truth—to plenty of witnesses. Marney came down the steps to join Ed.

"What was he hiding?" Ed asked.

"Something to do with this wall. I wanted to check, and Pel came to protect me."

"I was curious too," Pel added. "Why is this section disguised?"

"To keep nosy people away from it, of course." Ed came and tapped a release, causing the opening to widen.

Pel recoiled from the stench; Hallie gasped and stepped back. Ed triggered the door closed again, but not before Pel glimpsed a tunnel swallowed into darkness.

"It's a cemetery," said Ed. "A dead end, a go-nowhere tunnel where we can bury our dead without facing that wind. Nothing for you to make a big mystery over."

"Rumbo told me it was never built," said Hallie, "but here it is. Do you see why I have a hard time believing what I'm told? Rumbo lied to me. *You* made up stories about us."

Marney's face turned stormy, and Pel stepped in. "Can you blame us for investigating when no one will tell us anything?"

"You make a good point," said Ed. "Rumbo will be interred here when Orenda has completed her examination. And Hallie is right," Ed said, surprising Pel. "It was my initial mistake, misjudging your reasons for being here that got us off on the wrong foot."

Hallie tilted her head toward Ed. "Gardner said *you* were in the greenhouse yesterday, not Rumbo. Did you pick up Pel's noter?"

Ed nodded. "Yes, I wanted to see what he had recorded. And I spoke with Rumbo about—" He grimaced. "All right. I told him he was letting a pretty face make him forget his duties."

"And then?"

"I left him. Whatever happened came afterward."

"You were the last to see him and you blamed Pel?"

"Easy, Hallie." Pel nudged her shoulder with his own. The man had explained, and Pel didn't expect to hear any more apology than that. He felt her relax.

"I still don't like your blaming Pel."

"It brought out the truth, didn't it?" Ed said.

"If you're satisfied, why don't we all get some rest now?" said Marney.

With the adults looking pointedly at them, Pel and Hallie headed up the stairs. Pel put his arm around her shoulders. "You want to help me sort through people's stories tomorrow?"

"Sure. But they're still not telling the truth. I have my own ideas of where that door leads." She glanced at Ed and Marney behind them. "I'll tell you later," and she entered Melody's rooms.

Wondering what else Hallie suspected, Pel waited at Ed and Marney's door. When they arrived, he asked, "Do you want me to find another place to stay? Seems like I'm an awful drain on your space—and your peace of mind."

"Not tonight," said Marney. "Maybe we can come up with something you'll be more comfortable with soon."

Him? *They* might be more comfortable. Pel patted his inner pocket for the reassuring flat shape of his databank. Soon. Let it reveal what he wanted to know. Let it name names, explain. Meanwhile, he could dream up rhyming words about an ancient ship crash.

No, he was through with playwriting.

Though rhyming did help put him to sleep.

Ran

The food fab's mocha milkshake gave Ran a surge of energy, though a nap might have served him better since he had nothing to do but wait for Roly to produce parts.

He considered that odd diagram on Roly's list of completed projects. The design was for a tiny nanite-filled cylinder, with instructions for the nanites to divide and then seal themselves off in two half-cylinders. He'd never seen anything like it but could only imagine one purpose for such a device—to achieve entanglement between two computers. A tangle-link. Except Wick claimed it was the only Brain on the planet.

"Get a move on, kid!" Wick shouted.

"Tell that to the hardware fab." Ran got up to check Roly's progress.

Roly detached its current assignment—a housing to protect the Wreck's fragile anti-grav cylinder—and proceeded to work on a replacement powerpack for Capshaw's analyzer. Ran got to work. With the last piece installed in the Wreck, he levered open the battered hatch and climbed in.

"Anti-grav on," he said. His heart leaped as the Wreck silently rose.

"Turn ninety degrees."

No response. He touched the manual control and the Wreck came around easily. *Yes!*

Saxon and Gooney moved to block his exit through the closed hangar doors. Did they expect him to ram the doors with the Wreck?

"Anti-grav off." Ran climbed out and popped open the propulsion compartment for one last adjustment. He walked and jogged around the hangar while waiting for Roly to complete the powerpack. The day had been long, and he regretted not napping when he had the chance. Except after being tied up for so long, he lacked the trust needed to let his guard down for sleeping. He planned to be out of here asap, even if he had to land somewhere and wait for daylight.

With a light clunk, the powerpack landed in Roly's tray. Ran collected it and ordered Roly to hover into the Wreck's storage compartment.

Then he headed back to the main room.

"What's taking so long?" snapped Wick. "Get a move on!"

Ran stared at the man with contempt. "I could have finished a long time ago. *You* tell me why I didn't." He stalked over to the food fab and ordered a supersized batch of crisps.

Wick began another rant which Ran ignored. He kept his movements slow and deliberate. Time to finish this job. Sleep sang its enticing lullaby. Beginning in early morning he'd worked through a long, full day.

Capshaw's analyzer was a delicate instrument, its nanite-driven sensor able to detect the minutest amounts of minerals. The explorers who discovered this planet must have wondered why they were detecting so much Beijingite. But Ran still couldn't understand why they hadn't investigated the source of the Rift.

An hour later, the analyzer completed its self-cleaning; its green *Ready* light flared.

"Great job!" Capshaw seized the boxy instrument's handle. "How about a game?"

"No thanks." Ran pulled his tired body up and went to the food fab to collect his crisps. "I'm leaving."

"It's dark out. You're not leaving without Wick's say-so."

Ran grabbed the supersized order. "Tell Wick I'm out of here."

Fatigue was a dangerous state to be in. He had transport, emergency rations, a vague idea of where he was headed. And a niggling doubt he'd overlooked something.

He opened the door into the hangar. The lights were bright. Too bright.

Crouched at the rear of the Wreck, Noland removed the anti-grav unit and rose, tossing it from one hand to the other. With a smiling bow, Noland threw the cylinder into the refuse pile. It landed with a thump, followed by a tinkling of shattered bits. "Wick wants you."

From the other side of the Wreck, Virile sneered. Einstein and Saxon leaned back against the big Trilby. The broken anti-grav cylinder gave another clink.

Four against one. Ran's hands balled into fists.

"We had a deal." One-syllable words. He couldn't keep his voice from shaking. "I kept my side of it."

Not another night here. If he couldn't fly, he'd walk, hauling the water stowed outside. But his first step took him toward the Wreck, drawn by its need.

The door to the living quarters creaked open. Ran turned. Wick, of course.

"You're not going anywhere, son."

"I am *not* your son," Ran shouted, "and I'll fix nothing more for you! You are a two-faced cheat and liar." He was beyond tired of this madhouse, these guards, and their irrational boss.

In the doorway behind Wick, a figure appeared. Ran blinked, wondering if he'd fallen asleep. A ragged figure. The man was still there, something familiar about his tall, lanky build, though Ran was sure he'd never seen him before.

Wick smiled with confidence as he approached Ran. "We've got to have fire power." He opened his arms, pleading. "*You* can get our weapons system going. They're our only chance to board that ship."

"The Brain has a block that I wouldn't remove if I could." Ran spoke more to the silent listener in the doorway than Wick.

Wick scowled. "We've got to have weapons. That ship refuses to transport anyone."

"There are worse things than being marooned, Wick." The ragged man's voice was husky, sounding as Ran's had when he reached the top of the ridge.

Einstein jerked as the stranger stepped into the hangar, but Noland didn't move.

"Delver!" Wick whirled around, pulling his Snub from its holster. "That ship is threatening to bomb us all. We'll be stuck here. You too."

"And there are worse things than being bombed." The man's eyes were on Ran, his voice even. "The Rift is on the move; this base is directly in its path."

"You're supposed to be dead," Wick said. "I thought that resemblance was too good not to be true. Did you come for your son?"

"I don't have a father," Ran said. But his tired brain made a sudden leap. *Delver.* It had been Delver on the ridge. Perk had denied his presence. So much for Perk's *I don't take sides.*

"Oh, I bet he's your father all right. Look at that resemblance, men."

Paying no attention to Perk's Snub, the tall, bony man looked back at Ran with bleak eyes and deeply grooved cheeks, his clothes were shredded even worse than Ran's had been.

"Now that I've got you," Wick said, "you can tell me where that B'ite is."

"You believe him about the Rift, Boss?" Einstein's bald head gleamed under the hangar lights.

Wick shrugged. "Never known him to lie, but there's always a first time."

Ran had no doubts. Delver was *not* lying, nor would he divulge anything he didn't choose to tell.

Wick changed his tactics and faced his men. "All right! Capshaw's got the analyzer. Soon as it gets light, I want you—all of you—out in the Trilby. Find the B'ite and load it up. Let me know when you find it, and

I'll meet you at the Shed."

"What about these two?" Noland asked.

"If Del won't free up the heavy guns, we leave him here with his kid. Let the Rift have 'em."

"Perk says the Rift is moving out of its former bed." Delver still spoke in even tones, devoid of impatience. "It's slowly cutting a channel aimed directly at the base."

"Where does that leave us?" Wick yelled, his face red. "We've got to get off this *shithole* planet. We need my heavy guns to convince that ship. You can unlock them."

Wick waved his Snub wildly.

Ran leaped for it.

Wick swung the Snub around and buzzed him, a direct hit to his chest.

Too slow. Too tired. Too stupid. By a light year.

Ran fell to the floor writhing, trying to expand his lungs, his ribs in full agony.

The buzzing began again. Another thud. *Now look what he'd done!*

"You shot Delver? He could have unlocked the guns," protested Einstein.

"Not likely," said Noland.

"Lock 'em both up. The Rift can have 'em," said Wick.

Ran couldn't move; his open eyes refused even to blink. Einstein and Noland hauled Delver past him. Not the man he'd pictured Delver to be—but something indefinable.

His *father?* Couldn't be.

Hands grabbed Ran's shoulders. Drool dripped down his chin; whoever was holding his upper body tilted his head to the side so he wouldn't choke. Capshaw, Ran thought. Familiar tremors ran up and down his arms and legs. Gooney, in the underwear he'd slept in, picked up his feet.

A door closed him into darkness, one of the storage closets off the central area. Wick had him trapped again.

At least he wasn't tied up—not that he was capable of doing anything right then.

DAY TEN

Delver

Aryn

After waking early, Aryn dressed and escaped the Warrens, stepping out into a windy, pinkish-gray dawn. Her sketch pad held newly made sheets of hemp paper. Clutching it close to her body, she headed toward the quiet of the greenhouse, with its lights and plants.

An airtruck growled overhead, its rare sound blending with the rush of wind through her hood. The truck was flying back and forth in a search pattern. As promised, Wick's men were back, looking for the Beijingite.

What did that mean for Ran? Where was he? *How* was he?

Inside the greenhouse, the air and scents of growing plants brought a degree of calm. She moved into a slow round of tai chi before settling with her sketch pad near the lighted section of tomatoes she'd fertilized yesterday.

ork's distant gong announced breakfast. Aryn straightened, stretched her cramped hand, and examined her drawing. The first strokes of tomato foliage had lengthened into a landscape, but not one she recognized—neither the dune-shaped hills among which the Warrens was located nor the similar landscape that included the base—though a hint of the Rift darkened one side. She slipped the sketch into her pad and hurried to find food.

Aryn slipped onto the bench across from Hallie and Melody. Pel also arrived with a warm smile for Hallie.

"Something's about to happen," Melody said in her deep voice.

"Yes," agreed Aryn. She looked with meaning into Hallie's eyes before turning back to Melody. "Ran is coming. I want to show you Ran." She opened her pad to the last page and flipped it around to show Melody the sketches of both mother and son.

Melody stared. She touched the paper in the vicinity of Ran's cheek. "He looks like his father."

Hallie

Ran coming? Aryn's announcement startled Hallie. "Are you sure?"

Aryn nodded.

"How? Everyone's saying Wick is hunting for the Beijingite. He's more likely to hold Ran hostage than drop him off here."

"They're hunting now," Aryn said. "I saw the truck going back and forth over the silk plant area earlier this morning."

Hallie came alert. "Now would be a good time to rescue Ran, while they're busy." She just had to locate those vehicles.

But Aryn shook her head. "I think he's on his way."

Pel brought a comforting warmth against Hallie's side as he leaned toward Aryn. "How do you know?"

"The sketch I made this morning," Aryn said, "and a strong feeling."

"Listen up," yelled Ed. "All you kids, go off to your jobs. I need to talk with the adults."

"I need silk," Melody said. She returned Aryn's sketch pad with its drawing of Ran.

Hallie said, "We're supposed to be in the greenhouse."

"I'll help Gardner," Melody said. "You two can make up the time later."

Surprise upon surprise. Melody was being amazingly decisive! But why wasn't she going for silk herself? *Ran!* She must want to be here when he came.

Hallie looked at Aryn.

"Let's go," said Aryn, getting to her feet.

"All right then." Hallie said. They cleared their dishes and claimed two wind coats. "We'll need baskets."

"We could borrow some from the greenhouse."

"You think we'll be safe, with them out looking for the Beijingite?"

"They already searched there," said Aryn. "I had no idea showing her Ran's picture would make her want silk."

"But"—here was something the all-knowing Aryn didn't know— "the silks and her son are intertwined in her mind. She discovered the silk when she was looking for him, sleepwalking or half out of her mind. She weaves for . . . I think weaving helps her focus on something other than her pain."

They took the trail toward the mine office, leaning into the gusts of wind that pulled at their baskets.

"You are amazingly astute about people," said Aryn.

"Me?"

"The way you know exactly what to say. The way you defended Pel. The way you understand Melody."

"I just blurt. I was always in trouble as a kid."

"You have a real gift. I've always had trouble putting anything into words."

"But you have a gift of knowing." Hallie had envied Aryn's hair, her serenity, her many abilities. Nice that Aryn returned some admiration. Maybe they could be *real* friends, not just two people thrown together.

They rounded the hillside. Wind carried the same scent of creosote Hallie had noticed on landing, back when she'd felt that sudden, terrible guilt—*that* had been Ran blaming himself for *her* exile here. She *did* feel what other people felt, if only she didn't misinterpret it.

"I always thought if I were grown up, I'd know who I was," Hallie said. "And I hated being pushed to act in plays for the Arts Guild, because acting was me becoming other people, not myself. But by coming here and discovering that I want to be a public defender, I would really enjoy acting in Pel's melodrama. Isn't that strange?"

They veered from the trail onto the narrower path leading to Melody's silk plants. Warily, Hallie approached a stem still holding its boll. Melody needed silk. She loved Melody. She loved Pel. She . . .

The plant released its prickly hold and the boll dropped into her cupped hands.

"Thank you!" She hadn't even begun to ask or to make promises! Maybe the magic wasn't in the promise at all.

Melody had found her own kind of peace, even in this terrible situation. Aryn had an inner core of steadiness. Even though everything was chaotic, nothing as Hallie would choose, deep inside was something she chose to call happiness. Maybe all it took was happiness or serenity for the plants to respond. She *was* happy. So weird to say, in the middle of this exile.

Hallie moved down the row of rooted creatures. She no longer considered them plants, or rather, not *only* plants. They were aware.

"Time to go back," said Aryn.

"So soon? Oh!" They'd both filled their baskets. "I didn't notice." A thought struck Hallie as they headed back. "These plants are dying. Do you think they might make good paper?"

Aryn looked thoughtful. "It's worth a try. We could come back with gloves. The soaking process might dissolve their prickers."

"Isn't that the most amazing place?" Hallie said.

"I think the silk plants are teachers," said Aryn. "They're so peaceful to be around."

"They definitely have an awareness." Hallie hugged her full basket. "Do you see the universe as aware?"

"Physics calls it *entangled*. That's always been too big for me to grasp, but I've noticed some kind of . . . of sense or order in my own life—*when* I pay attention."

"You mean some purpose to what happens to us? Like, we blame the NODE for sending us, when instead we should ask why are we here? But it seems rather hard on Leif to come all this way and find out his parents are *still* dead."

"Leif has found friends, and a love of exobiology, and the truth of his parents."

"Truth isn't always comfortable." Hallie had discovered that one over and over. Pel had been such a comfort. "Oh! I've got to take Pel's lunch to him. I wonder how long we've been gone." With the wind at her back, Hallie picked up her pace.

Pel

Pel left for the mine office following Ed's orders for the teens to move out. Behind him adult voices erupted, not waiting for the room to clear. At least people were talking to him now, but why did Ed have such a need of secrecy? If there was danger, everyone—including the teens—should know about it and the plan of action.

Pel's morning repeated the previous day's pattern of watching bots scrape the sides of the Rift via the monitors.

At noon, Hallie's smile brightened the whole room as she entered with their lunches.

"How was the silk expedition?" he asked.

"Wonderful! Those plants are sentient! Or"—she corrected herself —"I'm not sure what *sentient* means, but they definitely sense emotions. The first time I tried to harvest silk, I was all mixed up inside and couldn't catch a single boll. This time, I . . ." The sparkle in her eyes held him entranced. "This time I knew myself to be happy in spite of everything, and the silk bolls just dropped into my hand."

Here was the real Hallie, fully revealed. "Seems you've harvested something more precious than silk."

Her lips parted in realization. "You're right. And I'm starved. I have to get to the greenhouse, so let's eat our lunches. How was your morning?"

"Rather quiet. I've been waiting to show you something. I was emptying out old data from my noter to make space to record more interviews. *And . . ."*—he picked up the noter.

"I haven't told her anything! What are you so worked up about? And what difference does it make in the long run?"

"That's Rumbo's voice!" Hallie said.

"See to it that you don't let a pretty face distract you, that's all I'm saying."

"And that's Ed," said Pel. "So Ed was telling the truth about talking to Rumbo after picking up my noter."

"Friends. I nursed him back in the starving time"—

Pel grabbed the noter and shut it off as the recording moved on. "Just a moment."

He checked the monitors and came back to pick up the noter. "That's another fascinating one. Remember that first morning when we talked to Ursa and Starving Satch? Listen to Ursa."

"I watched your faces, you and your girlfriend's, when you first arrived. You think he's a coward. Well, so are we all. We each find ways to not think about our fears. Let me tell you—Satch knows himself as well as anyone. He lets himself whine—but when the chips are down he sacrifices himself. And even his suggestion to send you all to the base had its merits. Lots of beds, and a food fab."

Hallie's eyes widened and an almost sinister look crossed her face. "*Ooh!* Think of it, our thirteen to their seven. Especially if Wick decided to hold us hostage."

Pel grinned. That would certainly be a different plot for his melodrama. Remembering his duties, he went to check the monitors. A motionless bot.

Pel slapped the red button. "Bot frozen in Mineshaft Three."

No more than a minute went by before Ursa entered from whatever job she'd been doing and scanned each monitor in turn. She also slapped the red button. "Everybody out now. Bot down in Mineshaft Three." Ursa jerked her head at the door. "That goes for you too. Move out."

"What's the danger?" asked Pel.

"We're out of business, and we're not risking another human dissolving. We leave the bots and get far away."

Pel grabbed his databank from the shelf and pocketed it along with his noter.

"What's doing it? Is that alien ship alive somehow?" Hallie asked.

Ursa goggled at her. "Something is. How'd you—" She shook her head. "For now and for good, we're out of business. Take your gadgets. Go live with them in the greenhouse if they're not charged yet. Or splash more energy paint on something. Go!"

They went, accompanied by Ursa. A small aircar was sitting at the entrance to the Warrens. Ursa said, "That'll be Perk." She brushed past Pel and Hallie and clattered through the door slats. The lunch crowd had only partially disbanded, and a sizable group was gathering around the geologist.

Ursa joined them. "We had to shut down the mines just now. What's going on, Perk?"

"It's from that crashed ship, isn't it?" said Nick.

"Who's been talking out of turn? Simms?" Ed looked accusingly at Nick's father.

Simms put his hand on his son's shoulder. "I never heard any theory about a ship," he said. "You keeping more information from us, Ed? I thought the kids were dreaming up their own explanations."

Several teens spoke at once, and Perk held up a hand. "Just one of you, please."

"It's from Aryn's drawings," Luisa said. "She drew a picture of a ship crashing."

"Well, a ship crash seems exactly what did happen," said Perk. "I don't know why you have to keep everything a secret, Ed."

Pel exchanged satisfied glances with Hallie. Finally some truth.

"Ed, you never did pay attention to basic physics," Sam added. "The universe is entangled. If someone—like my daughter—has a gift of seeing, there's no world-changing event that won't reveal itself, if it chooses."

"That's a big *if*," said Aryn. "I never know what I'll draw, and most of the time I don't know what it means."

Ed threw up his hands. "Accounting's my game, not science, Sam. And I never asked to be in charge."

Perk cleared his throat with a deep rasp. "People can't make decisions without the facts. We've a lot of decisions ahead. Something—intelligent or not—is moving up the Rift following the scar of the crash and digging deeper as it moves. That alien ship crashed into the sea as much as a century ago or longer. It's never been a secret, but DeWarg wanted to keep it quiet that he was mining a ship's hull, and Wick followed suit. Near as I can tell, some kind of nanotech from the ship took over with swarms of messengers or seekers."

Perk looked around at his audience. "And they don't recognize life forms in their path." Tilting his head toward Ursa, he said, "You'll have to let everything go. The Rift is alive all the way to the sea, and something is moving fast up the trench. There's no telling how deep it's gone into the heart of the planet. We may have more tremors."

Perk paused. "Delver volunteered to warn Wick."

That brought a gasp from several listeners. Hallie gave a start and Pel grasped her hand.

Orenda came away from the infirmary door. "You're not leaving him there, are you?" she challenged, her arm around Melody.

"*Everyone* has to be warned," Perk said, "and he thought he might find a son there. If Del doesn't show up shortly, I'll go find him."

Pel caught Hallie's smile of satisfaction as her hand tightened on his. Ran had parents, *both* parents.

"Where can we go?" asked a woman.

"We'll have to move back to the base," said Satch.

"The Rift is moving toward the base as we speak," Perk grated. "At the rate it's going, it'll be there in three or four days. That's why they got first notice."

"Assuming they have the sense to listen to Del!" said someone.

"Only place left is the Shed," Perk said. "Start packing up."

"Are you sure?" Gardner's hands went to her hips. "Leave shelter and crops and cram ourselves in there to starve?"

"We need to get to the base to call for help," argued Geraldine Ramirez. "Gear up that raiding party. Use the plans we made before."

Except, thought Pel, the base was in the most danger. He touched the databank in his pocket with his free hand. Whatever the gadget was doing, whatever work it was performing, he hoped—and hope was no basis for a researcher to live by—he hoped someone out there was listening.

A growing Rift eating away at the planet, *the only ship at hand manned by enemy band, what hope had the Warrens to carry the day? No choice in the matter. They all had to stay.*

He was going to pay attention, see what would happen next.

Ran

GG **W**hat d'you mean, you didn't find it? You've got the analyzer."

Wick's roar woke Ran. Still in the dark closet, he was surprised he'd actually slept. He must be stowed near Wick's office. His body shook, his injured ribs throbbed as the stun wore off.

Capshaw's voice came clearly through the transceiver. <"It didn't pick up anything except the Rift, Boss.">

Wick had spoken of sending them out in the Trilby. Fixing the analyzer hadn't found the Beijingite for them after all.

"I should've gone myself," said Wick.

<"It's not there. The analyzer works. It picked up the old cache at the Shed just fine. And the scattered bits of B'ite near the Rift.">

<"And nothing else,"> added Einstein's voice. <"You think the Warrens quit mining without telling us?">

"Rumbo would've told me if they had. Why is the man dead? What natural causes? If he had a problem, he should've told me that too!" Wick's voice rose. Ran pictured him stomping around his office. "They've buried the B'ite deep, that's what."

<<"AstroTwo to base, do you hear?">>

And now AstroMining calling, making the base a nexus of communications.

"Base here, AstroTwo," Wick answered.

<<"Is the pickup ready to go?">> The delay was briefer, the ship much closer.

<"Ask about that other ship, Boss,"> urged Capshaw from wherever the Trilby was.

"*AstroTwo*, you see any sign of another ship out there? The one that brought the kids?"

<<"You mean it actually arrived?">> The speaker sounded surprised.

Ran scowled. *AstroTwo* had known the *Orpheus* wasn't meant to arrive. Which firmly linked AstroMining to the *Orpheus's* sabotage.

<<"Have the B'ite ready to go. We're on a tight turnaround.">>

"We'll have it ready, but the mine is played out. You've got to take us back with you, *AstroTwo*."

The pause lasted longer than its com lag. <<"Not possible. Astro Two out.">>

From the *Trilby*, Capshaw said, <"What are we going to do?">

"I'm coming, damn it. Give us time to load up the Mini. After we swing by the Shed, we'll meet you at the Warrens and take charge, threaten the kids, whatever it takes. We've got to find that B'ite and get off this planet."

AstroTwo had already said no to passengers, but Wick wasn't taking no as an answer.

Ran moved, bumped the closet wall, rolled back the other way. His ribs flared, and he lay still, waiting for the pain to dissipate. Time to find a way out of his prison.

A hand shook his shoulder. "Can you move?"

Ran grunted. He hadn't meant to fall back to sleep. The tingling had gone. He rolled over. Awkward and self-conscious, he got to his feet.

"They've gone and left us?" Ran clung to the door jamb, getting his balance, blinking in the light. Delver had changed to one of the base's brown coveralls, no longer ragged, though he still looked like a starvation victim.

"Yes. You ready to travel?"

"The Wreck'll take us. One adjustment's all it needs."

"Good. But I'm staying behind. I want you to take something to the Warrens. If you start now, you might be in time to warn them before Wickham arrives."

"You can't stay here!"

"I've got to. If your Mini's transceiver still works, we can talk as you fly."

With Delver at his side, Ran staggered toward the hangar. "You were on the ridge with Perk, weren't you? Why didn't you—"

"I had something to do before going back. I still have to do it."

Ran scarcely took in Delver's interruption. "Was Wick right? *Are* you my father?" He didn't know what answer he wanted to hear.

"I think I must be. But you said you had none."

The hangar was empty except for the Wreck. Ran's eyes snagged on the pile of discards—broken bits, anti-grav cylinder, bot parts, tools. Unwanted, uncared for, deserted . . .

"I never had a father, did I?" Still facing the refuse pile, Ran's shout echoed. "We almost meet and you disappear. You finally show up and then send me off like one of those throwaways. Just another broken tool."

He turned to face Delver. "When I asked him who else was on the ridge that night I arrived, Perk said he was talking to himself. Why couldn't you let me know you were there?"

"I wish to god I had," the man said. "I didn't know you. My mission was secret. But your arrival changed everything. *Everything.*"

That last word, along with something in Delver's bleak eyes, moved Ran more than he wanted to admit. Unlike his foster fathers, this man didn't yell back, or fight.

So he'd be a tool. Be useful. That was what tools lived for, wasn't it? Walking through a blur, Ran reached the Wreck, opened the storage hatch where the hardware fab waited. He was surprised to see the large packet of crisps stashed there too. Hadn't he dropped them when he leaped for Wick and got zapped?

From Roly's cavity, he pulled out the replacement anti-grav cylinder and installed it.

"Slick," said Delver. "You'll need that fab. I'm curious how you got the Brain to cooperate." Ran opened his mouth but his father didn't allow him to speak. "Get to the Warrens and give this to your mother."

Ran started, jolted by a word. "My *mother?*"

"Melody. She'll know what to do."

"Why aren't you coming?" Ran slipped the small bundle Delver handed him into his pocket.

"I've got to stay with the Brain. You need to hurry," his father said.

Ran's chest ached this time, not his ribs. He had too much to say. And no words. He took a long look at Delver. At last, he said, "I'll be back for you."

But Ran couldn't move.

"Good," said Delver in a husky voice. He opened his arms. Ran walked into them and clung, his sore ribs pressing against his father's bony torso.

Too soon, he was being pushed into the Wreck.

"Anti-grav, hover," Ran said.

Delver went to the hangar doors and opened them. Operating with hand controls, Ran directed the Wreck out into not yet heavy winds. The Wreck bumped up and down.

"Increase lift."

No response.

Manually, Ran increased altitude and headed back the way the Trilby had come.

A minute later, the transceiver spoke. <"Son, do you hear me?">

Son. His heart leaped. "Loud and clear."

<"Good. Listen. Do not cross the Rift. Stay as far from it as possible.">

"You do know I've never been to the Warrens?"

<"Head toward the ridge. You'll cross that riverbed, then follow as it leads into the hills. The mining office will be the most recognizable structure, but it's almost too near the Rift. Better if you can spot the greenhouse roof."> The measured instructions were calming.

"You're staying to ensure entanglement between computers?" Ran asked.

There was a pause. <"You're carrying the key. I'll know when Baby connects. How did you guess?">

The transceiver crackled; Ran descended a bit but the crackling increased.

"I saw the design in Roly, the hardware fab, and wondered if it was a tangle link. Is the Warrens growing a secret Brain? How were you going to get it to the Warrens if I wasn't there?"

<"I'd have used someone else, but this is better—you're better.">

He was leaving his newfound father to find his mother. A family. Him? He'd been a terrible foster son. What did he know about being a real one?

"I don't even know your name."

<"Delwyn Durant.">

Durant. Ran's mind flashed to the time he took down the school's VR system. "Enhanced virtual reality? The Durant Effect? Is that you?"

<"Is that what they call it? Your mother discovered a genetically induced link that allows an organic brain to data-mine other brains. We developed it together.">

"It's in universal use, applied to every virtual recording." With a sense of wonder, Ran added, "I named my model boat *The Melody*."

His father's laugh warmed Ran. A family? A *real* family!

Turbulence had the Wreck bouncing. Ran increased lift. "There's the Shed."

With the black scar of the Rift off to his right, he steered toward a break in the hills. He was on his way to meet his mother. The mother he'd lost. The mother stolen from him.

The Wreck juddered with the change in direction. Wind noise increased.

Below him was the riverbed. And another flying object.

"I'm being tailed."

Hallie

Perk was already leaving after making his announcement about the Rift and its dangers.

Filthy spamguts! Hallie's stomach roiled, twisting and churning. Some choice he offered, to starve at the Shed or stay and be swallowed by the Rift! What if they never got back home?

Her throat ached with longing. A familiar sensation. Just days ago, she'd felt the same while looking out at this planet from the lander. Unknowns.

No whining allowed, not after bragging to Pel that she was happy. She *was* happy to be back with Pel. And happy she had a purpose—as if studying law was possible this far from Earth.

Hallie took a deep breath. She couldn't control the Rift, or that ship up there, or the threat from the base. She didn't know where the Beijingite was hidden. So. Do what had to be done.

They had to eat. Get back to work.

She looked around. The lunch crowd had thinned and Gardner was nowhere to be seen. Nor Aryn. They must already be in the greenhouse. She turned to tell Pel she was going to work when the growly hum of an airtruck sounded outside.

Nick galloped up the ramp and looked through the flaps. "It's a Trilby," he called.

"Back away then!" ordered Ed.

Several adults shoved Nick down the ramp and ordered him to the far end of the room. *Now what?* Hallie's mind froze.

Scowling from behind his counter, Bork hit the gong, drawing more adults into the gathering room,

Bork! He would know. Followed by Pel, she went to the serving counter. "What's happening?"

"It's not *our* Trilby." Bork polished the countertop and arranged a row of short, heavy bars along it. Then he came out from the kitchen and stood in front of the counter with folded arms.

"Aren't those hardware fab inserts?" Hallie whispered to Pel.

"Looks like."

"Won't they shatter?" She remembered the mess at school when a student had dropped one of those compressed rods.

"Not much use as clubs," Pel agreed. She realized he had positioned himself protectively between her and the entrance. But protecting her from *what*?

At breakfast, Aryn had said Ran was on his way. Was he on that Trilby? And what was the Trilby waiting for? No one entered.

The adults at the foot of the ramp shifted restlessly. Ramon drummed his hands on the teen table in an impatient patter. Blocked from the entrance by the adults, the other teens gathered near him, scanning the room, the ramp, each other.

"Move or we zap you!"

Hallie 's heart thumped. She hadn't even heard the slats clatter. Men stood at the top of the ramp, their Snubs aimed at the room, ready to zap whoever got in her way. Her impulse was to duck behind Bork's counter, but she also wanted to watch.

The adults at the foot of the ramp held their positions. "You'll use up your charge on us. Then what?" challenged Fletch.

"We outnumber you," added Nick's father.

From the top of the ramp, the bald one said, "Tell us where the B'ite is, and we *won't* use up our charges on you. Seven guns are plenty to take you all down."

"I count five, Einstein," said Simms. "That'll shut us up all right." Simms was *daring* them to act. No wonder Nick was always in trouble; he'd clearly inherited his recklessness from his father.

The five intruders looked at each other.

Wick wasn't with them. Hallie wondered where he was. It looked like the intruders were wondering the same. She counted teens and grabbed Pel's arm. "Leif and Amado aren't here!"

Too late. The slats rattled, Leif's voice preceding his entry. A Snub buzzed. Leif's voice broke off. The Warrens' adults roared in outrage. Those guarding the base of the ramp pressed forward, then froze. Slowly they backed away, revealing Leif writhing from the effects of being zapped. But it was Amado, a knife held to his throat by the pale man, who inspired horror.

"We now have two hostages," the pale one said.

The other four aimed their Snubs out at the crowd in the room below.

"Let me get to my boy!" cried Leif's stepmother.

"You don't have any kids, Layla," said the one Simms had called Einstein.

"I do now! Barbarians!"

They allowed her to pass. "We now have three hostages," said bald Einstein. "Tell us where the B'ite is."

Ignoring them, Layla knelt beside Leif, making sure he wasn't in a position to choke.

Amado's parents clung to each other silently, anguish on their faces.

Hallie felt sick. The remaining adults held steady at the base of the ramp.

Do something! she told herself fiercely. She looked for Bork and discovered him surreptitiously handing out hardware fab rods, which were then passed hand to hand until every third person held one. There was going to be a battle.

She thought hard. What could she do to help?

Ran

Ran kept one eye on the trailing Mini as he steered the Wreck toward the hills. Wick had said they were going to the Shed and then on to the Warrens. But he'd slept through Wick's departure. Wick never went anywhere without a guard. Which one was with him?

Wind funneled through the hills, causing increased turbulence. Ran descended farther, but wasn't sure if it helped.

His father's voice was breaking up. <"[crackle] Wick . . . control . . . crashed.">

<"Give up. You're mine!"> Wick's voice came through clearly, his Mini now flying directly overhead.

"I'm not yours, Wick!" Ran shouted as he fought against whatever tugged the Wreck toward the Rift.

<"MiniTwo. Anti-grav override."> Wick ordered.

The Wreck gave a sudden nosedive.

"Whoa!" Ran grabbed the control stick. "Anti-grav, resume."

The Wreck continued its fall. Not the time for the Wreck's faulty computer to obey Wick's aircar! Ran fought to level the Wreck. Delver's crackly message now made sense. Wick's override controls explained the Wreck's previous crash.

A couple of feet above the ground, the anti-grav took hold with a jerk, but wind gusts slewed it sideways and shoved the Wreck into a channel between two hills.

Wick still loomed overhead. <"Give it up. You're mine!">

"You said that already. You're insane, and power mad!" He was going to sever Wick's blasted override control the first chance he got.

Wick's voice blared. <"Turn around, damn you!">

But the Wreck refused to steer. Though maintaining its distance two feet from the ground, it headed up the hillside—toward the Rift.

Only one thing to do. "Anti-grav, cease." The Wreck settled on the slope with a tooth-clacking thump.

<"What th"> morphed into a wordless yell. Wick's scream broke off. MiniOne tilted and disappeared over the hill.

Ran pried open the stubborn hatch and climbed out. He'd walk the rest of the way.

Behind him, his transceiver crackled. <"Ran, I need your help!"> Noland's voice.

Now what?

Filthy sludge! Ran had a delivery to make. Leave them both to the Rift! He had no time for this.

It was an SOS.

Gah! Ran was already moving up the hill, brainwashed by sessions too numerous to count—while the rest of his class got the same message virtually: *Never ignore an SOS.* Too many had died in the chaos of the Change with its storms and epidemics and refugees.

Cat-o'nine-tails whipped at his legs, shredding another pair of coveralls. How did these plants manage to slice smart cloth when his little knife made such hard work of it?

The dark Rift came into view. And Wick's Mini inching downward, scraping a shallow protest into the ground. The slope wasn't that steep!

Noland, on the uphill side, struggled to haul Wick out as the Mini slid away.

Sludge and blast! Ran broke into a trot and grabbed Wick's other arm to help drag the man clear.

"Thanks. Wick just couldn't wait to crash your flier again." The contempt in Noland's voice caused Ran to flick a glance in his direction. "Let's go, kid, before it pulls *us* in." Noland heaved the stocky Wick upright and got under his left arm. "Move!"

Wick sputtered, not making much sense, mostly swearing.

"What's wrong with him?" Ran got under Wick's other shoulder.

"Either a heart attack or too much Rift."

Wick's bulk was a deadweight. Ran's ribs howled at him.

"And *you* call on *me*," Ran panted, "to help the creep who zapped us. After destroying my anti-grav regulator."

"You should've acted angrier." Noland sounded amused. "You know I tossed the broken one. You put it back in as a decoy."

Wick's language grew more abusive.

Ran's mind did a reset. "I was too tired." He kept moving. Noland must be his father's accomplice. *I'd have used someone else, but this is better—you're better*, Delver had said about the package he carried. Noland must be the answer to how Delver had escaped the base in the past and how Delver escaped from whatever closet he'd been locked in last night.

On the crest of the hill, Noland looked back at the Rift below. "I thought it was only the other side of the Rift doing that. *That's* what Del was warning of."

The far side of the Rift was a flat, windswept plain, its smooth downward slope in stark contrast to the hills on their own side. The Mini continued to slide.

The Rift was sucking in the entire hillside. "It's alive?"

"Whatever. As you see." They descended to the Wreck. Panting, Noland shoved Wick into the Wreck's passenger seat. "You fly him in. The Warrens is straight ahead. I'll walk up."

"Whose side are you on?" Ran asked, remembering how Noland had prevented his nighttime explorations.

Noland's grin was a flash of white against his black beard. "My own. Thanks for the help. I couldn't stop him. MiniOne was coded to his voice. And"—with a wry twist of his mouth and a nod toward the Rift—"I'm glad to be out of that trap. *Oh!*" Noland slapped his pocket and pulled out a Snub. "Here. It's Wick's. The rest of the base is already there, so be careful."

It took three attempts to get the Wreck's saggy hatch closed. Beside Ran, Wick groaned.

"Anti-grav. Lift." Without MiniOne's influence, the Wreck responded nicely. He was off to meet his mother.

<<"Base, this is AstroTwo,">> announced the Wreck's transceiver.

Wick's swearing stopped. He lurched upright in his seat. "*AstroTwo,* this is Wick."

Hallie

The room sizzled like a lit fuse, ready to go off. The blockading adults surrounded the ramp. Against the Snubs, they held brittle hardware insert rods. Plus, Hallie had noticed a few fist-sized rocks.

At the top of the ramp, the pale, skinny intruder held Amado in a choke hold. Leif lay twitching, his raging stepmother kneeling beside him. Though entirely on Layla's side, Hallie wondered that they didn't zap her for silence. The other four men kept their Snubs pointed at the blockade of people.

Pel's hand gripped hers, restraining her from the multitude of actions she envisioned—though she'd have to be a super ninja to rescue Amado from that evil man. There were only five men. They must be waiting for Wick and—

Hallie squeezed Pel's hand. "Stay here," she whispered.

"You can shoot us all, but you'll not find recharging your Snubs so easy," Fletch jeered.

Hallie sidled closer to Bork's counter. "You're going to need a distraction when the other two come." She tilted her head toward the musicians.

Bork barely moved his lips. "At my signal."

She edged back toward Pel. Feeling eyes watching her, she paused, trying to look as if she was maneuvering for a better view. She slid another step.

"You back there in the wind coat! Take another step and this kid gets his throat cut!" said the pale man who held Amado. His eyes gleamed with bloodlust.

Shocked, Hallie stopped. The wind coat slapped against her legs. Even Layla was silenced.

Long seconds turned into a minute.

And another minute. The intruders eyed each other.

A sound filtered through the wind slats. The bald one half turned. "I hear the Mini."

With that minor distraction, Pel appeared beside her. "Tell Ramon to play his loudest at a signal from Bork," Hallie whispered.

Pel ducked and was gone. She let out a shaky breath. *Done.*

Ramon turned his attention to his electronic music collection and brought his musicians to attention.

Everyone was listening intently to the faintest hint of voices coming from outside. Even from the back of the room Hallie could hear the crunch of approaching footsteps. Bork gave a single nod to Ramon.

Crash! Ramon's composer blared a hammering of drumbeats, the chorus of "Wanting You." He was using every bit of charged storage in his device.

"Take 'em!" shouted Leif's stepfather.

With a loud roar from the blockading adults, every rod flew in the air, thudding against targets.

The front line of blockaders fell, zapped like Leif.

The hardware inserts shattered; some ragged bits boomeranged back at the defenders.

Hallie's hand flew to her mouth as the bald man wiped blood from his face; his inattention allowed Layla, still kneeling over Leif's limp body, to snatch his Snub. She turned, zapped Amado's captor, then swung back to point it at the bald man who raised his hands.

Amado, freed from the knife at his throat, grabbed his captor's Snub and lobbed it into the crowd of defenders before ducking down beside Leif.

Well done, Layla and Amado!

Even as Hallie thought that, Pel yanked her back behind the counter. A second volley flew, this time of stones. Rocks clattered against walls and floor. She lost her view of the three remaining Snubs, but they sounded fainter, with lessened charges. For once, the lack of ambient energy was serving the Warrens.

The room became quiet. Hallie peeked over the counter. The invaders were bleeding—some badly. Amado's relieved mother yanked him down the ramp while two men carrying Leif crunched through the bits of hardware bars.

Pel grabbed her in a hug. "It's over! Victory."

Hallie leaned against him. But the current silence felt ominous.

Now controlling the top of the ramp, two Warrens defenders pointed their newly acquired Snubs at the wind slats.

"Maybe not over yet," Hallie muttered.

Ran

Following Noland's directions, Ran flew between hills, always keeping the Rift at a distance. Wick was no help as a guide, his attention wholly on pleading with *Astro Two*.

Ran found the base's Trilby parked at the foot of a low hill. He landed behind it and climbed out, leaving Wick arguing over the transceiver. He didn't bother to close the Wreck's wonky hatch, but as a precaution he detached the anti-grav cylinder so Wick couldn't take off.

Now he had only one question on his mind—how to recognize his mother.

The level area where he stood, with its lack of plant matter, indicated plentiful traffic. The Warrens was underground.

Correction. His first question was *where* was the entrance to the Warrens?

His feet crunching against sand and gravel, Ran circled the Trilby. A muted roar brought his head around. *There.* A well-used path sloped down into the hillside, its entrance blocked by vertical slats. The sound of real people, yes, but something was going on. Ran patted the Snub in his pocket, remembering Noland's warning.

The noise dropped away. His heart thundering, he descended to the entrance.

Next. Find his mother. *Melody.* Would she know him? He pushed between the slats—and froze, staring at the business end of a Snub held by a total stranger.

"It's Ran!" cried Hallie.

The Snub was lowered. Ran stepped through. Below, the room seemed littered with bodies. His feet crunched. He looked down, looked again. Hardware rods? What a waste.

Ah. Familiar faces. Einstein, Capshaw, Gooney, and Saxon on the near bench, most of them bleeding. Virile twitched at the far end. Zapped. How appropriate. Ran was pleased to see a massive bruise on Virile's cheek as well.

Seeing the men from the base reminded him. Ran pushed back his errand again, saying, "Wick's outside in the Wreck. I had to bring him along, since the Rift was busy sucking up MiniOne after he crashed her."

A woman shoved through the crowd to ask with fierce urgency, "Where's Noland then?"

"Noland's walking up. He's not far." She grabbed a white coat from a pile and left with a clatter of slats. Ran's assessment of Noland rose another notch.

"And you say the Rift—?" began a long-faced man with baggy eyes.

"I don't know if it caused Wick's crash. He was trying to force me down at the time. But both of our cars were acting strange. When he crashed, his Mini just kept on sliding."

Which reminded Ran of another matter. He raised his voice over the chatter. "*AstroTwo*, the mining ship, is transmitting over the Wreck's— over my Mini's—transceiver. Wick is trying to bargain with them. They're making threats."

Several people pushed past and outside.

Now maybe he could make his delivery. "Where's my mother? Where's Melody?"

A space opened up. Hands pushed him into the room toward someone in a patched white coverall. Drowning in her gray eyes, he walked into open arms, shutting his own eyes against leaks. A family at last.

After a long time, without loosening her arms, she asked, "Where's your father?"

It was Ran who had to let go. "He sent you this." He pulled out Delver's small package. "I said I'd go back for him."

"The tangle link. This can't wait." The wind slats rattled. Melody glanced at the ramp and smiled. "Someone else wants to see you. Come to the infirmary as soon as you can."

Aryn was coming down the ramp, followed by a tiny woman.

Pel charged up to thump him on the back.

"*Ow*, mind the ribs," Ran protested. "Good to see you!"

Next, Hallie grabbed him for a hug. "I wanted to go rescue you from that place, but Aryn said you were on your way."

"She did? That's good." *Stars*, how'd she know? Maybe there was a chance she liked him. Then Aryn was there, smiling.

"How's your hand?" he asked, his cheek warming where she had kissed it days before. His face grew hot.

"Healing." Aryn waved her wrapped fingers. "We were in the greenhouse and didn't know all this"—she indicated Wick's defeated men with her chin—"was going on until we heard your aircar land. Then we saw the Trilby. Gardner insisted on coming to fight, but it's all over. How are your ribs?"

"Still sore." His eyes darted around at the watching crowd. "My mother wanted me to follow her to the infirmary."

"Come on. This way." Aryn started across the room.

The infirmary was a small room off the main area. A tall, dark woman was settling Wick onto a narrow bed in one corner. When had they brought Wick through, he wondered.

Melody—*Mother*—moved out of a closet wearing a cleangown.

Seeing him, her face brightened like the sun. She beckoned. He crossed over to her, feeling gawky.

Come see." She handed him a cleangown, which he triggered on. Her voice conveyed her own shyness. "I need an interface clip to attach the link."

What had seemed a closet was a cleanroom smaller than the one at the base. The pale, young Brain, covered with a tough, muscular membrane, rested in its container on a waist-high stand. Though it didn't breathe, the Brain conveyed a sense of aliveness.

"Looks healthy." Ran examined the link Melody was holding. "Let me put the hardware fab to work on a clip. Won't take long." His father had said he'd need Roly.

Ran stepped out of the closet and shut down his cleangown. He had a family?

He had a family!

Pel

Clean up was under way. Some Warrenders guarded the bloodied invaders, some hauled their zapped people into the corner near the infirmary, and still more were sweeping up the shattered hardware rods. Meanwhile, the mining ship was broadcasting through the vehicle transceivers.

Pel doubted he could get near enough to listen in on the mining ship but decided to see. He had a foot on the ramp when Ran emerged from the infirmary and caught his eye. Ran grinned. Pel joined him mid-room.

"Pel, you ever get that databank to work? I've got to get something out of the Wreck."

Pel grunted and pulled it out of his inner pocket. "I sat a day and a half in the mining office charging it before they chased us all out. Even then it only gave out a tiny fraction of data before quitting." He handed it to Ran.

"That doesn't make sense." Ran looked at the device in his hand. "It *is* still working."

"Working how? What's it doing?"

Ran stopped and frowned down at a stone table. Catching Pel's eye, he said, "There's only so many options. Calculating, or stuck in a loop, or downloading. Or—"

Ran handed Pel his devise and headed up the ramp. "A ship's communication drive can send at light speed, but the energy required can be astronomical."

"*Ha!* Good pun," Pel said. "No, *wait.*" He speeded up. "*Uploading?* I thought maybe the Orpheus but you think it's signaling Earth? It would take years for the data to arrive even at lightspeed."

"With that cover, your databank soaks up ambient energy from your body and everything else it can find," Ran said. "The power's going somewhere."

They clattered out through the door slats, Pel trying to grasp the implications. "The last time it really worked was on Earth when Turner, the Tech Department head, gave it to me. *The man with the code!* I bet he set it up to report to the NODE. Can we shut it off? At least long enough for me to access the data—assuming it actually holds my data?"

"I don't know." Ran looked around. "I've got a hardware fab in the Wreck. I need to bring it in."

Pel followed on Ran's heels past the crowd surrounding the Trilby. Another group had gathered at the front of a battered Mini. Ran popped open the Mini's rear hatch.

"Emergency rations," Ran said as he handed Pel a large container of wafers in multiple packets like the ones they'd lived on in the Shed, except these were orange.

"Yuck. But any food is nothing to complain about. We're on a starvation diet." Pel opened a packet and tried one. All the crunch of a corn chip with the zing of a pizza or spaghetti with sausage or—

"Wow! *That's* not a wafer. You must have been living like kings out at the base."

"Those are spicy crisps," said Ran, "and you've got to be kidding! You wouldn't believe what we had to eat. We didn't starve, but if you listened to the men, you'd think starving was their preferred choice.

"Roly, anti-grav on." Ran grabbed the fab's handle as it floated out of the Mini. "Someone convinced the base's Brain to only act in emergencies—like transmitting ship contacts. None of their tools worked, and they wanted me to fix everything, but most of it needed reprogramming, and they wouldn't let me even *see* the Brain for the longest time. Their food fab produced glop, or slop, or— You don't want to know what the men called it."

Enthralled, Pel crunched another spicy crisp.

Ran's lopsided grin reappeared. "I tell you, Pel, those passwords you used in your NODE question were a wonder! Whedn I finally did get to visit the Brain, one of the passwords got it to respond. And then the Brain cooperated to reprogram the fabricators."

He picked up speed, Roly floating along beside him. "Let's get Roly inside. I ordered a scanner to find out what they added to our chips at the spaceport."

"A scanner! Great! Let's get it printed out, if you can find enough ambient, that is."

They clattered back down the ramp. Quiet musical notes stopped as they reentered.

Roly landed with a thud.

"What?" Ran's jaw dropped. "Its power unit ran out, but don't you have—?"

"What I said," said Pel. "*Major* lack of ambient energy."

Hallie, Aryn, and Ramon's musicians converged on them.

"What about painting those?" Ran nodded at the wind slats. "You have the nanopaint, don't you? Plenty of action without too much wind."

"Nano on the wind slats. Brilliant!" Ramon leaped onto the ramp. "Welcome back, Ran! But we don't have any applicators to spray with. Stupid hicksville planet."

Pel added, "We've had a rotten time of it, charging devices in the greenhouse."

Ran shrugged. "If we can find a spot where Roly *can* work, I'll line up orders. Sorry, but it's set to respond to my voice, and I've got to go back for my father asap."

"Bork seems to have plenty of energy piped down to the ovens," Pel suggested, "*if* he'll share. Otherwise, it's the greenhouse."

"I'll talk to him," said Hallie. "Come on." In the kitchen she put on her sunniest smile. Pel didn't know about Bork, but *he*'d do a lot for that smile. "Emergency, Bork. Ran just arrived from the base. He needs power for his fab."

Bork scowled. "So now you want to take over my kitchen."

"Just one little corner," said Hallie.

Pel handed Bork the crisps. "Ran brought these with him."

"Spicy crisps! We haven't had those in years."

He'd never seen Bork smile before.

"That corner." Bork pointed to a narrow space next to the ovens. Ran rolled his fab over and knelt beside it. "I understand you're Melody's long-lost son. Where's your father?"

"He stayed at the base, business to do with the Brain."

"We need Del back here."

"I'm off to get him, as soon as I've printed out an interface clip for your Brain."

"There's no Brain here," Pel said. What was Ran talking about?

"Yeah, there is. Named Baby. In the infirmary."

"Behind that wall? Of course! Look to the energy." *More* secrets. Pel wondered how many people knew. *Huh!* Bork had been protecting far more than just the kitchen.

The hardware fab beeped.

Pel accepted the newly fabricated scanner Ran handed him. "*Brilliant!*" Even if he couldn't access his databank, he'd find out what was on their implanted chips.

Ran

Ran bent to feed Roly his requirements. Clip. Nanoenergy paint applicator. What else did he need to queue up for Roly while he was gone? From the larger room, loud voices erupted—Wick's men arguing with Warrens people.

Behind Ran, holding the newly made scanner, Pel asked, "Ready for a reading?"

"Go ahead."

"Wayland Randal Durant."

Ran swung around to stare at Pel. "Wayland? No way! Where'd *that* name come from?"

"Plus a string of digits."

"What? My chip held more than that before I left Earth." School records, employment office, that Security arrest . . . "There must be files attached to those digits," Ran decided. "Where'd Aryn and Hallie go?"

"Back to the greenhouse. They're making up time they missed earlier. Food is in desperate shortage around here. No one is ever satisfied. And now Perk has given warning that the Rift is on the move, and we have to get out of here. We don't know how we'll eat. Gardner doesn't want to leave her plants." Pel held out the scanner.

Just then Roly spit out the interface clip. "Keep it." Ran waved the scanner away, and circled the counter with the clip.

Near the infirmary door, the Warrens' injured were recovering. He spotted Leif among them. Only last night he'd been in that same zapped state. On the far side of the room, Capshaw raised his voice. Wick's men were still demanding access to the B'ite, promising nothing.

Ran entered the dimmer light of the infirmary. Wick's bed in the corner was empty.

Melody clawed against hands gripping her throat, while blocking Wick's access to Baby's closet. Wick slurred, "Tell me where the B'ite is."

Ran hissed.

"Tell me or I spit on that Brain you're hiding. That Delver. No business having a Brain. Should've finished him off."

In rapid succession, Ran considered wringing Wick's neck, slugging him, throwing him into the biggest stand of bullwhips— He pulled out the Snub.

Taking careful aim to avoid his mother, he fired. Wick landed with a thud. Repayment for zapping him and his father.

"Are you all right?" he asked Melody, who rubbed her neck and smiled.

The woman who'd tended Wick before entered. She took in the Snub in Ran's hand. "What have you been up to, Wickham Dickerson? Out of your bed like this."

"I won't have him here," Ran said. "He was strangling my mother."

She shook her head. "He does press his luck. I'm Orenda, by the way. Let's get him back on the bed till he recovers."

"Only if you tie him down." Ran helped Orenda haul Wick back to the bed while his mother attached the link to the young brain in the closet. They had secured Wick to his cot with strips Orenda provided by the time Melody finished.

"We're going to need a transceiver to talk with that ship up there," Melody advised.

Ran groaned. "I've got to get going." He returned to the kitchen. Making a transceiver would take way too long. Plus time lost waiting on Roly's queue.

The teens had gathered at the counter eating crisps, giving Ran a better idea. "Does anyone have a com I can dismantle?"

Reba handed hers to him. "Even if we had energy, there's not much they can do here anyway," she said.

"Thanks!" A generous gift, even if they didn't work here. Ran settled on a bench, and pulled out his little knife to dissect the com. Fortunate that electronics were no longer solid state.

Reflecting Ran's thought, Pel said, "You couldn't have done that a century or two ago."

"Yeah, everything a throwaway back then. What a wasteful world," Ran agreed.

An hour later, he clipped the tiny transceiver to the interface link. "There."

<<"This is AstroTwo, calling Lodestone Base. Our ETA is now nineteen hours. We will expect to find the shipment ready and waiting. Out.">> The voice came through Ran's implanted chip as well as through Baby's newly installed transceiver.

"It's done," said Melody. "Entangled."

Two men, the one with the bags under his eyes, the other who was probably Nick's father, came in and took up positions near the closet door. Guarding Baby from Wick?

Melody nodded to them and gripped Ran's arm tightly. "Be careful."

"The Rift, you mean?" It was going to be a tricky flight avoiding its pull.

"No, the Brain. Don't let it trap you. It's lonely." She reached up to hug him.

Lonely. He'd had that same thought when he touched it and got caught in that whirling vortex. Maybe the Brain's link with Baby would be a remedy for loneliness.

He'd been at the Warrens too long, his stopover here more eventful than planned. He tightened his arms around his mother, hating to leave her. But his father had also been alone too long. The sooner he left, the sooner they'd be back together, a real family.

Aryn

<< << GGThis is AstroTwo, calling Lodestone Base. Our ETA is now nineteen hours. We will expect to find the shipment ready and waiting. Out.">>

In the greenhouse, Aryn straightened, startled by words coming directly into her head, and dropped the brush she'd been pollinating squash blossoms with. Several rows over, Hallie looked at her, eyes wide.

Aryn didn't bother to collect her wind coat or wait for Hallie, allowing the winds to buffet and scour her as she raced back to the Warrens. Ran came out of the infirmary with an intent expression. Spotting her, he corrected his course to meet her as she slipped between stone tables.

"Did you do that?" she asked, circling her finger near her ear.

"Make our implants relay communications, you mean?"

She nodded.

"No. It just happened. Baby and the Base Brain are now entangled."

Entangled, yes—but why were their implants also receiving?

<**"This is Simms at the Warrens on Planet Lodestone."**> She winced as Nick's father responded to the starship. <**Wick is no longer in charge of this planet. You will have to deal with us and our demands if you want your Beijingite."**> Simms was as small as his son, and just as fearless. But these pronouncements in her head were intolerable.

"Can you make it stop?" It was going to drive her crazy—and *soon*.

Ran grimaced in agreement. "It's coming through from the base Brain. I'm leaving now. I'll request it to stop when I get there. We should be back in a couple of hours."

"I'd go with you, but you'll need the room coming back."

<<**"If you know what's good for you, you'll tell us where the B'ite is."**>>

<**"This is Fletch at the Warrens. As Simms told you, Wick is no longer in charge on this planet. You will have to deal with the Warrens and our demands if you want your Beijingite."**>

Ran tilted his head in acknowledgement of this latest implant invasion. "You're going to be listening to a lot of threats flying around."

"Threats. That's all they are. Go get your father." She wished she had her pencils to draw his expression.

"And you?"

"I'll be here."

"I'll be back." But he looked uncertain.

Aryn closed the gap to hug him fiercely. He bent to kiss her cheek and she caught part of it on her lips. "Go. Now."

He turned and pushed through the wind slats.

<"This is Lodestone planetary geologist Perkins. The situation is indeed critical. These people need removal stat. The following warning is set to repeat every hour.">

Yikes, no! Not every hour!

A machine-originated voice began: <"Do not approach the Rift. It has gone live. It is a killer. Any and all remaining Beijingite is inaccessible to humans or robots. All mining on this planet is at an end. Repeat, do not approach the Rift.">

Two hours, Ran had said. Aryn looked at the room full of worried adults. A hostile ship up there. An encroaching Rift down here.

Do what comes to you to do. There was nothing for her here. She'd go back to work in the greenhouse. Whatever happened, they needed to eat.

And Ran would be back soon.

Ran

Keeping the Wreck as low to the ground as he dared, Ran headed out to retrieve his father.

To Be Concluded In

QUANTUM QUEST

You can learn more about the author at
KateHarringtonWrites.com